NO QUICK FIX

MARY CALMES

MARY CALMES BOOKS, LLC.

No Quick Fix

Edited by Desi Chapman

Line Edit/Proofing by Lisa Horan

Proofreading by Jenni Lea

Assistant Jessie Potts potts.jessie@gmail.com

❀ Created with Vellum

ACKNOWLEDGMENTS

It's funny that it's called self-publication when there is a whole group of talented people behind you helping in the process. I have amazing support from friends, fellow authors, and of course my wonderful readers. Thank you all so much from the bottom of my heart. My life doesn't work without you.

NO QUICK FIX

A retired SEAL is about to face his toughest assignment yet. As a nanny...

Fixer. Bodyguard. Advocate. Brann Calder is expected to play all these roles and more as a member of Torus Intercession, a security firm guaranteed to right what's wrong. In the military, catastrophe was his specialty. Five months out of the service, Brann is still finding his way, so a new assignment might be just what he needs. Unless it includes two things sure to make a seasoned, battle-trained veteran nervous: life in a small town, and playing caregiver to two little girls.

Emery Dodd is drowning in the responsibility of single fatherhood. He's picked up the pieces after losing his wife and is ready to move on now, hopeful that his engagement to a local patriarch's daughter will not only enrich his community but will grant his daughters some stability too.

The only thing standing in Emery's way is that he can't seem to keep his eyes—and hands—off the former soldier he's hired to watch his girls until the wedding.

Emery's future is riding on his upcoming nuptials, but being with Brann makes him and his family feel whole again. Too bad there's no way for them to be together.

Or is there?

ONE

My Thursday had gone right off the rails, and it was all because I was late.

I was the last guy into the office on the third floor of the Scoville Square building in Oak Park, and when I reached my desk and flopped down into my chair, very hungover and in dire need of far more caffeine, it took a moment before it hit me how quiet it was. Normally the office was noisy. Normally if I showed up at eight forty-five in the morning, wearing a pair of aviator sunglasses and my Cubs baseball cap, not bothering to take either off at the door, I would have caught some serious shit. The fact that no one said a word meant only one thing—I was already dead.

"Crap," I muttered, girding myself for the worst, knowing it had to be so much more than bad. "Where the hell do I hafta go?"

No answer from anyone, which was an even worse sign. When I finally looked around the office, the three men on my team who were there at the moment—there were two others still out on assignment—all stared at me like I'd drawn the short straw.

"What?" I asked no one in particular.

All three glanced away quickly, no one wanting to meet my gaze. It was like I had the plague—or worse.

"The hell is going on?" I groused at the room.

It was a big room.

The office was basically four sets of two desks, each butted up against the other in the center. In one corner were French doors that led to a huge, ornate, polished-mahogany and leather conference room. On the other side was a door that opened into a short hallway, with the bathrooms, supply closet, and breakroom. In the corner closest to the main door, so you had to walk by it to get to your desk, was my boss Jared Colter's office. I had long suspected that it was positioned there because he liked to keep tabs on our comings and goings—like whether we were in or not, awake or not, or what time we dragged our asses in—and to basically be a mother hen. But Nash Miller, who had been around the longest, told me that Jared really just enjoyed seeing us safe and sound every day. Apparently he'd lost someone important a while back, and seeing all of us was like keeping an eye on his kids.

To be honest, it kind of bugged me.

The only man's kid I would ever be had died when I was on a mission on the other side of the world, so it chafed a bit that someone thought they could parent me—or that I needed it—at this late juncture. But I kept my mouth shut since I liked my boss and the guys I worked with. As I hadn't thought I'd ever have that again after leaving the Navy, I didn't want to screw up and have to start over somewhere else. Though being late, and not a hundred percent sober, for a morning meeting was not doing me any favors.

"Someone better speak the fuck up," I warned everyone in general, sounding even surlier than I felt.

"We rock, paper, scissored for this," Shaw James said irritably from his desk across from Croy Esca, who appeared absorbed with whatever was on his monitor, doing his damnedest to avoid looking me in the eye.

"Coop!" I called out.

The man who sat across from me, who also happened to be the guy I was closest to at the firm, Cooper Davis, snickered, and I turned my head to give him my attention.

"Speak," I commanded.

He winced like he was about to tell me I was dying. "This is why I've told you a million times not to be late."

"Yeah, I know, but just spit it the fuck out."

He sighed deeply, then tipped his head and stared at my desk. Following his line of vision, I noticed the dossier sitting in the middle of the clutter in front of me. It had a Post-it note with my name on it.

After flipping open the folder, I read the first line that told me the location of the job. *Fuck.* Short straw was right. "Montana," I gasped, my head snapping up, my eyes meeting the deep blue ones of my friend.

His chuckle as he shook his head sucked all the air out of my lungs for a moment before I recovered and my brain kicked in. Every now and then, I noticed that the wavy brown hair that fell almost to my buddy's shoulders and the mustache and heavy stubble that passed for a beard were really fucking sexy on him. He looked like one of those undercover cops in a bad seventies police drama, but on him, it worked.

"Why aren't you going?" I asked, recovering, because as hot as the man was, he was not for me. I'd made a different decision the second I walked into the office for my interview.

I looked out across the room, he glanced up at the same time, and bam, that was it, lust at first sight. I had gravitated to Cooper at a more normal pace, and he to me, bonding over hockey and dive bars and horror movies. There were also the occasional nights out spent eating great food at the best restaurants in the city. Those were my favorite. Of course they had been few and far between lately, as he'd gotten serious about a guy only to have it unravel in spectacular fashion. A guy who didn't want to meet your mother was bad news. "I thought you were all about being out of town," I ventured, not adding the last part that only I knew. Cooper had been ducking his ex since May, so perhaps running off to a different state was a no-brainer.

"Not that far outta town," he assured me with a squint and a shake of his head.

One down. "Crap," I muttered, not worried yet but definitely annoyed.

"That's all kinds of fucked up," Shaw James chimed in from his desk a few feet away.

"Shaw," I wailed plaintively, willing my buddy who loved to camp and hike to chime in that it was a joke and he was going. "This is right up your alley, man."

He swiveled around in his chair and caught me in his dark emerald-green gaze. "Not on a bet, Brann."

"Why not?" I sort of whined and pleaded at the same time.

"Kids," he said, shivering like that was the worst thing he could think of. "Read it all, Brann. You're babysitting a parent, so there's no way in hell you don't have to deal with the children. That's a big no for me."

I scanned the document quickly. "It says they're six and eight. You could teach them to fish—you love to fish."

"Not with kids I don't," Shaw assured me, clearly

revolted as evidenced by the second shudder as he turned back around.

"You love the outdoors," I pointed out, grasping for anything to get me out of going to Montana at all, but definitely not now, in September. If it wasn't cold there already, it soon would be, and then I'd be there through October and November, and God knew what the temperature would plunge to, plus... Montana, for fuck's sake! "You're always saying how—"

"It's a three-month-long job," he said over his shoulder, "in a one-horse town named after a fuckin' bear, Brann. I would lose my goddamn mind."

Like I wouldn't?

"And you won't have any privacy. Seriously, the job is to live there *with* the family," he continued. There was no mistaking the horror in his voice when he said *with*. "I honestly can't think of anything worse than that."

"No, c'mon, it'll be fun."

Nothing.

"Please?"

He said nothing, just rubbed his hand over his ginger buzz cut and ignored me completely.

Fucker.

Turning, I focused my attention on Croy Esca, who looked sympathetic even as he shook his head. Pretty boy, looked way younger than twenty-eight, came from a rich family who cut all ties to him when he came out as gay as a senior in high school. He was lucky because he'd gotten a full ride to some college in California, and moved there from Boston. Somehow, he'd ended up in Chicago. I didn't know the whole story, and I'd never asked. I didn't like people prying into my life, I figured I'd extend the guys I worked with the same courtesy.

"Montana?" I said hopefully, smiling for good measure.

Croy arched a white-blond eyebrow and replied with that silky tone of his, "Whatever would I do there, Brann?"

"You could paint," I said, pouring on all the cheerful enthusiasm I could muster. He was an artist, that much I knew.

Croy's grimace gave me his answer—clearly I was deluded and no way in hell was he driving his ass northwest.

Spinning slowly in my office chair, the concern becoming real, I caught Cooper with my stare. "Let's really think about this now," I said seriously.

"I'm givin' that a hard pass. Way too much nature," he informed me. "And it's gonna get really cold there by November."

But it was only the second week in September now. "It gets a bit cold here too," I reminded him. It was Chicago, after all.

"Yeah, but here I have pizza and the Blackhawks and my bed," he shot back, grinning. He was being nice about it, not snide like Shaw, but still, he wasn't going. And he was right. There was a lot to be said for being in your own bed.

I tried to look pitiful.

"I think the puppy dog thing only works on guys who wanna fuck you."

I was thinking that was accurate.

"Do you even know what's in Montana?" he asked, pinning me with a look.

"No," I answered miserably.

"Well then, just think, maybe it'll be an adventure."

"Fuck," I muttered under my breath.

"Again," he said, sounding tired but gentle. "This is why we never, ever, sleep in, especially toward the end of the week. You have no idea what kind of bullshit job Jare got talked into taking on Monday or Tuesday that he'll dump on you and then start his weekend early."

At Torus, we specialized in what Jared Colter called, *intercession and alignment*. It was a fancy way to say *fixer*. Basically, we were intermediaries. We interceded on a client's behalf, and by the time we left, their life would be, or should be, in order. It was what my boss called *syzygy*, connected things that lined up just right. When Jared hired me, he gave me a whole speech about positive energy and good karma and crap like that, but for me, it was all about helping people out. I was happy to do that and, bonus, I got paid—a win-win situation and, in theory, it was easy.

What we did was never the same. We operated as assistants, instructors, contractors, everything from seeing someone through the first few days of an acrimonious divorce to checking on kids living across the country from their separated parents to overseeing a home renovation to plain-old standard protection. But the jobs were never long. Certainly one job never took a month, let alone two, and holy God, not out in the middle of nowhere. What my boss was asking me to do wasn't even humane. "I'm gonna go tell him I can't do it," I announced, a headache starting because I'd had no opportunity to either caffeinate or hydrate yet.

Cooper's brow furrowed as he stared at me—in a way he had that made me unsure of my life choices. "I had no idea you have a death wish."

I let my head slump onto my folded arms.

"It could be worse."

"How could it?" I whimpered.

"At least it's not snowing there yet."

"That you fuckin' know of," I grumbled into my desk. I had to think of something, anything, to change Jared's mind.

"Oh, shit, look who's back!"

Lifting my head, I saw Locryn Barnes and Nash Miller walk into the office, both all scruffy and tired from their month and a half away.

It was nice to see Nash. He was a good guy and would have sympathized with my current predicament and maybe even gone instead if he hadn't just gotten back. The other man, the guy I had been secretly sleeping with since I started working at Torus five months ago, him I wanted to run over with my 1983 Toyota Land Cruiser. And yes, since there weren't a lot of those still on the road, someone probably would have noticed when I hit Locryn and then reversed back over him for good measure. But truly, it would be a small price to pay for the supreme feeling of bliss I was certain to experience once Locryn Barnes was splattered all over the pavement.

If I were being honest with myself, I was the one who deserved to be run over for being such a fucking idiot. How stupid could I possibly be, thinking that a guy who was keeping me a secret—from everyone—wanted anything serious? I'd been there for sex, a booty call from the jump, and nothing more. When he left six weeks ago on a job with Nash, he didn't even bother to say goodbye. I hadn't heard a peep from him in all that time, and now here he was, back without warning. He hadn't even asked me to water his plants or feed his fish, for fuck's sake. Locryn couldn't have made things any clearer, and suddenly, just like that, Montana sounded really good. So good in fact that I had to wonder if somehow, someway, though we'd been super careful about the affair, so secretive, so cloak-and-dagger, that maybe Jared Colter knew anyway. The man had been a spook with the CIA, after all.

After getting up, pushing in my chair, I took the folder,

put it under my arm, and smiled at Cooper when he looked up at me.

"I'll call ya from Montana, and when I get back from this stupid assignment, I'm gonna need you to take me for Thai at the good place with the beer I like, all right?"

"You got it," he said, grinning at me. "Pack a parka. You'll still be there in November."

I groaned and turned for the door.

"Oh ho, pretty boy, can't even say hello," Locryn called after me.

Flipping him off over my shoulder, I could hear everyone laughing as I reached my boss's door. I knocked softly on the glass before leaning in.

I noticed then exactly what I had when I first met the man—that the silver flecks in his dark charcoal-grey eyes, and the laugh lines accentuating them, were amazing.

I had never been one to notice older men, but his height and powerful build, the gray-and-silver strands in his thick blond hair, and the way he carried himself—commanding and not to be fucked with—had stolen my breath away once or twice. Really handsome man, and though I'd never understood what the term silver fox meant before I met him, I had a firm picture in my mind now.

Jared was on the phone and said something quickly before putting his hand over the handset. "Are you going home to pack?"

"And then get a plane ticket, yeah," I told him. "I'll start reporting once I've been there a couple days."

"I would drive," he suggested.

This was news. "Drive?" I almost gasped but caught myself in time, so it came out sounding a bit gruff and less like a squeak. He nodded. "Yeah. It'll give you time to clear your head, and that way you won't have a three-month car rental to deal with."

Was he kidding? Drive to Montana? And what was I clearing my head from? "I... you know it's probably like—"

"Driving is good," he said, sort of steamrolling over me, closing the door on me saying no, like I could have, to begin with. "You'll see."

"Okay. I'll get there as fast as I can."

"Take your time," he said, grinning. "It's a boring job, but Harlan Thomas, he's the sheriff there, he's an old friend of an old friend, and he thinks there might be trouble if the two people in question don't successfully tie the knot. It sounds like the town might be dependent on the nuptials happening, or something else getting worked out."

"No pressure on the bride and groom, huh?"

"It seems like an antiquated idea to me," he said, his deep voice, drenching me in calm, so I took what felt like my first breath all morning. "It's like back in history when two countries sealed an alliance by having their children marry. This is the same thing, except with companies not kingdoms."

"Well, I'll make sure it happens, then."

"Or not," he countered, his tone and the shrug both suggesting he was leaving it in my hands. "I trust your judgement. Just do whatever *should* be done. You'll figure it out."

Should be done? What the hell? "I won't let you down," I said, because either way, that was the important thing.

"I never thought you would," he said, giving me a warm smile, which was my cue to get the hell out of his office.

I turned to leave and was almost at the door.

"Calder."

Pausing in the doorway, I looked back over my shoulder.

"No matter if you were first in this morning, you were the one going. Don't let those guys tell you any different. This assignment had you written all over it."

I had no idea what that meant. Middle of nowhere? Kids? Small town? How the hell was that me in any realm of the imagination? "Yessir," I said instead of arguing with him for a second. "Thank you, sir."

He gave me a fatherly nod of dismissal, and I bolted. Once I reached my car, my phone rang, and I saw Locryn's face pop up on my screen.

Well, he could go directly to hell. And yeah, I'd allowed him to treat me like a piece of ass, but that didn't mean I had to let it continue. I could actually live and learn from my mistakes.

Letting the call go straight to voicemail, I climbed behind the wheel of my Land Cruiser and wondered again if maybe Jared insisting I have time in the car, to clear my head, was code for him wanting to make sure I was good and over Locryn Barnes. He didn't have to worry. It had never been love, just infatuation, and so it had died quickly without nourishment. My heart was whole, not bleeding a bit.

I wish I could have conveyed that to him before he signed me up to make a long-ass drive out to the middle of nowhere.

Maybe it was time to start working on my faulty communication skills.

TWO

L ong and boring didn't do the horrific drive justice. Even stopping overnight to make sure I was rested, having done half on Thursday so there was only the other half on Friday, it was still an endless slog from Chicago up I-94, then to another highway and another, eventually to MT 200 that set me on course to Ursa, Montana. The town was twenty minutes out of Whitefish—which, of course, since I had never been anywhere near the entire state of Montana, didn't help me figure out where I was one little bit. In the file, my boss had made a notation, clarifying that if I reached Canada, I'd gone too far. The man clearly thought he was hilarious.

Not surprisingly, the town of Ursa was every bit as bad as I figured it would be. There were only two lanes through downtown, if it could even be called a downtown, and everywhere I looked were snow-capped mountains, pine trees, and sky that was so blue it made my eyes water. No skyscrapers, no office buildings—just fucking nature. It was horrifying. Whitefish, which I'd passed, was only a few miles from Glacier National Park in Flathead County, which, according to the still stupid GPS, was an amazing place to visit, famous for Going-to-the-Sun Road, Logan Pass and Avalanche Lake. Also, from where I was, apparently, I could throw a rock and hit Canada, which was what had prompted Jared's oh-so-funny comment in the file.

Super.

I was in complete and utter hell.

Traveling out to the home of Andrea Cahill, on that early Saturday morning, was an adventure. There were no road signs, and I was sure the annoying GPS would have given up, but I had an Iridium Extreme that all the guys in our office carried if we were going off the grid. It wasn't our regular phone. It was the auxiliary one, but I was glad to have it, or I would've been so very lost. Everywhere I looked, there were trees and grass, hills, more trees and more grass. There wasn't a gas station or a dive bar to get my bearings from.

The longer I drove, the more I had to begrudgingly admit the scenery was not horrible. If I was passing through, I probably would have even thought it was nice. After I took a right, following directions, I was impressed by the two-lane road lined with enormous pine trees on both sides. I was guessing it would be stunning in the winter.

Speeding down a small hill, I saw a wooden arch with the name Cahill on it and took a sharp left there to begin the long trek toward the house. The winding gravel driveway was seemingly endless, and I could only guess what a pain in the ass it was to navigate once it was covered in a foot of snow. It was as scenic as the rest of the journey and the closer I got to the house, I noticed there were other fences, some around large oak trees, which made no sense until I saw the horses.

I passed a barn that was bigger and nicer than a lot of

homes I'd seen in my life, and then I saw the main house that resembled a log cabin—if those came in mansion size. It hit me then that I was looking at money. Big money. It also didn't escape me that Cahill Lumber was probably what kept the town alive.

When I was finally parked in the paved circular drive-way, I got out and stretched at the same time I saw a man coming down the front steps toward me.

Extending my hand, I was surprised when the man in the black suit, crisp white shirt, and tie, holding a thick leather binder, only scowled.

"Are you Mr. Calder?"

"I am," I said, squinting, crossing my arms, annoyed that fast. I was still stiff from driving for two days, and this man was about as welcoming as a porcupine and seemed just as prickly. I needed food, a shower, a bed, and mostly, a warmer goddamn greeting. I was there because I'd been asked to be there, after all.

"You're at the wrong address," the man informed me, clipping his words.

This was news. "I'm sorry?"

He cleared his throat. "I'm Mr. Cahill's personal assistant, Mr. Duvall, and our contract with your firm, Torus, is for you to oversee the household of the groom, *not* the bride."

I was lost. "I'm here to facilitate the wedding of Ms. Andrea Cahill to—"

"No." Duvall shook his head. "It's *Miss* Cahill, *Miss Lydia Cahill*, who has never been married, and she's engaged to Mr. Emery Dodd, who was married before to Andrea Darrow-Dodd, who passed away three years ago."

Wait. "Who do the kids belong to?"

Duvall made a face like I smelled like dog crap or something. "There are two girls, Olivia, who is six, and April, who is eight. They are Mr. Dodd's children, and he will retain sole custody of them even after the marriage. That is a prenuptial stipulation."

None of that mattered to me. "So Mr. Dodd has the kids, and I'm supposed to be at his house, helping him out until the wedding."

"Not *helping out*," the older man said, like I was stupid and he had to use small words to communicate with me. "Keeping an eye on him and making certain the nuptials go forward without issue. The wedding is very important for the town, and Sheriff Thomas was happy to refer us to your firm, as we are in need of outside assistance to ensure a smooth transaction in both the marriage and the merger of Cahill Lumber and Darrow Holdings."

I had no idea what was going on, and at the same time, I had a moment to wonder how well my boss's friend knew the sheriff. Maybe *old friend* translated to someone he hadn't seen or talked to in years. I would have to make a call the second I was back in the car.

"Okay, then," I said, walking back around to the driver's side door. "Could you tell me exactly where Mr. Dodd lives?"

"Oh," Duvall said quickly, his brows furrowing. "Perhaps you would like to come inside and meet Miss Cahill and have some refreshments?"

It was like all of a sudden he remembered his manners. I would have sooner gargled glass than step one foot into the log cabin mansion. "No, I'm good, thanks. Could ya just point me in the right direction?"

"At the end of the drive, you take a right, go back toward town, and the Dodd home is ten miles in the opposite direction."

"Great," I quipped, and got into my SUV and left without another word.

Once I was halfway down the road, I got on the satellite phone and called the office.

"Torus," Locryn answered, because of course he was the one on call since it was the weekend. I could have kicked myself, but I'd forgotten it was Saturday morning and called there on instinct. What an idiot.

"Shit, sorry," I said quickly. "I was hoping to get hold of Jare. I'll try him on his cell."

"Wait."

I cleared my throat. "I gotta go 'cause—"

"Just wait," he barked.

There was hold music a second later, "Ode to Joy," which was funny, and I let out a deep breath, because given Locryn's brusqueness, he didn't give a crap that his fuck buddy was on the phone. We were over and done, and we weren't even going to have to discuss any part of it. How great was that? Clean breaks were a blessing, and—

"Why the hell haven't you been answering your phone?" Locryn snarled a second later.

Well, shit.

Not clean. It was going to be gross and messy. "I need to talk to Jare," I insisted.

"What the hell, Brann?"

"What the hell? Are you kidding?" All alone in my SUV, I still felt the heat of embarrassment on my face. It was humiliating, even if only the two of us knew.

"Oh, for fuck's sake, you can't possibly be pissed that I didn't call you before I left. It was two in the morning. What was I supposed to do, wake your ass up?"

"Yeah," I croaked out. "That's what you do when you give a shit. You wake people up."

"Oh, gimme a fuckin' break. We're not dating."

"No, I know we're not. You made that perfectly clear," I conceded, trying desperately to keep the hurt out of my voice, not wanting him to hear at all that I'd been wounded.

It was funny, but it turned out I couldn't sleep with someone over and over and not get attached. I was weak. I was needy. And though I didn't want to be either of those things, I'd fallen fast for the guy who slept with anyone and everyone who gave him a hard-on. It had been a mistake from the start, but I'd missed the warning signs, too infatuated with the man's wicked smile and his cocky swagger, the sexy whiskey rasp of his voice, and the whole bad-boy charm. Between the motorcycle and the sinfully tight blue jeans and how he wanted to be manhandled in bed, held down while I fucked him, I was a goner.

But listening to him now, having seen him two days ago with fresh eyes after over a month of going cold turkey without him, the detox was complete, and the ridiculousness of my situation hit me square in the face. Again. Like a hard slap. In case I'd missed it the first time.

Funny how quickly feelings lived and died when they were not deeply rooted. My interest, infatuation, fixation had withered on the vine, which made it so much easier to talk to him.

"Listen, you need to—"

"It's fine, Loc," I assured him, suddenly feeling the long hours of driving, the lack of food, the need for more sleep, and the desire to be under the spray of warm water. "Find a new fuck buddy. I'm sure you've got people on speed dial."

"Just don't be a prick, all right? We'll talk about it when you get back."

I scoffed. "It's okay. Let's not."

"You're never gonna talk to me again?" He sounded surprised.

"Not about this," I said, yawning. "It's not necessary."

"Brann—"

"Listen, you've been gone more than a month, and in all that time not one word, not one call or—"

"I was with Nash the whole goddamn time. When was I supposed to—"

"It doesn't matter. Again, it's fine. I'll be here a couple months, so by the time I get back, I'm sure you'll have a whole parade of people in and out of your place, and that's fine. But right now, I really need to speak to Jare."

"Fuck you, Brann. Like you were celibate or some shit while I was gone."

I owed him nothing, and definitely not the truth, but still... it was what was real, after all. "Actually I was busy missing you, so no... there wasn't anyone else. I waited," I confessed and then hung up. It was enough. There didn't need to be any more.

It was no surprise that he didn't call back. His pride would never allow that. What did surprise me, though, was that I didn't have to calm a racing heart, and that, more than anything, told me I was over and done with Locryn Barnes. Before he left, it was like I could never catch my breath around the guy. Getting a call from him used to make my pulse race, which I was smart enough to know was infatuation and lust, nothing deeper than that. But that too was gone, so now, I was good. It was always nice to have closure, even if it was only in your own head.

As I drove I savored that fact until I made it back into town, parked, and used my regular cell to call Jared on his.

"Calder?"

Jared didn't say hello, instead using my name as a question.

"Sorry to bug you on a Saturday, but I needed to talk to you real quick."

"Let me walk inside," he directed me, "I'm getting the oil changed in my car, and I was out here talking to Owen."

Or more likely, Jared was talking and Owen Moss was listening. I couldn't remember a time when I'd heard Owen talk. Ever. The first time we'd met, there had been an awkward handshake before Owen clearly forced a smile and walked away. There were rumors as to what led to the silence.

Shaw claimed it was social anxiety. Nash said Jared had saved him from a cult, and Locryn told me there was trafficking involved and Owen's mother had traded him for drugs. I didn't believe a word of any of it. But since I knew better than to delve into Jared's private business—and Owen was definitely off-limits and under Jared's protection—I had no hope of ever learning the truth. Again, with Jared being ex-CIA, the roadblocks to even inquiring were formidable.

Honestly, it wasn't that important. I was much more a live-and-let-live kind of person, which meant I didn't need to know why Owen was there, he was a good guy, and that was all I really cared about. What was cool about him was that Owen Moss was the mechanic who took care of not only our cars but our tech as well. He was the man responsible for getting us the best surveillance equipment, phones, laptops, and my freaky home alarm system, which I never had to turn on or off; it just knew, somehow, when I was home or when it was me coming through the door. I worried he had cameras in my place, but at the same time, I knew he didn't care enough about me to put in that much effort. I felt the same about him. Truly, the only part I found interesting about Owen was that he fixed cars on the weekends.

"Okay," Jared said briskly, returning my focus to him. "Tell me what's up."

"Is the car all right?" I teased him. "Is oil change code for mounting a flamethrower on the roof?"

"You're funny," Jared deadpanned, which made me smile, parked there on the side of the road. "And I would remind you that one small alteration does not give you, or any of the others, the right to give me crap about my vehicle."

Vehicle. He made it sound so benign.

My boss drove a tricked-out Hummer H3 to work every day that I was certain he would be safe in if the zombie apocalypse ever hit. The last time it was "in the shop," Jared came out with a grill on the front that looked more like a battering ram.

"Now, talk," Jared ordered, and I understood he had better things to do with his Saturday than shoot the shit with me.

I cleared my throat, nervous suddenly, not wanting to tell Jared that maybe his friend, the friend of the sheriff, didn't know what the real deal in the town was. "The file is wrong. I'm actually staying with Mr. Dodd, not Miss Cahill, and the kids are his, not hers."

Jared was silent, and when it stretched out for more than a minute, I began to worry.

"Boss?"

"I know all that," he said slowly, sounding unsure. "It seems like maybe you only skimmed something you should have read much more thoroughly. Take some time and read that file before you do anything else."

He hung up, and if he was right, which he usually was, I

had made a fool of myself in front of not only the client but my boss as well.

First there was my being late to work on Thursday, and now being uninformed on Saturday. Could I be a bigger fuckup?

Pulling over on the side of the road, then grabbing the file folder from the passenger seat, I flipped it open for the read I should have done the day I left Chicago. There, inside, I read all about Emery Dodd and his wife, Andrea, who suffered an aortic dissection three years prior. She'd had high blood pressure related to pregnancy after giving birth to their second child, but it was never considered life threatening, and the flaw in her heart had gone undetected. She died in her home one morning and was discovered by a friend who came by to return a casserole dish. Her family—husband and girls—had been devastated.

Andrea Dodd, born Andrea Darrow, had been the sole heir to the holding company that her great-grandfather had begun. She'd met Emery in graduate school, fell in love, and brought him back to Ursa with her. When she died, everything became his and, eventually, it would belong to their daughters. Darrow Holdings owned rangeland, acres and acres, which was used by ranchers for grazing cattle and sheep.

Cahill Lumber, which Lydia's father, Grant, started thirty-five years ago, needed more trees and land. The merger, once she and Emery married, was in everyone's best interest. Cahill, which by all accounts was a good company committed to sustainability, would take over the land management and daily operations, while Emery would continue to sit on the board of directors. The one thing he stipulated was that no strip mining occur on the land, and everyone had concurred.

It was, all in all, a perfect arrangement. Emery got a new wife, the girls a new mother, and Lydia got a ready-made family that, of course, she and Emery could add to. And because Cahill Lumber was the lifeblood of the town—the mill employed half of the population—Sheriff Harlan Thomas had requested that his old friend, some retired Army colonel, ask Jared Colter to send out a babysitter for Emery Dodd and his girls until the man said his *I dos*. Thomas had requested someone far more capable to watch over the family because if Emery and Lydia didn't tie the knot, the town was in trouble. Firepower was needed to watch over the Dodd family. The whole job made sense now, and as I started my car, I understood precisely what I was there to do, and it was infinitely worse than I'd imagined.

I was there to keep Mr. Dodd in line so nothing got between Mr. Cahill and his land acquisition. But most of all, I was there to help the man with his children. Torus had been contacted by Sheriff Thomas on a query from Cahill Lumber, and I was being paid by Darrow Holdings on behalf of Emery Dodd. At least I knew who I was actually working for. I really should have read the file cover to cover before I left.

It was just like Shaw said; I was going to live with them. I was going to take his kids to school and make them dinner. I was going to be the one picking up the slack in Emery Dodd's life.

And that quickly, the thought of having to deal with Locryn Barnes and his bullshit didn't seem like such a bad idea at all. I could have stayed and lived through that, it was way better than babysitting, and as realization hit, I really wanted to go home.

I was sent to be the nanny.

THREE

Without a doubt, the street Emery Dodd lived on was really beautiful and as was the case everywhere else in town, there were a lot of mature trees. It looked like a postcard, or what you thought of when the words *picturesque small-town neighborhood* were spoken. I could imagine kids walking to school and Christmas carolers and block parties.

The homes on the street were lovely, built close to one another, and were either colonial with wide porches and shutters, lots of windows, and wood accents, or ranches that were long and flat, some L-shaped and others a U, all with uninspired attached garages. I figured the Dodd house would be similar, but I was happily surprised to find it was different.

The house was nestled between giant cedar trees and ponderosa pines. It was a cottage style, which looked a lot like the Craftsman style I'd admired growing up in California. It was gray with white trim and a small second story. There was a charming white picket fence and a driveway that ran along the right side of the house, leading around back to the garage. The front yard was a lush emerald green, cut through by a cobblestone path leading to six wide front steps and up to a front porch that ran the breadth of the house. I doubted I had ever seen a more welcoming little home.

After getting out of the car, I raked my fingers through my hair a couple of times, adjusted my leather jacket, checked my pits really quickly to make sure I didn't reek, and then yawned so loud that my jaw cracked. Once I was sure I could see straight, I locked the car and headed up toward the gate. Halfway there, I stumbled over what I assumed was a crack in the pavement.

"Just don't lemme fall on my face," I said to the universe, hoping somebody or something was listening. "I need to at least make a decent first impression."

At the door, I knocked softly. It was early on a Saturday morning, after all.

I was surprised by how quickly the front door was thrown open while, at the same time, a man yelled out, "Ask who it is first!"

It was good advice, but the little girl standing in front of me, had not been listening at all, and probably thought her father—had to be him calling after her—was giving her a suggestion instead of an order.

"Hello," I greeted the short person, smiling down at her. She was very cute with her dark auburn curls tumbling around her face, big brown eyes, and a dusting of freckles across her nose.

"Who are you?" she asked sharply, giving me a scowl for good measure.

Squatting down, I faced the cherub. "I'm Brann Calder, and I'm here to help your dad."

She tipped her head, studying my face. "Oh, yeah, he said you were coming."

"Doesn't sound like you were too pumped about it, huh?"

She was still studying me. "That depends. Can you braid hair? Lydia can't braid hair, and she's a grown-up." It was not lost on me that the judgement in her voice could peel paint.

"No, but I can watch YouTube videos and figure it out later," I assured her honestly, because it was always the easiest thing to just tell it like it was. That way you didn't have to worry about it later. "In the meantime, though, I can make balls."

She let go of the door and crossed her arms. "How do you mean *balls*?"

"You know those balls of rubber bands that people buy at office supply stores?"

"Maybe. I'm not super sure."

I loved how serious she sounded, and I couldn't help smiling. "Well, I can make two perfectly round balls of your hair if you have any of the soft elastic ones."

"Huh," she said, like she was on the fence about that being a good idea or not.

"For serious, they'll look just like ears," I assured her, adding that in to tip the scales in my favor. Resembling an animal had to be good. Kids liked animals.

That did it. Her face lit up and she gave me a toothy grin. "How many hair ties do you need?"

"Three, maybe four per side," I said thoughtfully.

Turning fast, she darted back into the living room in a dead heat, not bothering to stop to say anything to the man who came flying into the room. She was too intent on her quest.

"Where are you going?" he called after her.

"Gotta get hair ties!"

"Of course," he murmured to himself and then turned and gave me all his focus.

I almost said "Wow," under my breath, but stopped before I made a complete and utter fool of myself and came up with "Hey," instead. Emery Dodd was a beautiful man, with deep, dark, warm brown eyes, sharp-chiseled features, and short, tousled brown hair. His lips looked like they were made to be kissed, soft and delectably curved.

I. Wanted.

"Good morning," I managed to get out.

"Good morning," he echoed me, staring, wondering, I was sure, where the hell I'd come from. It was probably a bit disconcerting.

I needed to get it together, because having a hard-on for the guy I was supposed to be helping with his kids was in really poor taste.

"You're Mr. Calder, aren't you?"

"I am," I said, pleased he'd spoken first. "And you're Mr. Dodd."

"Emery, please," he corrected softly, rushing forward to offer me his hand.

His grip was warm, strong, and I relaxed when he grabbed my shoulder with his other hand. It was like just that bit more contact was soothing.

"I assumed it had to be you, but you look so different."

He lost me. "Different?"

"I have your file from Torus," he apprised, as he eased me forward, across the threshold and into his home. "Five months out of the military looks good on you."

I didn't know what to say to the man who was gazing at me so kindly, like I was something special. It was unnerving and made me feel amazing at the same time. Whatever I'd done to make him gaze at me like that, I had to figure it out quick because I wanted it to continue.

He let my hand go and closed the door behind me. "Your hair got long."

"No, you just have an old picture," I informed him, knowing the one Jared Colter included in my file for clients. It was taken before I became a SEAL, when I was still sporting a buzz cut. He'd meant to update it, but there was always something more pressing.

"It's better like this," Emery assured me, "as well as the rest."

"Thank you," I said, raking my fingers through the dirty-blond strands. My hair hadn't grown out much since I left the Navy, maybe a few inches, but between the added length and the stubble gracing my jaw, the soldier I'd been was certainly gone. "It's easy to get out of habits you never liked to begin with."

"Oh, I'm certain of that," he said, chuckling, starting through the living room. "Come have a seat. May I pour you some coffee?"

I almost whimpered. "Yes, please."

Apparently I was funny, because I got a laugh over that.

The house was charming, to say the least. As I followed him through the living room and toward the kitchen, I couldn't help but feel the sun pouring in through a wall of floor-to-ceiling windows, warming the space and inviting me to curl up on the overstuffed couch or settle into its comfortable chairs and kick my feet up on the enormous ottoman, maybe watch some TV. The knickknacks and abundance of books strewn about felt settled, like this house could tell the story of the people who lived there. The art gracing the pale yellow walls was eclectic, the exposed-beam ceilings were rustic, and as we moved into the kitchen, a strange, eye-catching chandelier took pride of place. I stopped walking and stared.

Putting a pod in the Keurig, he paused and turned to me. "You're wondering about the chandelier, aren't you?"

"I am," I replied, smiling at him. "Are you reading my mind, or does everyone find it weird?"

"The latter," he said, chuckling. "Everyone wonders, and I know it's strange, but it has always been here," he told me. "When my wife and I first moved in, we kept thinking as we did our renovations that we'd sell it or give it away, but then —I forget who was here," he said, squinting, like he was trying to remember, "but they said it was actually cut crystal and that the style of it, waterfall something, was worth a small fortune, and he, or she, wanted it, so we left it up, thinking we'd trade it out for whatever they brought over, but that never happened, and... it just sort of stayed."

He was lost in thought, and it was nice listening to his voice, the low, husky timbre of it, as he spoke.

"I remember when April was about six months or so, we were right here, she and I, standing next to the chandelier, and she lifted her little hand like she wanted to touch it. I think she was watching the sunlight make rainbows on the wall, and I thought... I'm having a perfect moment."

I'd never had a perfect moment, not yet, but the dreamy expression on his face, the softness in his eyes and the wistful tone were making me think this was close. Man, was I having a weird reaction to him, the house, and even his cute kid. What the hell was up with that?

"Well, it's really pretty," I threw out lamely.

"It is," he affirmed with a sigh, turning back to the coffee maker. "So tell me, what do you take in this?"

"Nothing," I husked, admiring the long back muscles flexing and moving beneath his tight t-shirt. He wasn't as lean as I'd first thought; his shoulders were wide and his chest was defined. Between his long legs and tight, round ass, I was beginning to think I'd need to remind myself— over and over—that the man was straight.

"I'm sorry?" he said, sounding startled, clearly horrified as he turned to look at me over his shoulder. "Did you say you take nothing? Was that a joke?"

I read the disgust on his handsome face and couldn't miss the glower he was giving me, so I smiled wide. I liked him so much already. He was adorable.

"Just hot bean water? This is what you're telling me? Seriously?"

I snorted. "Listen, I learned to drink it that way or no way at all," I explained, walking into the kitchen I felt more at ease in than I had since I'd been back in the world.

"Well, how about this once, you try a little vanilla creamer and see if you go from coffee being something you require to something you actually enjoy."

I grunted.

"No?"

"Real men drink hot bean water," I teased him.

"I think real men drink whatever the hell they want to." He shook his head like I was ridiculous, and I watched him go to the refrigerator and then come back and doctor my coffee before he passed it over.

He waited as I drank some, and I had to give it to him, it was better.

"Well?"

I grunted again.

"All right," he said, grinning at me, "I'm counting that as a win."

As he moved around, getting out granola bars and the milk, I wondered if this was breakfast but didn't ask.

"So, how was your flight?" he asked as he emptied the dishwasher.

I leaned on the counter and watched those muscles of his some more, honing in on the strip of tan skin showing when his shirt lifted as he put bowls away on the higher shelves.

"I drove, actually," I clarified for him, sipping from the huge mug he'd given me while taking in more details of the room. I never thought I'd be a fan of a white-on-white kitchen—white cabinets and white tile countertops—but somehow, along with the stainless steel appliances, rather than sterile and uninviting, the heart of this house was simple and comfortable. Again, there was a rustic quality to it all.

"All the way from Chicago?" He stopped to glance over at me. "Whyever would you do such a thing?"

"My boss likes us to have our own cars when the assignment is as long as this one."

He was still squinting at me as he moved closer. "But that's what expensing something is for. That's a ridiculous drive. You must be exhausted."

"I started on Thursday," I explained, "drove some, and then did the rest yesterday. I'm good."

"Well, if you need to lie down, you let me know." He leaned into me and gave me a gentle pat on the chest but then didn't immediately pull away, instead leaving his hand there, lingering close. I had no idea what to do. Normally I would. Normally I would have jumped him, but this wasn't that. He wasn't stroking my chest or admiring the definition I owed to daily trips to the gym instead of soldiering. Emery wasn't feeling me up. He was just there, close to me, in my space, the two of us in a weird, quiet bubble that I wasn't totally comfortable with but liked, nonetheless.

A moment later, the spell was broken and he went back to unloading more dishes as though nothing were amiss, scowling at some of the items he was pulling out, like a hairbrush and wooden spoons and a Barbie.

I chuckled, watching as his expression went from concerned to confused.

"Clearly these items had to be sanitized for whatever reason," he said, putting the blonde beauty on the counter. "At least whoever put these in here had the good sense to place them on the top rack."

"Sure," I said like that made sense.

His grin, like he knew I was out of my depth, threw me off-balance. "Brann, I know this is all new for you. I read your file, after all, so please, know that I'll help you find your footing here."

"Footing?"

"With what you have to do," he clarified, which didn't help at all.

"What am I gonna do?"

He arched an eyebrow, and with his smile still in place, playful and sexy at the same time, I felt the flush of heat run over me. I took an inadvertent step forward, responding to what felt like an invitation into his space, a familiarity that at the same time was new but not, right before I stopped myself.

I never, ever, had this kind of reaction to anyone. It wasn't me. I never reached toward anyone new. It had to be safe first. Locryn had to invite me over to his place for a beer and throw me up against his front door before he got a reaction out of me. In the course of the short five months that we'd been fucking, he must have said a million times, why didn't I ever initiate anything? Why did I have to wait for him to kiss me, grab me, before I took over and held him down? Why couldn't I put myself out there?

And I knew why. Half of it was the dread of being turned down, of not being wanted—which turned out to be warranted, in his case—but the rest had been plain old me being careful. In the Navy, I had sex when I was on leave and no other time. There was the fear of being outed, if anyone found out, but there were also actual safety concerns in countries where being gay could mean a jail sentence, or worse. I was always on my guard. Up until I took the first step into this man's home.

"Are you all right?"

My gaze met his and I realized that there, in his kitchen, I felt utterly safe and secure and it was... overwhelming. I'd been all over the world, I'd been armed to the teeth, been the fuck buddy of a guy who would have actually killed anyone who tried to hurt me, and yet here, now, was where I felt grounded, like everything was solid under my feet?

What the hell was going on with me?

"Scared of what you're going to do here?"

Again with that. "I don't—what?"

He laughed, and normally that would have pissed me off, as though he were having fun at my expense, but I was so off-balance, off-center, that I just grinned like an idiot. He broke me, and I suspected he wasn't even trying to.

"You know you're the nanny, don't you?"

"I—yeah. Sort of. I mean... in theory yes, but really, no."

"Oh, that wasn't confusing at all," he said sarcastically.

"No, then. Firmly."

"No?" He sounded skeptical, crossing his arms as he regarded me.

"Well, no, because I shouldn't be."

"And why is that?" Emery pressed me, the rakish arch to

that eyebrow again making my stomach twitch. He was daring me to say something brilliant. "Do you hate kids?"

"What? No," I said quickly, defensively. "Who hates kids? That's nuts."

"Then clearly I'm missing the issue."

What was I supposed to say? "Okay, so I'll tell you that I never really got to be a kid myself, so I don't know how much help I can be."

"And why weren't you allowed to be a kid?" he asked, and I read the concern on his face and heard it in his voice.

My fault. I opened the door for that. I had no one to blame but myself. "It was just me and my dad after my mother died, and he drank some, so... I had to step up a bit."

He nodded. "So you're telling me that you grew up too fast."

I had to think. "Yeah. No," I said, finding it hard to commit to an answer. "Maybe."

He was smiling at me again. "You speak in circles, did you know?"

"I maybe got that memo once or twice."

Again with the gleaming eyes, like I was something special. It was a brand-new thing for me to have someone look at me like that, and I wanted it to go on and on and on.

"How old were you when your mother passed?"

"Two, I think." I couldn't remember. I had seen photos of her, had all of her and my father's scrapbooks in storage, but at this point it was hard to separate my true memories from pictures I'd seen of the two of us.

"You were very young," he said softly, those sweet, dark eyes of his missing nothing.

"Yeah, I was," I rushed out, nervous, because I wanted him to like me and I was worried I was blowing it but also thought I owed him the truth and not the sugar-coated version of who I was. "And because she died, my dad needed more help than normal parents do, and so I'm really not sure if you want me to be the one who—"

"Well, I think that perhaps since you missed out on having a true childhood, having a redo with my girls might do you a lot of good."

I'd missed that he was insane when I walked in the door. "I dunno about that," I said, coughing softly. "I wouldn't wanna mess up."

His attention remained focused on me, so I plowed on.

"Which is why my plan was to take care of all the other crap you've got going on so you can focus all your attention on your girls," I said cheerfully, and the *ta-dah* was implied. Clearly, I would be doing him a favor.

He nodded. "Which would be marvelous, except that where I'm failing right now is doing all the things I'm supposed to do for them in addition to my regular job, plus serving on the board of Darrow, plus this three-ring circus of a wedding."

His nuptials needed a ringmaster was what he was telling me.

"The day-to-day running around is where I'm failing," he said, sounding sad.

"Like how?" I pushed, wanting to know.

He shrugged. "You don't want to hear all my—"

"No, I really do," I assured him.

He stared at me, and it would have been unnerving, but I read it on his face—he was deciding about me just as his daughter had.

Quick breath. "All right, so two days ago, I was at a board of directors meeting, and even though I left on time—which everyone on the board was peeved about—I got stuck in traffic coming home and was late to get my kids."

"So you need a chauffeur for your girls is what you're telling me."

"Among other things, yes," he admitted, his grin almost embarrassed. "Because if I could have you sit on that board instead of me, I'd be thrilled, but that's simply not possible."

"Why don't you just quit?"

"Because then they could take the company away from the girls, and I don't want that."

"Why not?"

"Well, for one, the money I make there will send them both to college someday, which is vital, and it's also their legacy. Darrow is the company their grandfather started, so I want it to stay in the family because it's what Andrea wanted."

Which all made sense except that it seemed to be making him miserable. "Is it more what she wanted for you and the girls, specifically, or about the land?"

"She wanted the land to be protected."

I squinted at him. "Seems to me that if you gave the land to the state of Montana on the stipulation that it be turned into a park—I mean, wouldn't that solve all your problems?"

"It couldn't be mined that way, no, but neither could it be used by the ranchers who let their cattle graze on it now," he pointed out. "Plus, the federal government might be able to come in and overturn the designation of state park status and allow the land to be strip mined."

"I see." I sighed, giving him a hint of a smile. "So you're protecting it for your wife because that's what she wanted."

"Yes."

"And so Cahill is your best bet long-term, then."

"I believe so, yes."

"Which is why the merger," I concluded logically.

"Exactly."

How did I ask any more when it was none of my business?

"You find this antiquated."

I'd been staring at the toe of my right brogue boot and not at his sharp-angled face, but when he made the statement, my eyes returned to him.

"Arranged marriages still occur in this day and age, Brann," he murmured, and my name sounded rich and warm, almost like a caress coming out of his mouth.

"Yeah, but not for trees and cattle," I said, shrugging.

"I suspect for much less in certain parts of the world."

"Yeah, but not in Montana," I said, scowling at him.

"Regardless, Lydia is very nice, and she's invested in the growth of the town and in being a caretaker of the community."

He sounded so logical, and yes, she sounded great, but it was still not a good enough reason to marry her.

"The marriage is smart," he said, and I had a feeling that maybe I wasn't the one he was trying to convince. "It's for the best."

"I didn't say anything."

"No," he agreed. "But you're judging me."

"I'm not," I said honestly. "Only you know what's best for your girls."

He leaned on the counter, watching me. "We're friends already, Lydia and I, which is an excellent starting point for any long-term relationship."

"Sure."

He shook his head and huffed out a breath. "Why in the world am I standing here trying to convince you?"

"I have no idea."

His self-deprecating smile wrinkled the laugh lines in

the corner of his eyes, and I felt an utterly unexpected flutter in my stomach. "You're very easy to converse with."

"Not normally," I told him, being honest, having already surprised myself that I was listening and not talking over him. I had a bad habit of doing that, of telling people what I thought was wrong with them.

"Oh, no?"

"I've been called self-absorbed."

He chuckled. "Really? Do we find that in our military? Self-absorption?"

"You're funny," I assured him, hoping the sarcasm was there instead of the weird tremble of want in my voice.

It was already important that he liked me.

"Well, anyway...." He sighed, making himself another cup of coffee. "The marriage is for business reasons, yes, but it will help my girls and me, and no matter what they tell you, they both need another person in their lives besides their father."

"Well, sure," I said, because of course that made sense. "When one parent gets tired, the other takes over and vice-versa. If you can't pick up the kids, then your partner does. That's how it works, right?"

He nodded as he turned back around to face me instead of going to the refrigerator to pull out more vanilla creamer.

"Can I ask why you never hired anyone before?"

"You mean why did it take the sheriff in the town I live in to suggest to my soon-to-be father-in-law that I hire someone?"

"Yeah," I said with a chuckle. "That would be the question."

"The short answer is, my girls weren't ready to have anyone who wasn't their mother in their home," he said honestly, his voice hitching with sadness and memory. "And

I wasn't about to push that, no matter how far under water I went."

"It would have been better in the long run, though."

"Yes, but at first it was too painful even having one of my sisters here, or my mother, and then later we just fell into this rut of making do. I think it's like when you get hurt and you figure out how to do things around your injury."

"I get that."

"We got used to things not working, being forgotten, or--"

"For example?"

"Well, like last week I was running late because I got caught behind an accident, and April was upset."

"Why?"

"It's the same old argument; she says I'm always late."

"And are you?"

"I am a lot, yes, as I told you earlier," he confessed, and I watched the way his shoulders fell and how he bit his bottom lip. "But that day was an uphill grind from start to finish, so when I got there, I offered her pizza to make up for it, which you should never do. It's better to accept whatever your child wants to dish out and not try to placate them."

"Pro tip," I said, winking at him.

His chuckle made me smile.

"Placating gets you nowhere because not only are they still upset but now they feel like they can't be honest. You've given them what they said they wanted so they'd get over it, and everything gets all bottled up."

"Seems legit."

"Oh, well, thank you," he teased with a roll of his eyes.

I shrugged and he laughed, and the sound, like he was actually enjoying himself with me, guard down, wicked grin, all warm and disheveled from sleep, sent a pulse of arousal straight to my cock.

Fuck.

I needed to run. I should have run. Because even though I was a retired SEAL, nothing in my life had prepared me for being in this house with this man and his children. Already I could tell they were going to change me.

He reached for me then and squeezed my arm and held on like he was holding me there, keeping me from flying back out the front door. It was gentle, friendly, and I had the fleeting thought that he could read my mind.

"What happened when you got to school?" I asked so I didn't stand there like an idiot and just stare into his eyes.

His hand tightened on my arm, and I felt bad because I knew it was him remembering something he didn't want to. "I told her starting this weekend that you'd be here to help me, and she said she didn't want to live with a stranger, and I told her she didn't have a choice and she'd be living with Lydia soon anyway, and then there were more words back-and-forth that weren't kind as we were both frustrated."

"I'm sorry."

"Yes, but that wasn't the end of it because I'd missed the underlying cause of her distress," he said, huffing out a breath. "When I finally turned around in my seat to look at her, I saw that she was about to cry."

I nodded for him to go on.

"And it hit me then, what day it was," he said hollowly, letting go of me, staring out the window and appearing absolutely stricken.

Shit.

"So I suggested we go by Mr. Arnello's," he whispered, "and pick up some flowers for her mother."

"Mom's birthday?" I offered.

His gaze met mine. "Yes."

"And she wanted to get there before the flower store and the cemetery closed."

"Yes," he rasped, and I heard the pain in the way his voice cracked.

"Did you make it?" I asked because that would move the conversation along and hopefully get him out of the guilt pit he'd fallen into.

"We did."

"Good." I reached out, took hold of his shoulder, and squeezed gently.

"I need to be a better father," he told me.

I was thinking that just him, worrying about everything like he did, made him better than a lot of fathers I'd met in my life.

"I really appreciate you being here to help me," he told me, his hand covering mine.

He was the kind of man who wasn't afraid to touch, and they were a rare breed. So many men didn't think to, and others were afraid to. But not Emery Dodd.

When his daughter finally reappeared and stepped around him to offer the hair ties to me, he let go so I could give her all my attention.

"That took forever," he griped at her playfully. "Perhaps you need an organizer in your bathroom. What are your thoughts?"

"Like the one I'm supposed to be using?" She made a face. "Is that where you're going with this?"

"That's precisely where I'm going," he said, bending to kiss her.

She slipped an arm around his neck, kissed him back, and then when he straightened, she took hold of my callused hand and tugged.

"Where am I going?"

"You have to sit down."

"Okay," I said quickly, taking a seat on the bench on one side of the kitchen table, the chairs on the other, just as worn.

It was funny, because normally I was a fixer, a crisis manager, I was a retired Navy SEAL, for crissakes, but now, here in Ursa, in this scenario, I was, in fact, the damn nanny.

"Hell," I grumbled under my breath, and Emery, because he heard me, couldn't stifle his chuckle as Olivia stepped in close to me, between my parted legs, and turned sideways to give me access to her hair.

"I'm Olivia Dodd, but you can call me Ollie. Everybody does."

"Can I ask a question?"

"Yeah," she answered as I began separating her hair at the part down the middle before taking the wide-tooth comb she passed me.

"Do you like to be called Ollie?"

She turned her head to me as her sister, April, walked into the room. "No," she told me. "I like to be called Livi, but only Mommy called me that."

"Sure. But you miss it?"

Quick nodding.

"So we could try it out, and if it gets weird, you say 'Brann, knock it off,' and I'll call ya Ollie like everybody else."

She was quiet, her gaze faraway for a moment, considering my words, I could tell, and then the big brown doe eyes were back on my face. "Yeah, okay, let's do that."

"All right, then."

Emery caught his breath, and when I checked him, his

hand was shaking so hard he had to put the cup down for a moment.

"You okay?" I asked.

He cleared his throat. "You're very straightforward, and whereas I've been afraid to ask certain things, you're not."

"If you don't ask, how do you ever know anything?"

"Very true." He sighed. "And very wise."

I didn't know about that. I was possibly the most opposite of smart he'd ever meet, but I'd take the compliment.

She turned her head, and I got to work making perfect round balls of her hair, passing her back the comb, because of course I didn't need it to basically make her hair into a giant snarl. It was going to be a pain to comb out later, but I could help with that too. The fact that she was letting me help her was the important thing.

"You're gonna have to help her take those down after," her sister informed me, walking into the room, almost snarling, pissed off for whatever reason.

"Of course," I agreed affably, turning to her and smiling, purposely overdoing it with the cheerfulness. "I'm Brann. Who're you?" I asked, even though I knew.

She squinted. "April. Duh."

Emery cleared his throat. "Honey, we don't—"

"Dude, I just got here," I told her, switching to annoyed that fast, glaring back. "Could you be any ruder?"

Her eyes got big, and her mouth dropped open in surprise.

I laughed at her, on purpose, loudly, and waggled my eyebrows as her eyes narrowed. She was pissed.

Emery remained silent, which made sense. He was probably deciding whether to hit me or fire me. I was being douchey to his kid, after all.

"Don't catch flies," I warned her, pushing it because that

was how I was made, and Olivia cracked up, putting both hands on the adorable round balls on top of her head and beaming up at me.

"You're pushing April's buttons," she said with an evil cackle.

"Awesome," I said wickedly, grinning for good measure before giving April an exaggerated wink. When I turned to look at Emery, he appeared bemused. "You realize, of course, I might not be nanny material."

"I don't think that's going to be an issue," he replied softly.

"I gotta go put on my uniform," Olivia announced. "Are you coming to my soccer game?"

"Can we eat right after?" I whined, which coaxed a smile from Emery. "I'm starving."

"Yeah, we always get pancakes if I play in the morning."

"Awesome," I told her, because it was my go-to word at times, and then turned back to her father. "This is your last chance to send me packin'."

"Not on your life."

"Okay, then, I'm gonna go get my bag outta the car. Can you show me where to put my stuff when I come back in?"

He looked from me to April, still standing there fuming, hands clenched into fists, trying to shoot lasers out of her eyes to turn her new nanny, me, to dust, then to Olivia, and finally back. When he smiled warmly, I felt something unclench in my chest, like the very last knot had been undone, and my whole body relaxed.

"Yes, Brann, I certainly will."

"I'll go with you," Olivia offered, her voice breaking our silent communion, her hand slipping into mine like it was the most natural thing in the world.

We went together to the car, and when I came back in,

Olivia still holding my hand, I flashed my gun case to Emery as we reached the kitchen, needing to remind him that it was coming into his house. He had been made aware of it, of course, and had only agreed to the presence of the weapon because of the combination-lock safe.

"Show him his room, Ollie," he directed his daughter.

"Come on, Brann," she said, tugging on my hand.

I was led out of the kitchen and down a short hall to the first room on the right. It was as warm as the rest of the house, done in earth tones, all mahogany, cream, and sepia.

"I gotta pee," I lied to Olivia, and she gave me an exaggerated wink, which was ridiculous and made me smile as she peeled away from me and waited as I closed the door to the room.

Walking to the closet, I pulled my Glock 19 out of the locked gun case and then placed it on the top shelf so neither of the girls would ever know it was there. Normally I wore a shoulder holster, but since I would be walking around a sleepy little suburban town, I put on my ankle holster instead. I had to carry the weapon, but I didn't need to alert anyone—especially the girls—that I was.

"Geez, Brann, how long does it take to pee?" Olivia groused from the other side of the door, which was hysterical as it hadn't been even a minute. "We're burning daylight out here!"

She cackled as she said the last, which made me smile as I bolted for the door.

FOUR

Emery drove, and as we pulled away from the curb, I had to move the seat back in the Toyota 4Runner, change the position of the drop of the belt, and then, finally, after all that maneuvering, I was comfortable.

"Lydia's gonna have to put all that back when she rides with us," April said snidely.

"Not sorry," I baited her, turning to look at her as she bumped back in her seat and crossed her arms to sulk.

"Why are you here?" she snapped at me.

"To help your father," I answered before flashing her my patented shit-eating grin, the one that most recently had prodded a Chicago PD patrol officer to take a swing at me, and before that, an Army Ranger in Kabul.

A moment later, she kicked the back of my seat.

"April," Emery scolded her.

"What? It was an accident."

I snorted.

"Really?" Emery asked me, but when I turned to look at him, I noted his grin.

He knew the score just as well as I did. She was testing

me, seeing what I'd take, and that was okay. He was clearly letting me know with his lack of interference that he was leaving things alone for us to figure out.

When we stopped in front of another house, April got out before Olivia, both of them bolting for the front door to pick up another one of the players on Olivia's team.

"I can be a grown-up if you want," I rushed out, knowing I only had a few minutes. "I can be more careful with April, and I won't—"

"No," Emery said quickly, hand on my thigh for emphasis. "I'm thrilled she's even speaking to you. All I've received are grunts and shrugs and rolling eyes for—what—months, except for on her mother's birthday." He choked, swallowing down his sadness. "I know that the wedding is painful for her, but it's good for both companies and the town and... good for my girls in the long run. They need help; I'm not enough."

"I think you're plenty."

He shook his head. "That's very kind of you to say, but I —April was five when her mother died, so her memories of Andrea are so strong, which is good, but I know the fact that the marriage is imminent is carving her up inside." He stopped suddenly, taking a breath.

"Tell me."

He explained that her anger and melancholy, though always strong, had become something she was nearly choking on. What was even worse was that every time he tried approaching her, she shut down. He so wanted to talk to her, but she was having nothing to do with the topic, or him. She had become so distant. It was getting harder and harder for him to bridge the gap.

"But she's responding to you." He finally turned to look at me, his eyes so full of a mixture of hope and pain that it took everything in me not to lean sideways into his space and kiss him.

He was hurting. I could fix it. Or, more to the point, I could normally fix it if the guy who was grieving was gay. There had been many times when I'd used my body to soothe and nurture, and it was funny, but guys who would never think of accepting a hug would give anything under the pretense of it just being sex. But that wouldn't work with Emery because he wouldn't be receptive to being mauled. For once, the quick fix wasn't an option. I would have to use my brain instead.

"I don't want to lose my daughter to grief, but me bending over backward, turning myself inside out, isn't accomplishing anything productive."

I nodded because I had no idea what else to do.

"The older she gets, the more closed off she becomes, but mere moments with you, and you're right under her skin," he said hoarsely, and his smile was tremulous and his chin wobbled.

And it hit me that this was a much bigger deal than me baiting his kid to react and thus talk.

"I'd love it if she opened up and talked to you—or even better, me—but I'll take what I can get."

"I'm not a miracle worker," I said flatly, because I wouldn't allow him to pin any type of hope on me or think something great could happen just by having me around. The opposite was much more likely. I was a good soldier, I could be counted on under pressure, and if lives were in danger, if people were shooting at you, I was the guy you wanted. But for me to be an emotional anything wasn't likely. Why Jared thought I was the one who should come out to Montana and be the nanny was beyond me. I had to wonder about him. What in my skill set said "good with kids"? How did he get caregiver from me being the guy you wanted in a firefight?

"I know that." Emery sighed, returning my focus to him. "But she's not grunting or ignoring you, so to me this is a sign of life, and I couldn't be more thrilled."

I really needed to reiterate that I was not a cure.

As his girls, and a third—Taylor, Emery told me—climbed into the SUV, I turned and looked out at the road. I had to wonder how the other guys at Torus did this job year in and year out and never got involved. I was quiet for the rest of the drive, trying to figure out what I was going to say to Jared to get the hell out of Ursa.

Once we reached the park and Emery found a spot in the crowd of other cars, I got out and watched Olivia throw off her seat belt and try and leap down onto the gravel parking lot. The problem was that her feet got tangled in the straps of her soccer bag, and she would have pitched forward and fallen, but I was there and caught her easily.

"Ollie!" Emery shouted.

"It's okay," I soothed him, leaning sideways so I could see him and make eye contact. "I got her. No worries."

He nodded, took a deep breath, and then turned away from me and bumped his forehead into the steering wheel. "Thank you," he said without moving, eyes closed.

I had no idea why something so small would shake him up so badly, but thinking it was a good idea to give him a minute or two, I gave my attention to the little girl in my arms.

"You all right?" I asked her.

"You didn't let me fall," she said as I carried her out of the way of an enormous puddle and put her down. "That was awesome."

It didn't escape me that I'd used the word awesome a bit

ago and now she'd said it. It was pretty damn cute. "You're easy to catch."

"But I'm big."

I snorted, thinking that her slight forty-five pounds—she couldn't have been any more than that—could have been any kind of strain. "You should slow down a little bit, huh?"

She made a noise and nodded. "That's what Daddy says."

"Daddy's right," I told her, grimacing. "It sucks, but he is."

She put both her hands around my left bicep. "You're pretty strong."

"You can be too. We'll work out together in the morning."

"And why would I wanna be strong?"

I squinted at her. "Why *wouldn't* you, is the better question."

She stared up at me, and I crossed my arms and stared back.

"Fine," she said, aggrieved, like she was doing me a favor, rolling her eyes for emphasis.

"Good."

"You know I get up early," she warned, shooting me a daring grin.

I shrugged. "That's all right. You can wake me up. I need to be gettin' up earlier anyway." Which was the truth. I'd been slacking off a bit lately, but I'd only been out of the Navy for five months, so I was still figuring out what my new normal was going to be.

"Yeah? You promise?"

"'Course," I agreed, bending to tie her right soccer cleat. "So what do you do out there?"

"I'm a forward."

"I have no idea what that is, but I'll watch and figure it out."

Enthusiastic nodding followed. "Can you get my bag?"

After rushing back to her still open door, I grabbed her FC Barcelona duffel from the floor and then closed her door. When I was standing beside her again, she slipped her little hand into mine and led me around the SUV to her father and April.

Immediately, Emery put his hand on Olivia's shoulder. "Please slow down, Ollie. I don't want you to break your arm again, okay?"

It all made sense then, his alarm, his near nervous breakdown in the front seat. If my kid broke her arm the last time she got out of the car, I might be a mess as well.

She smiled up at him. "I know. I'm sorry I was going too fast again."

"It's okay," he said, touching her cheek for a moment. I saw him notice her holding my hand, and when his gaze met mine, I was surprised at the concern I saw there.

"Can we just go already," April grumbled.

When we arrived at the field, Emery set up April's chair, which she plopped down into and immediately flipped open her sketchbook and started drawing. He readied Olivia's next. The last one, he opened and offered to me.

"Oh, that's nice of you, but I've been driving since Thursday, so standing is awesome."

His smile was warm, and I watched him deflate and relax. "Well, if you want it, it's there."

"I appreciate that."

I watched as he put on Olivia's shin guards, then sent her over to the coach. I stood beside him as the girls all put their hands together in a circle, yelled "fight, fight, fight"—maybe not super appropriate—and rushed the field.

After a beat, he said, "Ollie's going to get attached."

I turned to him. "I'm sorry?"

His brows furrowed as he stared at me. "Ollie. I can already tell, she's going to get quite attached to you."

He made it sound like a terminal illness.

"Because you'll be there, in our home, and she'll see you every day, and you're already getting along. She's going to develop feelings and when you leave, that will be hard."

"And what would you like me to do about that?" I asked him honestly. "Should I be a prick to her?"

He snorted. "No."

"Should I leave?"

"You're not going anywhere." He was adamant.

"Then?"

"I just have to deal with the fallout," he said miserably.

"Sorry," I teased him, trying to lighten the mood, "but when you're this charming, there's not a lot to do about your daughter falling in love with me."

"Are you always this helpful?" he asked as he scrubbed his eyes with the heels of his hands, rough about it.

I didn't answer, instead waiting while he took a breath and then gave me a trace of a smile. "If it's any comfort, I think April hates me."

"Oh, well, thank God for small favors."

I shrugged and he put a hand on my shoulder and left it there.

"Let's talk about something else."

"Like?"

He was still for a moment. "You seem really young to be retired from the Navy," he said to me but turned his head to watch Olivia bolt down the field.

"Yeah, well, I'm not all that young. I'm thirty-two."

"Really?" he said, giving me his attention again. "I would have said you were still in your twenties."

"That wasn't in my file from Torus?"

"No, but why would it? Your age doesn't, in fact, tell me a thing about you. Your life experiences are the important part. But really, I would have never guessed thirty-two."

"Well, it's true. I'm all grown-up and everything."

His smile made his whole face light up, and I felt a warm ball in the pit of my stomach. "So why did you leave the Navy?"

Some people wondered, most didn't, until they found out I was a SEAL, and then they didn't understand why, after earning my trident, I would leave after the six year contract was fulfilled. But I had been in the service for fourteen years; it was enough. "It was time. I know a lot of guys who are SEALs who reenlist, but I was done."

He was waiting for more.

"It's not like the movies," I assured him.

"No, I'm sure, but still. It seems like once you've made the commitment to begin with that the staying would be easier."

People who didn't know thought that seeing things got easier with time. It didn't. I had contemplated staying because I'd started to believe my own hype, that no one could do the job as well as me. My ego had fooled me into thinking that men would die—men I knew, men who I called friends—if I wasn't there. And I knew that for certain people, it was true. I had come across many individuals, on the line and off, who the unit would suffer without. But that wasn't me. I was steady, yes, commended often for being calm under pressure, but not the linchpin of the unit. When it came time to reenlist, I was smart enough to know my limitations. Of course, I had no idea at the time how long it was going to actually take to feel safe in my own skin once I was back in the world. That constant readiness just didn't disappear overnight. Waiting for the sky to fall, always checking, was getting old fast.

"Brann?" Emery prodded me. Apparently I'd been in my own head too long.

"It's a life-and-death job, and if you're beat-up over losing friends and seeing strangers on the worst days of their lives... well, it's best to go out on a record you can be proud of and not let anybody down."

"Of course," he murmured, and his hand, which was still on my shoulder, fell away. I missed the heat from his palm immediately.

I was touched that he didn't ask any more questions like so many people did. They weren't interested in me, of course, but instead in lurid details that I could never share.

There were noises behind us then, and we both turned to find a stunning blonde woman, her hair falling thick and wavy to the middle of her back, her enormous sky-blue eyes trained on Emery. She was in an oversized off-white shawl-collar sweater with a camel-colored wrap coat, knee-high brown leather lace boots, and leggings. The outfit, all effortless chic, was impressive as was her Hermès Birkin bag that I only knew about because I had loaned a buddy of mine the cash to buy his wife one for their tenth wedding anniversary. I was betting this woman, who I assumed was Lydia Cahill, had one in every color.

"Oh, Lydia, you didn't have to come," Emery told his fiancée, confirming her identity for me as he took hold of her hand.

It wasn't lost on me that he didn't call her *honey* or *love* or *darling*, but maybe that wasn't their thing.

"I want her to start liking me," she said, smiling at him. "Of course I'm going to come."

He nodded, taking a step sideways, closer to me. "Well, you definitely don't have to come for pancakes afterward. I know you don't love the Kitchen Sink."

Had to be the restaurant.

"Yes, but you all… do," she said, her gaze sliding over me. "I'm sorry, have we met?"

I offered her my hand. "No. I'm Brann Calder. Your father hired me to help Mr. Dodd with his—"

"Emery," he corrected me, hand between my shoulder blades.

I took a second to wonder if he had any idea that he was gazing at her and easing closer to me with every passing moment.

"To help Emery with his girls until the wedding," I corrected.

"You're the nanny?" she said, grinning. "Well, my goodness, this is quite the surprise."

"And why is that?"

"You seem like something far more glamourous than a nanny, Mr. Calder," she said, her eyes narrowing as she gazed at me. "My money would have been on race car driver or something equally dangerous."

I wasn't stupid. I knew people liked looking at me, and I had traded on that a million times when I was younger and only stopped once I was eighteen and safely enlisted in the Navy. Clearly, Lydia Cahill was enjoying the view, and that was okay. It was just kind of crappy with the guy she was going to marry standing right beside me. Not that he noticed, of course, far too involved in Olivia's game.

"You look like you work out, Mr. Calder," she said, letting out a quick huff of air. "I'm sorry to say there's not a decent gym in this one-horse town, so if you'd like to use the equipment at our home, please feel free."

"I appreciate that, thank you."

"We have a pool as well."

"And tennis courts," Emery chimed in absently, reaching for the leather jacket I was wearing over my gray hoodie, and tugging. "Look how fast she is."

Olivia was tearing down the sideline, the ball in front of her, going where she was driving it, and headed toward the goal. At the last second, though, another girl plowed into her side, knocking her off her feet and down into the soggy wet ground.

There was whistle blowing and yelling, and Emery bolted onto the field at the same time a man from the other side of the field rushed out as well.

"April, what did your father say about drawing those kinds of pictures?"

Both Lydia and I turned to find a woman standing over April, who had closed her sketchbook quickly.

"I think she likes getting grounded," Lydia said to the woman, smiling at her before she moved over beside April's chair. "Let me see," she said, and her tone was forceful but not sharp.

April stared up at her, eyes flat but not moving. When Lydia reached for the sketchbook, April stood up and put it behind her.

"Sweetie," Lydia began gently, switching gears. "I just—"

"You're not my mother," April said icily. "You'll never be my mother, so no. You don't get to make fun of my drawings."

Lydia's lips pressed together tightly. "I wasn't going to--"

"You don't get to see them," she finished flatly.

"That's fine. We'll see what your father says."

"No!" someone yelled.

Glancing back at the field, I was surprised when a man shoved the referee, who had a red card in his hand.

Emery put a hand up to stop the guy from pushing the referee again, and when he did, the man grabbed his arm, twisted, and put him on his knees.

"Call 911," I snapped at Lydia, who started digging into her high-end bag for her phone as I darted out onto the field.

I ran right up to the stranger and swept his legs out from under him, which immediately broke his grip on Emery. He was dumped ass-first into the dirt; it wasn't quite mud yet but would be soon. We were probably on the driest patch on the field.

"You son of a—"

"Kids," I snarled at the stranger as I helped Emery to his feet. "Watch your mouth, or you're gonna get hurt on top of talking to the police."

"The fu—"

"Kids," I almost yelled that time, turning to Emery. "Are you all right?"

"Yes, fine," he breathed out, hand on my forearm, shivering a bit.

I checked on the referee then, and he too was shaken but unhurt, and we all heard the siren at the same time.

I was impressed with how fast the response time was but then realized that it was doubtful Lydia had gotten through to the dispatcher that fast.

I glanced over at Emery.

"I'm sure someone just ran over there," he said, answering the question I hadn't voiced. "The sheriff's station is right across the street on the left."

"You had someone get Thomas?" The guy on the ground

was fuming, but when he tried to get up, I put my foot on his wrist, not pressing down but exerting enough pressure so he couldn't move it. "The hell are you doing?"

"Stay down," I ordered as Emery picked up his daughter and hugged her.

"Are you okay, sweetie?"

"I have dirt in my hair," she lamented, "and my uniform is gross again."

"It's always gross after soccer," Emery said, chuckling.

Olivia nodded, like yeah, maybe, before she buried her face in the side of his neck as he rubbed her back.

Moments later the deputy, David Reed—whose name I knew from the file—not the sheriff, walked out onto the field, and the referee began immediately yelling that he'd been attacked without provocation.

"How dare you attack this man in front of all these kids," the deputy accused Emery, jaw clenched as he pulled his handcuffs from his belt. "Put down your daughter and—"

"Hey," I snapped at him, grabbing his bicep and yanking him around to face me. And yes, I knew that touching an officer of the law was a no-no, but what the fuck was he doing? Plus, this was a small town in Montana and *not* Chicago, and truly, if things went sideways, I could drop the deputy just as I had the man who attacked Emery. "Do you see me right here with my foot on this piece of crap or not?"

Reed was furious, and it was there in his flushed face, his narrowed eyes, and his right hand that was on his gun. And no, he hadn't unsnapped it from its holster, and he couldn't pull it on me without doing so, but still, he was showing me he was ready.

What the hell? Anger issues much? That was exactly what I wanted in my law enforcement—hair-trigger tempers.

"Are you hearing me, Deputy?" I asked flatly, not

backing down, my voice rising, ready to put him on the ground as well if he even thought about pulling his gun on me.

He took a breath and turned his head to the referee. "What happened?"

"As I was trying to tell you," the man stressed, pointing at the ground. "Mr. Barr attacked me after his daughter nearly crippled Olivia Dodd!"

"She did not, and get this psycho off me, Reed!" Barr said as he struggled like a tipped-over tortoise under my boot.

The deputy turned back to me. "Could you let him up?"

Once I did, I moved so I was standing beside Emery, ready to shield him if the deputy got weird again.

"And you are?" Reed asked me once he had Mr. Barr back on his feet.

"Brann Calder," I answered, squinting at him. "The sheriff might have told you about me as he was informed I'd be here."

It took him a second, and then his face brightened. "Oh, yes, the bodyguard."

Not quite, but I'd take it at the moment. "Yeah."

He cleared his throat nervously, adjusting his duty belt. "Sorry about this, Calder. It's nice to meet you, and clearly it was lucky you were here."

It certainly was, I thought, but said nothing, knowing my propensity to add a sarcastic remark wasn't always appreciated. "Mr. Barr needs to be cuffed and taken to jail, unless no one's pressing charges," I directed the deputy.

He looked over at the referee, who nodded.

"Really, Jonas," Barr jeered at the referee. "You fu—"

"I'm serious about any words you're thinking of using," I warned Barr, my voice sharp, cutting. "I'll put you back on the ground in front of all these people."

Thankfully, he shut up and allowed Reed to cuff him without any further incident. It didn't escape my notice, though, as Reed led Barr away, that he hadn't said a word of apology to Emery. As I turned to him, Emery shook his head before telling Olivia to go with me. She leaned away from her father and toward me, arms open.

Taking her gently, I smiled as she wrapped her arms around my neck, and I carried her back to the sidelines.

"Oh, Ollie," Lydia cooed over her, touching her cheek and back. "Are you hurt?"

Olivia laid her head on my shoulder and just held on to me, tight, as I patted her back, and only then did I notice that April was sitting in her chair, head down, shaking, and the woman I'd seen earlier had her sketchbook and was leafing through it.

Never, ever, had I been diplomatic in the least.

Stalking over to the woman, I snatched the sketchbook out of her hands. "The hell do you think you're doing? That's private property."

Her gasp was loud. "How dare you take something out of my hands!"

"How dare you take something from a little girl!" I fired back, loudly, which caused her to take a step back and for Olivia, still in my arms, to squeeze my neck. I patted her back gently to reassure her, and it was sweet how she returned the motion, seeking to comfort me as well. "Did you steal anything else?" I barked even louder.

"I didn't steal any—"

"The hell you didn't!" I roared, and that time she retreated several steps, because if she thought she could be loud, she'd never yelled over open ground downrange in a firefight. I could get my voice to really carry when I wanted.

"What's going on?" Emery demanded as he was suddenly there, stepping between me and the older woman.

"Who is this man?" she snapped, pointing at me.

"He's the nanny," Emery explained, sounding absurd, as I pivoted and strode back over to April to thrust the sketchbook out to her.

She lifted her head, and I saw how red and puffy her eyes were. Seeing the sketchbook, she took it from me gently —didn't snatch it like I was expecting—and then continued to stare up at me, almost confused.

"Next time just come to me, and I won't let anyone take anything from you, all right?"

"Really?" she asked quietly, her voice strained and timid.

"Yes, really," I snapped so she'd know—from how irritated I was at her second-guessing me—that I was telling the truth.

"Okay," she murmured, then added, "Brann."

Taking a breath, I stood beside her chair, guarding her, glancing around, making sure no one even thought about coming near her or Olivia, who was still squeezing my neck tight. "Check through your book and make sure it's all in one piece."

She was quiet for a few moments, leafing through the pages. "I think it's fine."

"Good."

Emery came up beside me moments later.

"Sorry," I muttered under my breath as I continued to rub Olivia's back. "It's quite possible that I don't have the right temperament to be a nanny."

He coughed softly. "Perhaps not," he agreed, "but you certainly have the protective instincts."

I had no idea if that was good or bad.

FIVE

After Mr. Barr's daughter was thrown out of the game, the opposing team had to forfeit because they didn't have enough kids, so we got to go for pancakes earlier than expected.

Lydia wanted to join us at the restaurant, so Emery and Olivia rode with her in her Mercedes, and I drove the Toyota. April went with me, which I was surprised about. She sat in her same seat, behind the driver's, and stayed silent as I followed Emery through town.

"Just because you got back my book doesn't mean I'm gonna like you," she said once we reached the restaurant. Emery parked near the front while I looked for a spot farther away, as I needed a few minutes to sort things out with his oldest.

"I didn't think it would," I told her honestly. "And I didn't do it for you anyway."

"You didn't?"

"Nope. I hate bullies, plain and simple."

She sucked in a breath. "You think Mrs. Dabney is a bully?"

I was going to say, *hell yeah*, but since I knew squat about the woman, I had to refrain and change my wording a bit. "She sure acted that way, didn't she?"

April nodded quickly.

"Who even is she?"

"She's the school librarian, and she won't let me check out books anymore."

"I'm sorry?"

"She said my privileges were suspended."

"The hell for? What'd you do?"

"Why do you think it's all on me?"

I grunted. "Yeah, all right. Two sides and all that." But she didn't start talking, and more and more seconds ticked by. "So are you gonna tell me, or should we play charades?"

She took a breath and I heard the wobble in her voice. "She said that until I stopped bringing my sketchbook to school that she wouldn't let me borrow any more books."

"Did you tell your dad?"

"No."

"And why not?"

"Because he told me not to draw what I'm drawing too, and if he knew she was mad about that and that's why she won't let me use the library, then maybe I'd be in trouble."

"I think he'll be madder at her for not letting you read, but that's cool. If you don't wanna get into this with him, I'll go talk to her on Monday."

"But she already doesn't like you, and when she sees you, she'll just call school security on you."

"And then I'll have a talk with your principal, and we'll see who wins."

She was quiet for so long I thought maybe she was doing something else. "You'll talk to my principal?" Her voice was tiny and nasally, like maybe she'd started to cry again.

"Of course. You have freedom of expression to draw whatever the hell you want. Those are your First Amendment rights, so she can kiss your ass."

Her gasp made me smile.

"She thinks she can get away with treating you like that because you didn't say anything. That's how bullies win, when no one speaks up."

"It is?"

"Yep," I said adamantly. "You have to stick up for yourself in all things. It's necessary for life."

"But what if I'm not enough?"

"Then you tell someone," I explained to her. "Like in this instance, you should have told your father as soon as that happened."

"I was scared."

"'Cause you didn't want him to get mad."

"Yeah."

"Well, guess what, he's gonna get mad at you a lot in your life, and I bet you'll get pissed at him too. That's part of living, yeah? The important thing to remember is that he loves you and he's on your side no matter what. It's the whole parent gig."

"Gig?"

"Just—I'm having a moment, all right? Don't interrupt."

She snickered behind me, which was a good sign.

"Next time, you come clean with him, all right?"

"Okay."

"Okay, good. Now, in the meantime, we're gonna fix this shit on Monday."

A snort of laughter behind me made me smile. "You can't use bad words in front of me. I'm only eight."

"Shit's bad?"

Listening to her giggle was even better.

"Fine," I groused, getting more annoyed by the second at how many cars there were in the damn parking lot. More people meant more orders, which meant more waiting between me and the food I so desperately craved. I needed to eat. I could feel my blood sugar dropping, and I didn't want the headache that came with that. "Why the hell are all these people in this goddamn parking lot?"

"It's a really good restaurant," she offered in explanation.

I grunted as I maneuvered around cars.

"Brann?"

"Yeah?"

"What if Daddy gets mad at me about my drawings?"

"Then he gets mad," I told her, shrugging. "It'll pass, and you have no control over how he feels. I mean, if you didn't clean your room and he got mad, I'd say, dude, clean your stupid room so your father won't be bummed out."

"I do clean my room."

"Follow what I'm saying," I directed her, enunciating the words.

"You mean drawing pictures is different from not drying the dishes or brushing my teeth or like you said, cleaning my room."

"Correct."

"So if he doesn't like my art, then he doesn't like my art, and there's nothing I can do to change that because I can't just stop drawing."

"Exactly."

"Okay, I get it now."

"The important thing is that you spoke up and defended yourself."

"Sure."

I finally found a spot and parked the car. I then turned

around in my seat to look at her. "Can I see your drawings so I know what I'm fighting for on Monday morning?"

She passed me her open sketchbook, and the first thing I saw was a woman bleeding all over the floor. When I flipped through the pictures, which were really good for any age, I immediately saw the theme. It had to be her mother, over and over, dying in lots of ways that included absolutely buckets of blood.

I lifted my gaze from the pages to her face. "You know an aortic dissection is all inside your body, right? Nothing comes out, like, no blood. It doesn't look like this at all."

She was listening intently, studying my face, trying to figure something out.

"I know you must've asked somebody what it was, and they told you a dissection is like a big cut, so you figured it meant blood all over the place, right?"

The smallest nod answered my question.

"An aortic dissection is different. There's nothing outside your body."

"Really?"

"Yeah," I apprised her, using the gentlest tone I could manage. It was heartbreaking that she was fumbling around in the darkness, trying to figure things out for herself. I could help her if she'd let me.

"Are you sure?"

"I am," I told her, unclipping my seat belt and turning all the way around. "I have a friend, he's a surgeon in Chicago, we can Skype him if you want, and he can tell you all about it."

She unclipped her seat belt and climbed over into the front seat, then sat facing me. "I tried to read stuff about what happened to my mom, but the books in the library that I checked out were hard to figure out, and I can't look it up on the internet because where I wanna go my dad has it all blocked."

I gestured at her. "Well, yeah, of course, 'cause you're eight."

"But every time I try and ask a question, people think I'm sad, and I *am* sad, but I'm not *just* sad anymore. I wanna know stuff."

"Of course you do."

She searched my face, making the same decisions about me that her sister had, whether to trust me or not, have faith in me or not. "Everyone tells me to be happy 'cause Mommy's in heaven, but I don't wanna talk about heaven. I need to know what happened. I wanna know if it hurt when she died. I wanna know if it took a long time and if she was super sad and if she was crying because she knew she was gonna die and knew she was gonna miss us."

I shook my head. "What if it makes you sadder when you find out the answers?"

"Don't I get to decide?"

"Nope," I replied honestly. "That's up to your dad because he's the grown-up and you're the kid. It's his job to tell you stuff, and your job to listen."

She shook her head. "But if he just tells me to wait 'til I'm older, then I'll be the same as I am now."

"And that's a valid argument, but he might want that."

"I want to talk to your friend."

"We'll ask and see what your father says," and then I continued quickly when she opened her mouth to protest. "I think he'll say yes, because he wants you to understand, but if he's maybe not ready, you gotta be okay with that."

"I'll try."

"Well, your dad's a teacher, right? He wants you to know stuff."

It was unnerving how hard she was staring at me, like she was trying to see inside my head and make a decision.

"I know you're sad, and you'll probably stay sad for a long time, but it's okay if you're not sometimes too, 'cause your mom would want to hear you laugh and stuff."

"I don't believe in heaven," she informed me. "I don't think she's up in the clouds staring down at me, waiting to hear me having fun."

"I don't either," I agreed. "But I do think she's in your heart, and I think she's around in the things you guys liked to do, and not like a ghost or something, but you know, with you."

Her eyes filled fast, and I was not ready for her to launch herself at me.

She hit me hard, and I had to scramble to grab her and had just enough time to tuck her tightly against my chest before the dam broke.

All I could do was hug her as she sobbed into my hoodie, loud, racking sobs that shook her small body hard. She couldn't breathe, and I was worried for a second that she was hyperventilating, but her air came back in a rush and with it more crying that sounded almost like screaming, as high-pitched and broken as it was.

She'd been holding things in for a while, and I knew I wasn't some kid whisperer. I was, instead, simply in the right place at the right time to give her a gentle push in the right direction. When Emery came up to the driver's side door, I shook my head so he wouldn't knock on the window. He leaned close, saw April in my arms as I rocked her, then nodded and walked back toward the entrance of the Kitchen Sink.

After long minutes, she finally lifted her head and looked at me.

Pulling Kleenex from the console between the seats, figuring, as a dad that Emery's car was well stocked, I got two, and put them to her nose so she could blow. The kid was not delicate at all. She blew a ton of mucus into the tissue, so much so that I had to get two more until she was done.

"Dude, you just blew a snot ball outta your nose," I said, laughing softly. "Holy crap, warn a guy next time, all right? That was disgusting."

She laughed then through fresh tears.

"We should go in and talk to your dad so then, if he gives us permission, we can talk to my buddy later this afternoon."

"Okay," she said nasally, all stuffed up.

"When we get inside, I'll walk you to the bathroom and you can splash cold water on your face, all right?"

"People will still know I was crying."

"You can borrow my sunglasses, and then nobody'll know. I always leave mine on whenever I'm hungover."

"What's hungover?"

"I'll tell you later," I promised, catching the irony in my response to her, rubbing my eyes as they watered. They felt like they were full of sand, a sure indication I needed more sleep. Resting in motels was hardly ever actually restful.

Inside, there was a line already, but we bypassed it, and I walked her to the bathroom and waited outside, thinking how great more coffee would be. Everything smelled good, and I didn't normally go in for breakfast.

"Excuse me."

Looking up, I squinted at the woman standing in front of me in a Green Bay Packers sweatshirt, gray leggings, and worn Nikes.

"I'm Denise Richmond," she said gently, holding out her hand. "I was at the soccer game."

I took her hand and forced a smile. "I'm sorry about that, but that guy was—"

"No," she said briskly, covering our joined hands with her other. "You misunderstand. Mr. Barr is a menace, and all of us cringe whenever we have to play that team because we never know how combative he's going to get. A year ago he came at my ex-husband after one of the games, so I was very appreciative of the way you stepped in to protect Emery today."

I was relieved and gave her a real smile as I withdrew my hand. "It was no big deal."

"Oh, believe me, it was; we all agree."

"We?"

She turned and waved at a table near the back, and four other women there lifted their hands and waved back.

"Got it," I said, chuckling as I returned the gesture.

"What's your name?" she asked me.

"Brann Calder. I'm Emery's nanny," I said, giving up on being anything else for the immediate future. "At least until he and Lydia Cahill get married."

She grunted, and all the happiness drained from her face. "Like that's good for anyone besides her father."

Well now, tell me what you really think?

"Anyway," she said, seemingly brushing her concern aside. "We hope to see you next Saturday as well. I think the game's a little later, so we all don't have to be up quite so early."

She added how good it was to meet me just as April came out of the bathroom. I thanked Denise before squatting down in front of the little girl.

"How ya feeling?"

She shrugged.

I pulled my sunglasses from the case I'd been carrying in the breast pocket of my leather jacket and put them on her.

"Can you see my eyes?" she asked from underneath my aviators.

"Nope."

"Thank you."

"You're welcome," I muttered. "Now, can we eat before I starve to death?"

She smiled at me, took my hand, and led me back toward the front. Halfway there, Olivia slipped around in front of me.

"The table is on the other side," she said cheerfully, grabbing hold of my free right hand and tugging.

I reached the table with a little girl on each side, and before I could pull out a chair, Olivia told me where to sit. Emery offered April one close to him, but she sat down beside me instead, and once in her chair, whispered for me to scooch her over.

Sliding her closer to me, I yawned, and then I picked up the menu to check my choices.

Olivia leaned into my side and pointed things out that I should have.

"Sweetie," Emery said, "maybe give Brann a second to look for himself."

"But Daddy, he's never been here, and what if he gets something gross like that corned beef hash you like. That would be terrible."

I snorted out a laugh and bent down behind the menu with her. "What's good, Livi?"

She pointed, explained how the French toast seemed like a good idea but tasted weird, and told me which syrup to get.

Once we put the menu down, I smiled at Emery, who, after a moment, smiled back.

"April," Lydia said, "you need to take off those sunglasses at the breakfast table."

"No, I'm sorry, she can't," I chimed in protectively. "And of course, normally she'd listen and do as you told her, but we had a thing in the car, and it would be crazy embarrassing for anyone to see her looking like she got punched in the face."

"I don't—"

"I'm betting she looks like an MMA fighter at the moment," Emery suggested, disarming his fiancée with a winsome smile, "so I think we should let it go, don't you?"

All eyes turned to Lydia.

"Oh, well, yes, we—okay."

"Perfect," he said, smiling at her before his eyes flicked to mine.

I mouthed thank-you.

He gave me a quick nod before leaning across the table. "April honey, do you want to go home?"

"No, Dad. I'm starving like Brann," she assured him, leaning against my arm. "But can I ask you a favor?"

"Of course, love," he replied with such love that I wondered how anyone carried that much affection around for another person. No one had sounded like that when they spoke to me. Not ever.

"Is it okay if me and Brann call his friend who's a doctor later on and talk to him about how Mom died?"

He wasn't ready for that, and I felt bad he was blindsided, but I didn't think she'd bring it up over breakfast. Though, honestly, I should have guessed, because it was on her mind, so of course she'd want to fix it as soon as possible.

He took several deep breaths and then looked at me. "We'll discuss it when we get home, but for now let's all just have a nice meal."

The death glare I got told me I was a dead man.

I was starting to think the odds of me getting a handle on the whole nanny thing were probably really not all that great.

SIX

Breakfast was delicious. I ate six pancakes, four eggs, and a pork chop, plus finally drank enough coffee to allow me to see straight once more. In the military you learned that no matter what else was going on, when you got the chance to eat, you ate. There was no question about that. So even though I knew the man was not pleased with me, I scarfed down my food.

Since Lydia had to go to the Glacier Park International Airport to pick up her maid of honor, who was spending lots of time with her before the wedding, she said she would call Emery later to coordinate dinner plans.

I stayed quiet, and when we got into the house, April passed me my sunglasses before I flopped down onto the couch. Emery sent Olivia to change and April to her room until he got done talking to me.

Once we were alone, once he checked to make sure there were no little people lingering in the doorway, he tore off his parka and rounded on me. I saw the clench of his jaw, the furrowed brows, and realized I was about to be fired.

"How dare you mention something like that to my daughter!" he yelled at me.

I stayed quiet.

"Before you make plans with them, offer any course of action, an alternative, a choice—anything at all—you discuss that with me first!"

"Yessir."

"April is much too young to be—"

"Oh, no."

"No?" he shouted back, incredulous.

He was livid, and my personal communication style was, as usual, not helping. "I mean—she's not too young to talk about death, and I beg your pardon, but I have to wonder if you've looked in that sketchbook lately."

"Of course I—"

"How long ago did you demand that she not draw in it anymore?"

"I didn't demand any—"

"She said you did."

He stared holes in me, and I felt like one of those dissected specimens in a museum exhibit, with the pins holding the skin open so everything inside was on display.

"You thought if she didn't keep drawing death that she'd heal, right?"

His lips parted, but no sound came out.

"You guys saw someone—some therapist—and they said that was best."

"Well, yes, she—yes," he rasped.

I made a face that I was sure must have looked pained. "It's not fixing anything for her not to be able to share how she's feeling with you."

"You don't know anything about me or my daughter," he said coolly.

It hurt to hear how angry he was and to know how fast he could turn on me, ready to expel me from his life without a moment's thought. But I was new, so I got it. I hadn't proven dick to him yet.

"You're not allowed to judge a situation you just walked into."

I nodded. "That's valid, you figuring that I'm talkin' out of my ass, but I know the sketchbook is all about her mom," I said flatly, trying to watch where I was treading but also wanting to explain myself like I normally didn't. It never bothered me if people thought the worst or if they assumed I was being stupid or thoughtless... usually.

Looking up at Emery pacing in front of me, I realized I wanted this man to have a better view of me. And maybe it was the girls—because I liked both of them already—but it could have also been that being around all three of them, Emery and his daughters, I found myself not anxious like I was most of the time. Ever since I'd left the Navy, I'd been waiting for the other shoe to drop. I kept thinking that today was the day something worse would happen than watching my friends die. But being in the Dodd house, that feeling of dread was replaced with calm. Jared always said being grounded, settled, was one of the best feelings in the world, and I had to wonder if this, now, was what he was talking about. The moment I'd walked through the front door, I'd felt lighter, peaceful, and not being invited in right away had been almost physically painful. It was strange, but I was okay with him yelling at me because I knew I could fix it if he'd stop a second and let me speak.

"Are you listening to me?"

"Oh," I said, startled, "yeah."

He crossed his arms and glared down at me. I was

betting it was how he looked when he was talking to his students in class. "Brann, you—"

"She has to talk about it 'cause it's eatin' her up inside," I blurted out. "And if you don't do something quick, it's gonna get to where you won't be able to get her back from it."

He sank down onto the couch I was on and stared at me mutely.

"I think you didn't wanna talk to her about the specifics before because you were worried you'd scare her. Maybe you wanted her to focus on the loss and the grieving and not if her mother had suffered when she died. She was only five when it happened, so that's probably why you didn't have a discussion about it before, and that makes sense, of course, but now... now she's older, and she really wants to know."

He was so still, like he was waiting on me.

"She needs answers to heal all the way, and because you still won't talk about it, she's sorta been chasing them around on her own."

His eyes filled, and I felt like total crap.

"Aww, man," I groaned, leaning close, taking his face in my hands and using my thumbs to wipe the tears away. "I didn't mean to dredge up nothin', but your daughter has serious questions that are haunting her drawings, and her interactions with people, with you and Livi, and I'm guessing her dreams as well," I said, letting him go before I stood up. "And I know it's not my business, and I know I shouldn't've even offered to let her talk to my buddy before I asked you, but she's seriously grieving, and she needs some closure, at least, for her questions."

He watched me, eyes never leaving my face.

"If you let her have the facts, at least she can stick with the loss and not be worried about *how* her mother died anymore, but focus instead on that she *did*."

Since he wasn't saying anything, just continuing to give me his full and undivided attention, I plowed on, pacing now as he had been. "I think if you let her talk to a doctor and ask questions and have them truthfully answered, it will go a long way to clearing out her anger and frustration over being lied to."

"I've never lied to my—"

"Yeah, but you never sat her down and said this is how it happened, this is what she would have felt, this is how long she lived once the tear occurred."

"Those are gruesome details," he choked out, and I saw how broken he was inside, and heard the fractures in his normally gentle voice.

"Yeah, but your daughter wants to know, and she's frustrated that she doesn't."

"You can't know that."

I shook my head. "I lost a lot of friends when I was deployed. I carried guys out who didn't make it and then escorted their bodies home to their families, and once I was there, the questions were always the same. Did he suffer, was he in pain, did he call for me or his father—did you hold his hand?" I sighed deeply before I smiled at him. "They needed answers, and I gave them to them. It's what you do."

He took a breath.

I waited.

"How do you even answer questions like that? From their families?"

"You can't keep that stuff from people; they have a right to know. And you understand, those were the last words someone they loved would ever speak."

He was studying my face.

"There's no more time, and people need closure."

His eyes were so deep and dark and wet now with tears. I really wanted to simply ease him forward into my arms and hold him against my heart. It took a lot of control to keep still and not reach for him.

"Okay," he said after a moment. "But I want to sit with her."

"Of course."

He stood then, and I thought he was going to shake my hand, maybe, but instead he walked forward and right into me, into my space, his arms lifting to wrap around my neck as he leaned in and gave me his weight.

In my civilian life, no one ever hugged me to get comfort. It had been different in the service when everything was life-and-death and you had only your buddies to turn to. But back in the world, I got hugged only before kissing, which always led to fucking, but no one ever just needed me. Not until I came to this house.

I realized as he clutched at me that I really liked having him all over me. Only when he shuddered did I realize he was crying. His sobs were the same as April's had been earlier, except that instead of crying on my chest, he bawled into the side of my neck. I held him tight, one hand between his shoulder blades, the other on the small of his back, pressing him against me, trying to push whatever strength I had at the moment into him. "I think all you guys are having some trouble right now. Because you're getting married and so it's bringing stuff up all over again."

He nodded and inhaled, trying to calm himself.

"Please let me help you. It's what I'm here for, but more than that, I want to."

"I know," he whispered as he eased himself from my arms and then gave me a brilliant smile. "So," he said, sniffling before sighing deeply. "What else do you plan to fix while you're here? You should give me a list."

"Gimme a second and I'll figure it out," I said gruffly, really liking how I was being looked at. There was so much fondness there already, and I realized I had misread him earlier. He hadn't been planning to kick me out, to get rid of me. He'd been blindsided because he was already counting me on his side, and when he thought I'd turned on him and promised his child something he had not yet agreed to, *that* had been a betrayal. He was hurt. And I'd been able to do that because he'd already given me that power. It was a huge responsibility, the navigation between what the kid needed and what the parent could do, or would. I had no idea how people did it every day, the dance of parenting while also staying in sync with a partner or spouse. It was terrifying. And I knew right then that Olivia wasn't the only one in danger of becoming attached. The kind, soft-spoken man with the adorable daughters was giving me heart palpitations after only a few hours; what would it feel like after days or weeks?

I had to steel myself to walk away and remember they didn't belong to me. They weren't mine. I was only passing through. Distance was key as was the reminder that I was only there for a very short time. It was definitely something to keep in the forefront of my mind.

ONCE I SHOWERED AND CHANGED, I called my buddy who had quit during Hell Week when we were going through Basic Underwater Demolition/SEAL or BUD/S training. I had been sad to see him go but pleased he wanted to continue our friendship after he left. I was even more appreciative of our bond when I got out of the Navy and he insisted I give Chicago a shot instead of returning to San Diego where I started. His guest room became my temporary home as I looked for work in the Windy City. He was there because once his contract with the Navy was up, he'd returned to medical school and was now an attending physician at Northwestern Memorial Hospital. He was a cardiovascular surgeon and was building a name for himself in the medical community.

"Can you Skype with me later today?" I asked Dr. Anthony Leone. "I'm on a job, and there's a little girl and her dad who need some straight talk about what happened to Mom when she died."

"Define straight talk," he said, and I could hear the concern in his voice. "And how did she die?"

I explained about the aortic dissection.

"Oh for fuck's sake, Brann," he groaned like I was killing him.

"Listen," I pleaded with him. "She's eight and she's imagining all kinds of things that happened to her mother in the last few moments of her life," I continued with a sigh. "It's important that she hear the truth from a doctor who can explain things thoroughly but on her level."

"Holy crap," he grumbled. "Ask for the moon, why don't you?"

"Oh, come on, I have faith in you."

"I refuse to screw up a little girl's life by—"

"That's the problem, Tone," I confessed. "I'm worried if she doesn't get answers soon that what she's going through now is just gonna fester and eat her alive."

He was quiet on the other end.

"Please."

He exhaled sharply. "Of course I'm going to say yes to

you, because you've tripped my interest with her wanting to know and me wanting to teach."

I knew that, because I knew him. He was an amazing mentor.

"Where the hell are you, and what's the time difference?"

"I'm in Montana, so you wanna do it now, maybe?"

He told me to grab my laptop.

Olivia decided she wanted to sit with her father and sister, and even though she wasn't sure if she felt like staying the whole time, she was willing to see. Emery shot me a look, concerned with that, but when I grabbed hold of his bicep and squeezed, he took a breath and nodded, agreeing to let Olivia sit on his lap.

April was shaking, she was so excited. Emery seemed nervous and scared, and Olivia was uncertain as they all sat down at their kitchen table together. I pulled up Skype on my MacBook Air and called Tony. Once he answered and April saw him in his white doctor coat with a wall of x-rays behind him, appearing serious with his rimless glasses and beard and mustache, I watched her visibly relax. Her shoulders dropped, she unclenched her fists, letting her hands open as she leaned forward to better see the things behind him. And I understood. She'd thought maybe I was bullshitting her and that I was having her talk to someone other than a doctor or someone who wouldn't take her seriously. When she saw where he was, who he was, all that changed.

"Dr. Anthony Leone, this is my friend April Dodd and her father, Emery, and her little sister, Olivia."

"Good afternoon," he greeted them. "April, I understand you have some questions about what happened to your mother."

She nodded.

He then glanced at Emery. "And I understand that you've agreed to have me talk to your daughter, sir."

"Yes, I have," Emery agreed.

"Okay, then." Tony sighed and returned his focus to April. "I have a model of a heart here if you're okay to see that."

"Yes, please, and thank you for talking to me," she rushed out.

His smile was kind. "Of course. Now listen, if I go too fast or you don't understand something or if you want me to stop because you need a moment to process the information I'm giving you... if any of that happens, you just let me know, all right?"

"Yes," she agreed, and grabbed her father's hand and squeezed it tight.

Emery stared at his little girl's hand in his, and I saw his eyes fill instantly. I knew from what he'd told me that they had not had any father-daughter bonding moments in a while. This was exactly what he'd been hoping for, though probably not over something that was going to be so heart-breaking for both of them.

Walking out of the kitchen, not wanting to intrude on the family, I went to the living room and stretched out on the couch. It didn't take long for my body to get heavy, and when I felt a hand in my hair, petting me, I made a sound somewhere between a grunt and a purr.

"That's a good noise," Olivia said absently. "You have pretty hair; it's got lots of cool colors in it."

"Thanks," I mumbled into the pillow.

She was quiet, her fingers carding through my hair over and over.

"Were you bored?"

"Mm-hmm," she said, then yawned, wiggling around

until her head was next to mine on the throw pillow. "I know Mommy is in heaven, even if April doesn't think so."

It was good that she believed, and why would I contradict her? I couldn't say empirically one way or another.

"This one is gold," she said, back to looking at my hair. I could feel the tug of her fingers. "This one is brown. This one is... red. My mommy had red hair like me."

"Yours is auburn."

"It's red like yours," she contradicted me.

I might have had some stray colors in my dirty-blond hair, but red wasn't one of them. Thing was, though, I wasn't about to correct her because it was endearing that she wanted there to be similarities between us. She wanted us to have things in common. "Okay."

"This one is yellow, not gold, and this one is kinda white."

I was fading fast under her gentle ministrations.

"Daddy was supposed to walk me to Mariah's house to get my Wonder Woman lunchbox," she informed me. "Should I wait 'til he's done?"

I was quiet for a moment, thinking about what I would say.

"Earth to Brann," she teased me. "Come in, Brann."

"You know, being passive-aggressive is not a good thing," I told her with a groan. "Ask me straight out."

"What is what you just said?"

"When you ask for something or you want something, you should simply come out and say it. Don't do it in a roundabout way; nobody likes that."

"I still don't get it."

"If you want me to go somewhere with you, you say 'Brann, can you walk me to Mariah's house 'cause she's got my lunchbox and I want it back?'"

"Oh."

"Yeah, oh."

"So just tell you what I need."

"Yes, ma'am."

"Okay. Can we go?"

I wasn't about to do the *can we* versus *may we* bit with her, because I said *can* all the time myself. Once upon a time, I had a sergeant who used to say, "I dunno, *can* you?" whenever I asked him a question like that, but it never bothered me.

"Yeah. Let's go to Mariah's."

"Awesome," she agreed happily. "It's only to the end of the street."

"Lemme get my phone first," I lied, rolling off the couch to go back to my room so I could get my Glock back out of the locked gun case I'd put it in when we got home. I needed it, it was necessary, but I really didn't want either of the kids to know I was strapped.

It wasn't far, seven doors down the street from the Dodd house, but when we got there, Olivia went from holding my hand to clutching it.

"What's wrong?" I asked, turning to her.

She bit her lip but didn't answer me.

"Livi?" I asked, a ripple of dread slithering its way down my spine.

"Mariah's dad is here," she said in a tiny scared voice that I hated hearing. "She told me that he's not supposed to come here anymore."

I stopped her from moving as a woman from across the street came out of her house on her cell phone.

"You should take Olivia home," she told me, hand on her forehead as we both heard something break from inside the house.

"What's going on?" I asked her, crossing to her with Olivia in tow.

"I... I can't get the sheriff or the deputy on the phone, and Jenny has a restraining order against her ex, but a lot of good it's going to do her if there's no one here to—"

There was a yell and another crash and then a high-pitched wail.

"Poor Mariah," Olivia whimpered beside me. "She's so scared of her daddy."

And just for that, her father should have been beaten, but this was not the time for me to say what I thought of men who terrorized their wives and children.

"Who are you?" I asked the woman quickly, sharply, drawing her attention.

"Oh, uhm, I'm Susan, Susan Whitley," she said haltingly, clearly distracted by what was happening to her friend. "My daughter and Olivia and Mariah are all in gymnastics together."

"Livi," I said, taking hold of her shoulder and looking her in the eye. "I need you to stay here with Mrs. Whitley for a minute while I go get Mariah's dad out of the house, all right?"

"What?" Susan gasped and grabbed hold of my wrist. "Oh, no. Jenny's ex is a lumberjack, and that's not me screwing with you—that's actually what he does for a living. He's huge."

"Don't worry," I soothed her, patting her hand before I peeled her fingers off me and turned toward the house.

"Brann," Olivia called out, her voice rising, clearly scared.

"Stay right there, Livi, and don't move," I ordered as I darted across the street.

At the front door that was busted in and bent, I pulled

the Glock from the holster just above the top of my jump boot, straightened up, and slipped inside.

The living room was a riot of overturned furniture and broken glass, and farther in, there was a laundry basket that clothes had been thrown free of, and then a disaster of a kitchen.

"Mommy!" came a terrified scream.

Bolting down a short hall, I found a little girl pounding on a closed door. She was frantic, kicking it, hitting it, but she was small, fragile, and could only see out of one eye since the other was covered with blood.

I reached her and took her hand in mine. "Honey, I'm Olivia Dodd's new nanny. Is your Mommy in there?"

She nodded, clutching at my hand, shaking hard from fear and shock, I was sure.

"Is your daddy in there too?"

"Yeah."

"Okay," I said gently, pointing a bit down the hall. "You go stand right over there for me so I can get Mommy." Having no idea what I would find inside the room, I didn't want the little girl to have any new horror added to those already in her head.

She moved quickly, and I stepped back and kicked in the door.

I was instantly glad I'd made the little girl move. Her mother, beaten and bruised, was facedown on the bed, bleeding, held by the back of the neck while a huge man loomed over her with his dick out. He'd frozen when I came into the room, but I could tell from her shredded dress and discarded underwear that he was moments away from raping her.

I walked into the room, away from the destroyed door,

lifted the gun and levelled it at his chest. "Don't move or I'll shoot."

He took several steps back, and the mostly naked woman scrambled off the bed, ran to where the door used to be, and was out of the room in seconds, shrieking her daughter's name.

"Go outside," I barked at her, and when the man, who now had his dick tucked back in his pants, took a step forward, I moved to block his way. "Don't."

"Who the hell are you, and what the fuck are you doing in my house?" he thundered, and I realized then, with the slur of the last word, how very drunk he was.

"It's not your house," I reminded him, glancing away just for a second to make sure his ex-wife and his daughter were safely down the hall. "You're trespassing."

"I'll kill her!" he shrieked, and because he was sloshed, my gun didn't give him pause as he charged toward me.

Feinting left, I tripped him as he lunged for me and lost his footing, his momentum flinging him into the wall. Hitting it hard, the impact stunned him for a second before he bounced off and tumbled to the floor. I was on him fast, kicking him solidly in the side of the head. The first one stunned him, the second knocked him out.

I rolled him to his side to make sure he didn't choke if he puked, which he did a moment later. It happened to buddies of mine who were blackout drunks, and I always had to stay up all night when they passed out on me.

I used a discarded t-shirt and wiped his face, slid him away from the vomit, and then stood up and called the Montana Highway Patrol. I was fairly certain that Sheriff Thomas and Deputy Reed were not up for the task of securing the inebriated lumberjack.

Walking back out to the living room, I found the little

house empty, and so went to the garage to look for rope. The only thing there was twine and bungee cords, but since I'd been trained to use what was available, I made do.

I took pictures on my phone of the unconscious man before I started tying him up so there could be no question of the state he was in before I began. Once I was sure he'd have to be Houdini to get out of my knot work, I got up, walked back into the living room and out the front door.

The cheering was instant.

Holy crap.

The street was full of people, and they were all clapping and whistling. Olivia waved from across the street, looking at me with big eyes, the question obvious, so I gestured her to me and she bolted from Mrs. Whitley's side, reaching me as I sank to one knee, her hands on my face.

"Are you okay?" she asked, checking me over. "Are you bleeding? Did he knock out any of your teeth?"

"No, love," I assured her, giving her a hug.

She wrapped her arms around my neck and squeezed, and the clapping got louder as way too many people began crowding around us.

"You're a guardian angel," Olivia pronounced, and even as I groaned, I heard a little voice say that yeah, I was.

Turning, I had enough time to let Olivia go before her friend was in my arms, face in the side of my neck, crying and shaking. Her mother was right behind her, folding into me, sobbing, holding on tight, as Olivia pet her hair.

SEVEN

The highway patrol and the police in Whitefish both made it to the house before the sheriff, which was a sad commentary on what would have happened to Mariah Rubio and her mother if I hadn't been there.

"Those are nice knots there, Calder," one of the troopers assured me when he walked back out after a few minutes.

"Thank you," I said from where I was talking to his supervisor, Highway Patrol Captain Dennis Noguchi, who had explained to me that his commander, Robert Eads, in charge of District VI in Kalispell, was not thrilled that he was getting yet another call about an incident in Ursa. Apparently the sheriff was having trouble keeping the peace.

"It should just be rezoned," Sergeant Tavares out of Whitefish explained to me after he shook my hand and his men, four of them, carried Scott Rubio out of his ex-wife's home to one of their cruisers.

"He's not gonna fit," I yelled over, because the man was

at least six-five, so there was no way they were getting him into the car.

There was some swearing after that as they figured out what to do with the behemoth of a man.

"The Whitefish Police Department is more than capable of patrolling this postage stamp of a town," Tavares snapped at Noguchi. "It's stupid that we don't."

"You're preaching to the choir," Noguchi grumbled, still holding my license and multi-state CCW permit—which I was required to carry at all times—that allowed me to have my gun on me back home in Chicago as well as in Ursa. "Hell, you could swear in Calder here and be in better shape than with Thomas."

Tavares glanced at my two forms of identification still in the captain's hands. "What kind of background do you have, Calder?"

"No," I said simply. "I live in Chicago. I'm just here on a job."

They both looked up at me, waiting for an explanation. I knew the expression well.

"Basically we're licensed as private detectives slash bodyguards in Chicago, which is what's up with my conceal and carry license."

Tavares grunted.

Noguchi lifted an eyebrow. "Lots of PIs are PIs because they couldn't be cops. You got something in your record that would have prevented that?"

"No, I just never thought of myself as the cop type."

"And yet you went right in to help Jenny Rubio and her daughter."

"Because it had to be done," I said sharply. "There was no one else here."

"You could have waited for the sheriff."

"How? Jenny and her kid were in immediate danger."

The two men exchanged looks.

"What?"

"You were thinking about the woman and her child first, Calder, before yourself. What do you think being a cop is?"

I shook my head, because what the hell were they even talking about right now?

"Why do you think Mrs. Rubio went to Whitefish to get a restraining order instead of getting one in her own town?"

"I have no idea," I answered brusquely, already too deep into the conversation.

"I think you do," Noguchi insisted. "I think you know that she went to Whitefish because she has more faith in cops that are fifteen minutes away than in a sheriff and his deputy who are a minute—maybe a minute and a half— from her door."

I had to remember that Harlan Thomas was the friend of a friend of my boss.

"Because she knew if she got one in Whitefish that not only would the cops there protect her, but also Sheriff Thomas would have to comply as well."

"That's right," Noguchi agreed. "So don't you think that serves as a terrible commentary on her faith in her elected official to protect her and her child?"

I did, but it wasn't my place to tell them that.

"What would you have done as soon as she brought the restraining order to you if you were sheriff here?"

"Roll by here a few times a day just to check on her."

"What did you do before your PI job, Calder?" Tavares wanted to know.

I wasn't about to tell them. "I was in the Navy."

Noguchi smiled slowly. "What did you do in the Navy, Calder?"

Olivia joined us then, running up and wrapping her arm around my waist, leaning into my side. "Brann, I forgot that Daddy was supposed to take me to sign up for karate today, so will you take me?"

"Of course," I assured her before turning back to the two men, having given her all my attention. "I know you two have to stay here and wait for Thomas, but I certainly don't."

Tavares squatted down in front of Olivia. "Honey, do you know what Mr. Calder did before he came to take care of you and your sister and your dad?"

"He's just taking care of me and April, not Daddy, but he lives in the Windy City—that's what Daddy told me—and he was in the Navy, and he had a job training seals!" she said, squealing the last part excitedly. "Doesn't that sound fun?"

Tavares nodded and stood up, his gaze solid on mine. "A SEAL?"

In this instance, even the wrong story didn't help me. "Doesn't mean I'd make a good cop," I muttered, hoping the death glare I was giving him would work.

"And yet...," Tavares said, gesturing at the road where Sheriff Thomas and Deputy Reed had just appeared. It was the second time I'd seen the deputy, and he forced a smile and waved at me, jogging over, not waiting on the sheriff.

"Twice in one day, Calder," Reed greeted me affably, patting my shoulder. "Are you a superhero or something?"

He wasn't helping even a little bit.

"Not at all," I said brusquely, still unsure about him because of how he'd been with Emery. What I was certain of was that he would have been utterly out of his depth with Jenny Rubio's husband. It was annoying that he wasn't more capable, but I was probably being too judgy. From the size of the town, I was guessing homicidal rapists were not a usual occurrence. I shouldn't have been pissed at him for not being prepared for an anomaly.

Taking hold of Olivia's hand, I turned and nearly plowed into another man. It took me a second to see the badge and realize I was looking at none other than Sheriff Thomas.

"Mr. Calder," he said, hands on my biceps, smiling at me like I didn't think he would. If it were me, and some guy came out of nowhere and was showing me up, I would have been pissed. But the older man seemed quite pleased to meet me. "I hoped you would come by the office when you hit town, but I'm happy to get the chance to finally say hello."

Why in the world would I have gone by his office? I was in town to be a nanny, for crissakes. What the hell was with him?

"Stop in and see me as soon as you're able."

"Sure," I said, offering him my hand. "Thank you, Sheriff."

He took my hand, leaving his other on my bicep, and really, he looked way too happy. Why the hell was he so happy?

"Jared tells me that you were a Navy SEAL, is that right?"

Oh for the love of God. "Yessir," I almost growled at him, because didn't he know he was supposed to be talking to Tavares and Noguchi and not shooting the shit with me?

"And no family back in Chicago."

I did a slow nod. "No, sir. I—"

Bigger smile. "Excellent."

He made no sense. "I'm off to get my girl to karate sign-ups," I said, letting go of his hand and taking a step back.

"Of course, of course," he said kindly, patting Olivia's head before trotting over to the two men waiting on him.

I walked through a gauntlet of people who wanted to

thank me and pat my back and shake my hand, and then we were out of the throng, and Olivia was leading me down the street.

"We're walking?"

"Yeah," she explained as we turned a corner to a park. "We just have to take the shortcut."

It was a beautiful space, all lush and green and more for running and walking than anything else. As we went by a small duplex that had a sign up in front of it, a woman stepped out onto the porch.

"Ollie."

Both of us stopped and looked up at her.

"Sweetheart, I know we told you all Monday, but Winston's ready to come home if you want to pick him up now."

From the delighted squeal, I knew this was her pet.

Walking into the veterinarian's office—I finally actually read the sign—we were greeted with some barking, lots of cats in carriers, and two nurses beaming at us.

"Who's this, Ollie," the nurse sitting behind the desk asked, smiling at me.

"This is Brann, my nanny," she told them.

Their expressions were priceless. And I would have thought that they'd be confused or judgmental, but they both sort of melted and sighed. From their reactions, I was guessing that maybe men who took care of kids were high on their list.

I shook both their hands, and the second nurse held on a bit too long, her eyes mapping my entire frame, top to bottom.

The nurse who had called us in came out with a pocket-sized thing that was darling and lost his mind when he saw Olivia. She dropped to the floor and the two of them hugged and kissed and loved on each other, to the cooing of the entire room. No one was impervious to the adorableness of the cute little girl and her precious dog.

"What kind of dog is he?" I asked Olivia as Winston turned to me, started smelling my shoes and wagged his tiny little tail as I leaned over to pet him.

"He's a Westie, a West Highland Terrier, and we got him right after Mommy died."

"Gotcha," I said as the nurse passed first the leash to Olivia, then one of those plastic bones filled with poop bags. "Is there a balance on the account?"

"No, it's all paid for," she said, staring up into my face. "He's good to go."

Once we were outside, I started down the sidewalk because I could see the karate dojo now, but realized Olivia wasn't with me.

"What?" I asked as she caught up with me.

"All those ladies were staring at you."

"I'm sorry?"

"There were ladies watching you at soccer too."

"It's 'cause I'm new in town," I explained to her as she took my hand and Winston trotted along beside her.

"I think it's because you're pretty. Daddy said that people used to stare at Mommy too."

"Well, thank you for thinking I'm pretty," I said, chuckling over her noticing weird things. "Hey, what was Winston at the vet for?"

"Because he's dumb and he ate bees," she grumbled like she was really put out. "I told him to stay away from the flowers, but he wouldn't listen to me, and then he started eating them like they were treats and ended up with three stingers in the roof of his mouth."

I tried not to smile.

"His face swelled up like a balloon."

I looked down at Winston, and when we stopped at a crosswalk, he looked up at me. "Not too bright, are ya?"

He tipped his head sideways, all innocent.

"Grandma says that Winston does the best he can with what God gave him."

I snorted.

"Daddy says that Winston was born pretty and that if he was smart *and* pretty that wouldn't be fair to the other dogs."

"No, I expect not," I said, chuckling as we started walking again.

At the dojo, I had to hold Winston in one hand and fill out Olivia's application with the other while she talked to all her friends who were there. The man in charge, Sensei Ozumi, was very nice and came out to welcome Olivia to the Ozumi-Tanaka School of Martial Arts.

"Would you like to take classes as well?"

"I'm more a Brazilian Jujitsu and Krav Maga guy," I explained to the karate master.

He nodded. "You're in the military?"

"I was."

"Well, if you'd like to be certified to teach or if you become certified, please let me know. We don't offer those two styles here and would love to have an instructor."

"I actually live in Chicago," I let him know.

"Ah, so you're just visiting."

"Yeah."

His smile was warm. "Well, if you change your mind, please let me know."

If I changed my mind? About living in Montana? The hell was with everyone in this weird-ass town.

Once we were done and Olivia was carrying her gi home in a bag, she asked if we could stop for ice cream.

"It's like forty-five degrees out here," I groused at her. "Are you kidding?"

She shook her head.

"Fine," I said, yawning, giving up, because who was I to get between a little girl and saturated fat when I knew I'd want some later.

I got a pint for her father and a different one for April, and since Olivia and I both apparently liked double fudge brownie, we got that to share and then headed back.

We passed by the same scene we'd left earlier. The circus was still in town, and everyone waved as we walked by down the street toward home.

"How long does it take to clear everyone out?" I muttered under my breath.

"Everything takes a long time here," Olivia answered my rhetorical question.

I grunted, and as we approached the house, I saw Emery and April out on the front steps sitting side by side. He was holding her hand, his arm around her as she leaned into him.

"Winston!" April shouted, sitting up straight.

Olivia let go of his leash, and the dog scampered down the street and up to his people.

When we got to the steps, Olivia tumbled into her father's arms and showed him her gi.

"Brann signed me up, and look, April, we got ice cream, and I got the cookies and cream one you like and the Irish coffee for Daddy."

"You ran errands?" Emery asked, smiling up at me.

I shrugged. "The dog was a surprise, but I just realized I should have asked you about the karate before I—"

"No," he stopped me, reaching up to take my hand and

squeeze it. "I appreciate it. I was supposed to enroll her a week ago."

April stood up and bumped into me, arms wrapping quickly around my waist. "Thank you for setting things up so me and Dad could talk to your friend. He was awesome."

Now both kids were using my word.

I patted her back as I met Emery's warm gaze. Only then did he let go of my hand.

"He was," he assured me, his voice soft, caressing. "He was extremely patient, and even though finding out the truth was painful, I think we both feel a lot better knowing everything."

April nodded into my side.

"Brann saved Mariah and her mom," Olivia said, leaning back against her father as Winston jumped up into her lap so he had a kid and a dog in his.

Both April and Emery looked up at me.

"It's not really a thing."

"That's not true," Olivia corrected me. "It was a ginormous thing 'cause Mariah's mom was bleeding and crying, and so was Mariah when they were hugging him in the street. And Daddy, I wanted to go with him, but he made me stay with Mrs. Whitley until he came out."

Emery's eyebrows lifted in question.

"I promise it wasn't that big a deal."

"Everyone was clapping." Olivia added, deflating me completely. Hard to lie with the peanut gallery right there.

"Tell me the truth, Brann," Emery said hoarsely, "are you a closet superhero?"

"Listen—"

"Because you've tackled quite a few things since you've arrived, and I'm just wondering if you planned to take a crack at curing the common cold while you're here as well."

"It's not like—"

"And Daddy, all the ladies at the vet thought Brann was super pretty."

One eyebrow lifted as he gazed up at me. "Is that right?"

"Yeah. I think they want him to be their nanny, but I'm keeping him so he can't go."

"I think that's good thinking, Ollie."

She looked very pleased with herself.

EIGHT

B ack at the original place I'd rolled up on hours before, the log cabin mansion didn't look any more inviting the second time. Lydia had insisted Emery bring the girls and me, for dinner at her home. I, of course, thought that eight was a strange time of the evening for the girls to be eating, but Emery said it was fine since it wasn't a school night.

There were two men in uniform walking down the steps as we started the climb up, and I recognized Tavares instantly.

"Sergeant," I greeted him.

He stopped, and I watched the way his face went from wary and strained to relaxed when he saw me. Facing me on the steps, he offered his hand, which I grasped quickly.

"Calder."

"What're you doing here?" I asked him and the other officer with him.

"We're out here asking Mr. Cahill questions about a geologist who—" He stopped and considered Emery and the girls. "—just turned up and was last seen on his land."

"His land?" I asked, because my understanding was that there was a lot of it, so the question made sense only if Mr. Cahill knew what was happening on every acre every second of the day.

"Oh, sorry," he amended quickly, gesturing at Emery, "on your land, Mr. Dodd."

"On my land?" Emery seemed confused, taking a step forward. "Are you sure?"

Tavares cleared his throat and gestured for Emery and me.

"Stay right there, you guys," I told the girls. "This'll just take a second."

April nodded, still too happy with me not to agree with whatever I said. Even when I'd told her to clean her room earlier, vacuuming downstairs while Emery got the bathrooms, she had done so without any of her usual, her father said, kvetching.

Tavares waited until we were close and tipped his head at the other officer, who pulled his phone and read from the screen.

"He was on your land at some point, Mr. Dodd, because Mr. Cahill hired him to survey a small portion of it."

"What portion?"

"It's that small parcel where the Kingman stream forks off into that ravine that butts up right against Mr. Cahill's property."

"Oh, I know where you mean."

"Well, about a week ago, park rangers were called out by a couple of ranch hands who found a man chewed up by a mountain lion there, and when they took him to the morgue in Whitefish—because Ursa doesn't have one," Tavares explained to me. "—Lauren Tate, that's our ME, she says that the cause of death was not an animal attack but that someone severed his carotid with a blade."

"Cut him and left him bleeding, which is what drew the animal," the officer explained for our benefit.

"Oh my God," Emery gasped, glancing around at all of us. "We have a murderer here in Ursa? That's––"

"We have someone who had a reason to go after the geologist," Tavares said brusquely, hand up to stop Emery. "Don't make assumptions about anything beyond that."

Emery glanced behind him at his daughters, and I understood what he was thinking, so I reached out and took hold of his shoulder, grasping it tight until he turned and met my eyes.

"I'm here, yeah," I reminded him, my gaze steady, my voice level, hard, unflinching.

After a moment, he took a breath.

"Between your girls and the whole wide world," I said gruffly. "Keep that in mind."

He nodded quickly, and the way his shoulders dropped and his hands fell out of the clench, his tongue wetting his lips, and his eyes closing for a moment and then opening, all of that filled me with a surge of protectiveness that made my heart swell in my chest.

He trusted me. He trusted *in* me. What was better than that? What meant more?

"So now of course we want to know two things," Tavares continued, returning my attention to him. "Can you guess what those are?"

"First," I began, "what was the man doing on Mr. Dodd's land, and when was the last time Mr. Cahill saw him?"

"Precisely."

"So tell me something; if the geologist was in fact on Mr.

Dodd's land, why didn't you consider questioning him?" I asked Tavares, getting a weird feeling.

"Because when we checked with the deceased's wife, she provided us with an email sent from a satellite phone that we have not been able to locate, that he was out here on Mr. Dodd's land at the request of Mr. Cahill."

"Why?"

"She didn't know. Like I said, all she had was the email from Mr. Cahill asking her husband, Peter Bannon, to survey a piece of Mr. Dodd's land."

I turned to Emery. "Why would he do that?"

He shook his head. "I have no idea. Andrea told me years ago that when her grandfather had the land surveyed, there was nothing on it besides a tiny deposit of iron oxide. Apparently it was so small that when it was time for her father to make a decision about mining, he decided to let it be just as his father had."

"So then why would Mr. Cahill call a geologist out here now?"

"I don't see why he would."

"And so you think, what?" I asked, turning to Tavares. "That maybe the geologist found something more important, reported it to Mr. Cahill, and wound up dead?"

"That's not what I said," Tavares cautioned me. "So don't repeat that."

"What are you inferring?" Emery asked, grabbing my arm and turning me to him.

"That maybe Mr. Cahill knows more about this than he's letting on."

He turned to Tavares, stepping in close to me, arms crossed, like it was us against them. I doubted he even realized he was doing it, lining up like we were on the same team. "And what do you think?"

"We have no official comment, Mr. Dodd."

"No official comment," Emery repeated with a scoff, staring holes through him.

Tavares cleared his throat. "As far as we know, Grant Cahill conducts his business honestly and ethically."

Emery nodded at the officers and turned to me. "And you think he's not a stand-up guy?"

Me? Why the hell did he care what I thought?

"Brann?" he prodded, waiting.

"I know what I read," I answered, using the flat, devoid-of-feeling voice I used to talk to civilians when I was deployed.

"What does that mean?"

Fuck.

Why was he pushing me? All I knew was that I was not a fan of Mr. Cahill for one huge reason—it was his plan that Emery should marry his daughter, and I was not on board. I'd been in town less than twenty-four hours, and I already knew that having Lydia Cahill in that house was not the best thing for Emery or his girls. I was certain of it. The planned marriage of convenience was not going to do any of them any good.

"Brann?" He was insistent.

"I think maybe you ask him about the geologist, right?"

He stared at me a long moment before he nodded. "I think so, yes."

When Lydia was Emery's wife, his land would be hers, which made it all, technically, Mr. Cahill's. And just maybe, Cahill had gotten greedy and called for the geologist too early. But perhaps he had to know before the *I dos* were spoken.

"You know," Emery began, glancing at Tavares and the other officer before his focus returned to me, "he's been nothing but good to me since I lost Andrea, but that doesn't mean that I go blindly forward."

"Good," I agreed, forcing a smile. "Because being stupid and shoving your head in the sand won't help anything. I mean, if he called for a geologist, why did he do that without telling you? Without asking you?" I said pointedly. "That's weird, isn't it?"

"It is," he said, shooting Tavares and his officer a glare. "And I'm so glad you have no official comment or apparent concern."

"Mr. Dodd, I——"

He put up his hand to let Tavares know he was done and then pivoted and walked up the stairs toward his girls.

"I think it's weird," Tavares assured me as I turned to him. "But I can't tell him that. I mean, he's engaged to the man's daughter."

There was that.

"We're not dropping it," the other officer chimed in, letting me know. "Our investigation has just begun."

"Could you keep me in the loop," I asked Tavares, and he gave me a quick nod before I caught up with the others.

"Do me a favor," Emery said to me as we neared the front door. "Let me speak to Grant before you say anything to him."

"Of course. You're the boss."

He turned his head. "I'm not your boss. I simply—right now, you being here—we're partners taking care of the girls, and I'm enjoying having you here even for this short time. All I'm asking is that I be allowed to make inquiries before either of us jumps to conclusions."

"Fair enough."

He took a breath, and I realized how hard this all had to be for him. Here he was, navigating a wedding that would have repercussions for not only him but for his girls as well. Being a single parent was hard enough, and now on top of that, he had his nanny second-guessing him.

I was going to say something else, but the door opened, and there was the personal assistant, Mr. Duvall, from earlier in the day.

"Mr. Dodd, good evening," he greeted. "Girls, Mr. Calder," he continued, stepping aside so we could all walk inside the huge marble-floored foyer.

It might have resembled a log cabin from the outside, but inside it was a giant ski lodge, complete with an open ceiling so all the beams were visible, a giant light fixture made out of antlers in the great room, and floor-to-ceiling windows everywhere. It had to cost a mint to heat in the winter.

The polished hardwood floor was covered in rugs, there was overstuffed leather furniture in clustered groups, one near the fireplace, another by the windows that looked out onto an enormous backyard and farther toward a small stream, and another near an arch that led into the kitchen. It was not lost on me that there were no other children, and all the adults had drinks in their hands.

"Oh, you're lucky you brought the help," I whispered to Emery, and his smile, full of relief when he turned, made me grin back.

He lifted his hand toward me, maybe to touch my face, but thought better of it and let it drop back to his side.

Lydia appeared then, with a few women in tow, and rushed up to Emery, and kissed him on the cheek. "Oh, I'm so glad you're here." She sighed, eyes flicking to me. "And I see you brought your new nanny."

First they were surprised she wasn't kidding, and then

Lydia introduced Shelby, her best friend and maid of honor, as well as the other two, whose names I didn't retain.

Shelby was the one who stepped close and offered me her hand, saying how great it was that I was comfortable in a traditionally female role. "It's fantastic that your masculinity is not threatened working as a caregiver," she told me. "I know lots of guys who could never do it."

"I've never really cared much what people think of me," I assured her. "I got over that in high school."

Emery smacked me in the abdomen, calling me on my shit, because yeah, that had probably come off kind of assholey.

"Where do the kids go?" I asked Lydia.

"Oh, after dinner I have a room all set up with video games and movies for the girls," she informed me.

"I know where it is," Olivia told me, pulling on my hand.

"Oh, no," one of the other woman said, taking hold of my arm. "The grown-ups need to stay here, sweetie. You have to leave him here with us."

"I'm the nanny," I explained to her, smiling. "I'm only here so Emery can visit."

He opened his mouth to say something.

"I'll get right to work, Mr. Dodd," I declared, letting Olivia lead me away as April trailed behind us.

It was a nice room down a long hall, and I was certain it was chosen so the sound wouldn't carry out to the other guests. There were two large screens; on one, Mario Kart was queued up, and on the other Netflix was ready to go.

"You guys wanna go back outside and walk around the property?"

"But it's dark," Olivia explained to me.

"I'll protect you."

We went out the side door, and the kids were thrilled to

see that there were lightposts and even benches along the path winding through the property. I liked that there were strung lights near a fire pit and farther out over a small footbridge, a large picnic area complete with several tables and a barbecue grill now covered with a tarp.

We ran around and then lay down, all three together, on one of the picnic tables and stared up at the stars. I pulled up an app on my phone that showed them the constellations, and they were both amazed at how cool it was. Little kids were so easy to impress.

When we got back, it was time to eat, and since it was sit-down instead of a buffet, we had to all take a seat in the dining room at a long-ass table.

"Grant, I'd like you to meet Brann Calder," Emery said, taking hold of my bicep and drawing me close.

"Nice to meet you, Mr. Cahill," I greeted him, offering my hand as Emery kept hold of my arm. I had to wonder if he knew that he hadn't let go.

"And you, Brann," the tall man built like a linebacker said to me as he grasped my hand. He was smiling, yes, but it wasn't hitting his eyes. "I was just explaining to Emery that I had a man come out to take a geological survey of a parcel of my land that butts up against his because we were thinking about doing some mining out there, and though we thought we might have found something, it turns out it was nothing but a small vein of silver."

Even as I was listening, I knew it was crap. "So you're mining on your land but not on Emery's, since I know his wife didn't ever want that done."

"We won't be mining anywhere, as getting that silver out of the ground would cost far more than it's worth," he informed me with a chuckle, "but yes, you're right. We will always adhere to Andrea's wishes for the land."

"That's good," I said frankly, "'cause you wouldn't want to go back on your word."

"No, of course not," he said, smacking my arm before reaching behind him for the stunning woman standing there. She had to be in her late fifties, early sixties, her thick white-blonde hair pulled into a low, messy chignon, and her minimal makeup accentuating pale, flawless skin. The black maxi-skirt she was wearing appeared effortlessly chic combined with the loose white shirt and minimalist gold jewelry. It hit me then that compared to everyone else, elaborately coiffed and over-dressed, her elegance was luminous. "Calder, I'd like you to meet my companion, Anne Stratton."

She lifted her hand, and I took it in mine, just to hold, not to shake, and her smile was warm and kind. "Mr. Calder, I—"

"Brann," I corrected her.

"Brann," she repeated, her voice low, seductive, her dark hazel eyes holding my gaze. "It's a pleasure. Emery has needed help for so long, and it seems as though he finally has someone terribly capable that he trusts."

"Thank you."

She sighed almost sadly. "Trust is a rare commodity, don't you agree?"

I nodded. "I certainly do."

Giving my hand a final squeeze, she glided away, drawn off by another man, who I hadn't met as Cahill took hold of Emery's bicep to keep him at his side, all of them moving to the head of the table near Lydia, leaving me and the girls at the opposite end.

Dinner was an ancient grain salad, which was basically quinoa and pine nuts and bits of Romaine lettuce and strawberries, then seared salmon with what the waiter—because didn't everyone have Saturday night dinner catered—said was sorrel sauce and fresh sage along with a roasted red beet risotto.

I squinted at it.

The girls stared at it.

"Huh," I said after it was put in front of me.

April had one eyebrow lifted, waiting for me. Olivia was biting her bottom lip.

I leaned forward, and so did they, and when I spoke, I made sure it was low.

"I wish I'd had PB and J with you guys earlier," I grumbled.

"Told you so," April singsonged, very smug. "Daddy always has us eat something early when we have to come over here late."

"He's a very smart man."

She nodded like yeah, he was, giving me a patronizing smirk.

"We can't eat anything huge," Olivia explained, wincing as she caught a glimpse of her plate. "Because we're not supposed to be too full to try stuff, so we don't hurt Lydia's feelings."

"That's nice," I said, because it was. It was thoughtful, which I already knew was the kind of man Emery was.

"There were snails one time," April let me know, making the vomit face for my benefit.

I groaned.

"So what now?" Olivia asked brightly.

"Okay so just move it around, mush up the salmon, put the veggies on top of it, and then we'll all go to the kitchen and drop off our plates."

We all leaned back at the same time.

After I wiped all the sauce off the salmon, I ate that

because I needed the protein, but there was no way in hell I was touching the salad. Once I saw that everyone was chatting at the other end, I glanced at April's plate, then Olivia's, and was disappointed to see that the moving around of the food didn't appear all that convincing. Stealth was definitely not on our side.

"I think it's too big to hide," I said under my breath.

"Napkin?" April suggested hopefully.

They were the real thing and couldn't be thrown away. "Negative," I said, hiding the word under throat-clearing.

"We could run," Olivia whimpered. "'Cause if you make me eat it, I'm gonna barf it up, and then I'll be hungry again, and then you'll have to get me something else to eat, and holy cow, this could take up your whole night."

I was stunned and chuckling at the same time. "Holy shit, Livi."

"What?"

"Your excuse is that you're thinking of me?"

"Yeah," she said, her voice going way up. "Of course."

"Uh-huh."

"I agree," April chimed in earnestly, pinning me with her gaze. "This is serious."

It was so not. "You know people are starving in the world."

"Everybody always says that, but I never see anyone sending gross dinners anywhere on the news. And my teacher, Mr. Leonard, he says that even though he's not religious, that Jesus's point was well made that we need to teach people how to fish, not just give them fish."

"You see, Brann, those people need nets and poles, not gross salmon," Olivia summed up for me what April had said in case I was too stupid to figure it out.

"Really?"

"Yeah. We need to stop having wars and start planting crops. You never hear about Cro-Magnons fighting each other. It was hunting or gathering."

"That's because they were afraid of getting eaten by a dinosaur."

April rolled her eyes at me. "Oh dear God. You know that dinosaurs were dead for, like, millions of years by the time—"

"Yes, I know, shut up, I'm teasing you. It would've been saber-tooth tigers."

"People, let's focus on the disgusting salmon on our plates," Olivia chimed in, wanting us back on task. "What're we gonna do?"

"Follow my lead," I muttered, coughing again, getting ready to stand up. "On three."

I counted and we got up without anyone ever glancing at us, even Emery. We carried our plates to the kitchen and dropped them off with a woman who gave us all the evil eye.

"I gotta pee," Olivia announced, which was good since it gave us a reason to get away from the woman judging us on our dislike of quinoa.

Walking out the other side—who knew kitchens could have more than one way in and out—we made our way down a short hall, which, wonder of wonders, dead-ended at Mr. Cahill's office. I wasn't sure how I'd made it there, but I wasn't about to look a gift horse in the mouth.

Since there was a bathroom right across from it, I sent April in there with her sister and told them not to come out until I knocked. Once the door was closed, I went back to the open doorway of the office, flew into the huge space— seriously, my apartment could fit in there—and pulled a Kleenex from the box close to the phone. I laid the tissue over the mouse before I shook it and found the man's email up. Everyone knew if you left your computer, you signed out. But it was his house, so he probably wasn't expecting anyone to be snooping around in his business.

Quickly, I sent an email to my buddy Huck Riley, then made sure to delete it from the sent folder before wiping the keyboard with another tissue. I stuffed both into my pocket as I walked back out the door. The whole process took only moments. After crossing the hall, I collected the girls, and we retraced our steps back to the kitchen and out into the dining room.

"Did you guys get enough to eat?" Lydia asked us as soon as we emerged.

"Oh, yeah, so full," I lied, and April and Olivia both followed my lead, letting her know they were absolutely stuffed as well.

I didn't look at Emery because I knew he'd know it was bullshit, and I just grabbed the girls and went back to the playroom. As they started playing Spyro, I walked to the other side of the room and called my buddy, Huck, from the service, who'd been out only a couple of months. Apparently, after I retired, he'd started to drink as a means of coping with things. He hadn't hurt anyone or himself, but it had been a near thing. He was discharged quietly with nothing permanent in his file. I'd been begging him to move to Chicago; we could be bunkmates again. But so far he said that being home, back in Phoenix, was working out for him.

"Hello?" came the cold, sterile greeting. Clearly the man had not looked at his caller ID.

"Huckleberry," I teased him.

"Oh shit." His voice warmed instantly. "Brannigan, what the hell, man? You don't usually call until Monday."

We had a regular phone date and watched Monday Night Football together, because even though his mother and I were friendly and she'd call if she got worried about Huck missing too many Sunday dinners, I still made sure to check in. And it wasn't that he was weak or that I thought he'd relapse, but it was good to keep up with your friends. Especially the ones who had saved your life more times than you could count.

"No, I know, but I need a favor."

"What? Tell me. You in jail?"

I groaned.

"What?"

"Why is that the first thing everyone always says to me?"

"Oh, I dunno, buddy," he said sarcastically, "maybe because you were stuck in that jail in Pattaya for three days before we knew where the fuck you were."

"That's 'cause I got mugged in my civvies!" I protested.

He scoffed, and it was loud and made me smile.

"Are you home?"

"I am," he said with a yawn. "I got ahold of some bad carne asada last night, and—"

"No," I said quickly. "You know if you talk about barfing, I will too."

"I know," he said with an evil cackle. "I'm so great with the details, you can actually feel the chunks rising in your throat."

"Stop," I grumbled. "You're disgusting."

"Yeah, sorry, go."

"You'll need your laptop."

"I've got it. I was watching a movie."

"What kinda movie?"

"Oh, fuck you. I told you I was barfing all night, and it looked the same coming out as it did going in, and—"

"Stop," I said, breathing through my nose.

"Then you stop. I have my fuckin' laptop."

"Okay then, I sent you an email from Grant Cahill or Cahill Lumber—not sure how it came over."

There was clicking on the other end. "I see it."

"Well, I need you to hack the computer it came from for me, because I'm looking for anything about mining that Mr. Cahill is doing."

"Who are these people?"

"I'm on a job in Montana, and I think the guy our client is mixed up with might be dirty."

"Data mining?"

"No, regular mining, like for gold or whatever."

"Ah," he said, exhaling deeply. "Okay. Gimme a sec."

At first glance, people would think Huck Riley was a rock star, and if not, then maybe an actor, and after that, a cowboy. He was the guy you stood on the sidewalk and watched walk by. He was *that* stunning. I had seen normal people lose their shit simply talking to him. Between the dimples and the raspy, smoky sound of his voice, blue-green eyes, thick golden-brown hair, and the body of an Olympic swimmer, he had women falling all over him. I would have as well, but Huck bent one way, and that was for girls. The thing was, though, with the outside being traffic-stopping gorgeous, no one ever suspected that underneath was a scary hacker.

There was silence as I heard more key tapping.

"Where is this computer, Fort Knox?"

"No, it's his home computer."

"He's got some serious security here for a home computer."

"That's what I figured. I didn't think for a second I'd be able to get in fast."

"You wouldn't be able to do it at all," he snorted. "My ten-year-old niece is more techy than you, brother."

I had no doubt.

"Oh, yeah, here we go. This is brilliant. He's got video of you sitting at his computer."

So the man was not so trusting, after all. "Can you delete that, please?" I said drolly.

"Already did."

"I'm looking for a geological survey that had to have been done in the last few weeks."

"Why?"

"Because the survey guy was murdered and then fed to mountain lions."

Silence.

"Huck?"

"Fed to what?"

"You heard me. I couldn't make that shit up."

"Holy shit. Are you all right?"

"I'm fine, but you get why I'm looking into it."

"Yeah, I do," he said with a sharp exhale. "Okay, so there's something here about a possible carbonatite deposit, which would be interesting."

"And why's that?"

"Well, because if the geologist suspects some rare earth elements, like say Cerium or Promethium or Yttrium, or something even better, then that could be serious money."

"How?"

"Well, all those are used to make processors and chips for computers, and they're basically the building blocks for high-end tech."

"You're dumbing this down for me," I accused him, because he did that to me often. And usually it was for the best. He was a hardware guy all the way. I was not.

"No, it just doesn't matter, because according to the

report I'm looking at, something is there, yes, but there's no way to know what without getting it out."

Which is where the mining comes in, am I right?"

"Yeah. Mining, drilling, I have no idea the specifics, but it's invasive to the environment, without a doubt."

"Like you'd have to cut down a fuckton of trees to make this happen."

"Absolutely."

"Mr. Cahill told Emery that it was a silver deposit."

"Is Emery your client?"

"Yeah."

"So he lied, then."

"Yes, he did." I sighed because already Emery thought I was second-guessing Grant Cahill. This was not going to go over well, me digging around in the man's emails, no matter what he was hiding. "Which complicates things for me."

"I wonder why Cahill would say it was silver instead of carbonatite?"

"I'm not following."

"I just mean, why say anything at all?"

"Well, he has to say something. The geologist was there for a reason."

"But if he hadn't died—"

"He was killed," I corrected him.

"Yeah, but either way, someone would have seen him, right?"

"Possibly."

"I'm gonna say, in a small town, that it's probably likely."

"Fine," I conceded. "What's your point?"

"My point is that it's weird that Mr. Cahill wouldn't just tell Emery the truth. Why does it matter what's there, silver or carbonatite or whatever. I'm guessing it wouldn't matter either way to Emery. Mining is mining, and I imagine that's what he doesn't want."

"Maybe the process for mining one is less invasive than the other, and he's thinking he could sell Emery on going after silver if that's easier."

"I doubt it."

"Yeah, but you don't know."

"True," he agreed. And then he added, "It's terrible that this man is going behind your client's back like this."

"Yes, it is."

"Maybe he'll come clean."

"He had the opportunity tonight and didn't."

"That's too bad, but either way, carbonatite is mentioned in the report as a maybe but not a for sure. He talks about meeting with this guy—this Peter Bannon—to discuss in more detail so that's probably what he did."

It wasn't concrete and certainly not enough to get Emery to turn on Mr. Cahill. And was that for the best anyway? Just because Andrea Dodd didn't want mining didn't mean it was a deal breaker. And why was I thinking that the best thing for Emery was not Lydia? Who was I to say? I didn't know either of them well enough.

"Makes you wonder how this Peter Bannon ended up dead."

"And why?" Huck added.

"The why is the sticky part."

"I would think so."

"Which is why the police were out here tonight questioning him."

"You might need to tell them what you know," he apprised me.

"But Emery already knows Cahill met with Bannon, and that's all I know too."

"But you can provide a motive for Cahill to kill Bannon."

"Maybe. It's kinda thin if we don't know what exactly is in the ground, or if it's actually worth anything."

"That's true too."

"Can you just monitor his email for me, and if anything more is said about the land, you'll let me know?"

"'Course."

"Thanks, Riley," I said playfully, using his last name. "I appreciate it."

He grunted.

"What?"

"Nothing."

"Something," I countered, concerned now. "What?"

"You're fine, right?"

"What're you—"

"I mean, you're not doing something stupid, snooping around all by yourself."

"No. I have you for backup."

"I'm not close enough to be your backup unless you need me out there."

I thought a second. "Why don't you?"

"So you do need backup."

"Are you working?"

"Not yet."

"Well, then, take a vacation from looking for work and come visit."

"Yeah, but you're on a job."

"I've got all kinds of time. The kids go to school. My nights'll be free."

"I'll think about it," he said, but I could hear the worry in his voice.

"There's no pressure. If you're not up for it, it's okay."

"I don't like the idea of you all alone in a place where a guy was just killed and fed to wolves."

"Mountain lions."

"That's so much better."

I snorted. "It's a small town. Nothing ever happens here."

"Famous fuckin' last words," he growled at me. "What'd I tell you?"

"Never to tempt fate."

"You need to listen."

It had always been my weak spot. "Absolutely."

"Goodbye," he said, chuckling. "I've got this."

"Never a doubt in my mind," I said and hung up.

The girls were both staring at me. "What?"

"I think I'm gonna starve to death," Olivia assured me.

"You had PB and J," I reminded her, being as snarky as her sister had been to me earlier.

"Yeah, but that was a billion years ago, and I'm hungry again."

"There's an awesome diner that makes shakes and burgers and egg salad," April announced, looking up at me expectantly, eyebrows lifted.

Crossing the room, I crouched down beside them.

"You heard them earlier; they have some kind of dessert Lydia thinks you guys are gonna like, so how the hell are we gettin' outta here?"

"Watch the master," April said, waggling her eyebrows at me.

Olivia snorted. "She's really good."

Following them out and over to their father, who was sitting in a circle of chairs with everyone, April tapped him on the shoulder and waited. When he turned to give her his attention, everyone got quiet.

"Dad, I need to go because I forgot, but I have to do some more reading for my vocabulary test on Monday."

"Oh, but sweetie, we're having baked Alaska for dessert," Lydia said cheerfully. "You're going to love it."

"As much as the salmon?" Olivia choked out.

I bumped her, and she whined and turned into me, her face in my stomach.

"Kids," April said, shrugging, making her eyes big.

Everyone chuckled over that except Emery, who met my gaze with narrowed eyes. He knew we were up to something.

"So we'll just go and get out of your hair," I suggested with a grin that was way over the top before flicking April on the shoulder and taking hold of Olivia's hand to lead them back toward the front coat closet.

"Your family is leaving," one of the men said, and Emery was up and following us as I got the girls' coats and mine.

"You aren't fooling me one bit," he said as the three of us stood in front of him all bundled up.

"What?" I drawled innocently as I pulled Olivia's beanie down and passed April hers. "Up to? Dude... vocabulary, studying. You heard her."

"And you?" He put his hands on his hips as he scowled down at Olivia.

"Mr. Ozumi said that if Brann wanted to, he could teach crab manga and bazillion juggling at his school, so he's gonna show me some moves."

Emery's gaze lifted and met mine. "Crab Manga?"

"Small child," I said, giving him an exaggerated wink.

Reaching up, he slid his hand around the side of my neck and his thumb traced over my jaw. I had no idea if he knew how he was touching me. From the fond expression on his face, not infused with even a trace of lust that I could see, sadly, he did not. But I felt the connection of his gentle touch, regardless, and it went straight to my cock. There was no doubt about it. Emery Dodd could light me up like a Christmas tree.

My breath caught, and I chuckled to hide the cough of discomfort. And before my clothes got any tighter and my skin any hotter, and before I leaned in to give him a kiss goodbye—because I should, shouldn't I?—I took several steps back. I was leaving and taking his kids. It seemed natural to give him a peck, but before everything got weird —weirder—I bolted for the front door. I had to put some space between us.

"Come on, people, let's motor."

He was still standing there when we left.

I HAD ASSUMED someone would run Emery home at the end of the night, but maybe he'd sleep overnight with Lydia.

Which was fine.

Totally fine.

Utterly fine.

I had no problem with that.

Not a one.

"Brann, are you sick?" Olivia asked me as I drove us to the diner.

"What?" I snapped at her, defensive, wound-up, feeling like I couldn't breathe.

"You look like you're gonna barf," April seconded from the passenger seat.

"What?" I said like she was nuts.

"How come your voice went up so high?" Olivia wanted to know.

"You almost squeaked," April added, squinting at me.

It was just so weird. I didn't have feelings, and I didn't get attached, and definitely was never, ever, jealous before I even got laid!

What the ever-loving fuck was going on?

And fast. Holy fuckballs, fast. I never, ever, ever had any interest in anyone after less than a day. Yes, I'd taken guys off a dance floor and fucked them in a bathroom many times in my life, but this was not that. This was.... I had no idea what this was.

I tried to drag air into my lungs, but my skin felt hot under my clothes even as I shivered in the heated air blowing from the car's vents.

"Maybe we should pull over in case you gotta throw up," April said calmly before leaning over to pat my knee.

"I'm not sick," I grumbled, scowling at her.

She didn't look convinced.

At the diner, we had to wait, and as we sat there, April beside me with Olivia on my lap, people came by and said good job at the soccer field or good job helping Jenny Rubio or how wonderful I was for helping out Emery, as he'd been alone for so long.

A man and woman sat across from me with their three kids, and out of the blue, the man just struck up a conversation about life in Ursa.

"Don't mind him," his wife said, smiling kindly at me. "When you're the fire chief, these PSAs sort of come naturally."

It was funny, but I'd had some ideas about Montana before I got there, and the diversity I was seeing wasn't part of it. The man I was talking to at the moment was black, his wife white; there was Captain Noguchi and Sergeant Tavares, from earlier, and all the little girls at the karate school, who'd been a mix of skin colors and ethnicities. And while it was nice, I wondered if it was the norm, because that would go a long way to making me feel comfortable.

Ever since the Navy, I'd been surrounded by people in every size, shape, and color and found that I functioned best with diversity. It was just another reason why I liked Chicago—lots of different kinds of folks walking around. It was interesting, but the more I was in Ursa, the more I liked it.

"What's your most regular call?" I asked Chief Parkinson, who had introduced himself and his wife, Carla, to me.

He sighed deeply. "Cats in trees."

"You're serious?"

He grunted. "What I wouldn't give for a nice warehouse fire."

Carla elbowed him in the ribs, and he leaned over and kissed her cheek. "I'm kidding," he qualified and then looked at me and shook his head. So not kidding. I liked him already.

At the booth, I realized the menu was under the glass on the table and when our waitress showed up, on roller skates, I asked her about the special.

"Pot roast," she said with a smile, "but don't get it."

"No good, huh?"

She shook her head. "Have a sandwich or the chicken pot pie or the meatloaf. The meatloaf is great, and so is the gravy."

"I'll have that and a huge iced tea," I replied, turning to April. "Whatcha gonna have?"

"I can have anything?"

I scowled at her. "Within reason."

"Define reason."

"Maybe not a chili cheese dog with chili cheese fries, huh?"

"Why?" she asked, grinning up at me.

"Lots of gas," I explained, grinning back. "Think of all the farting."

She dissolved into giggling, as did Olivia.

The girls had shakes—April chocolate and Olivia strawberry—and Olivia ordered a cheeseburger that I was amazed at the size of. April got a pastrami sandwich that was bigger than her head. I had to help her clean up the pastrami, and I broke down and had a root beer float, and then we were all miserable on the ride home. To help, we took Winston for a walk, and once we were in, I sent them to take showers while I turned on the TV and flipped through Netflix.

Once they were both done, they joined me on the couch in their pajamas and socks, and I had a kid snuggled into each side with a dog in my lap, when Olivia told me to open Amazon on the TV so we could watch a movie. With how late it was, sometime after eleven, I knew they wouldn't make it long. We ended up on *Home Alone* and as I predicted, they were out cold minutes later. Since I didn't want to wake them, I stayed where I was.

Sometime later, there were fingers combing through my hair, over and over, and it felt really good, tender but with just enough tug to let me know that it was a man touching me and not a child.

"Hey."

My eyes opened slowly, and I realized Emery wasn't in front of me, but behind me, and his warm breath on my ear meant that his lips had to be only a hairsbreadth from my skin.

My groan was pure agony.

"I'm sorry I woke you," he said softly, his hand on the

back of my neck, squeezing gently. "But if you sleep like this, you'll be broken in the morning."

"Compared to some places I've slept, this would be heaven," I told him.

"Oh, I'm certain of that," he said with a sigh, coming around the couch to sit down on the coffee table in front of me. "But you're not in combat anymore, so you should treat yourself a bit better, don't you think?"

I grunted, and his smile was my reward, big and bright, all that warmth focused on me. There was so much genuine fondness, and it was a revelation because no one I'd ever met in my life showed their emotions so easily. He hid nothing, and it was refreshing, as I'd lived most of my adult life around people who either chose to or had to.

"Let me get up," I said, my voice gravelly because I was only half-awake. "I didn't mean to fall—"

"You're fine," he assured me, hand on my knee for a moment to keep me still.

It was amazing that he could simply sit there and be close to me and not feel awkward about being in my space. Like it was natural and comfortable and not giving him the heart palpitations that it was giving me.

Fuck my life. Being attracted to a straight man who was also a father was a recipe for heartache that I didn't need in the least.

"You all passed out," Emery said softly, lifting his hand from my knee, and returning it to his side. "Did you take them to eat?"

I cleared my throat so it would work. "I did, and holy crap can April eat."

He chuckled and nodded. "Oh, I know. Her mother and I used to wonder where she put it because she looks like a bird."

We were quiet then, the mirth dying slowly, awkwardly, as he stared at me and I stared back at him, both of us, I was certain, figuring out what to do.

"People asked me about you after you left," he said gruffly, taking a breath. "They didn't understand how I could simply allow my girls to leave with a man I just met today."

I felt myself glower. "I hope you told them to go to hell. I have been scrupulously vetted by Jared Colter and more importantly by the US Navy. I mean really, who could keep your kids safer than me?"

"I think they meant how could I let them be with you. Alone."

And I heard what he was suggesting that time. "Oh, that's disgusting," I barked at him, and both girls twitched and moved restlessly.

"I know, I know," he soothed me, hand back on my knee. "I read your file when Grant, Mr. Cahill, first suggested this to me, and then today, seeing you with both of them, how fast they warmed up, how much they missed having a moth —having a person in the house with us— that was really touching to see."

"I'm sure it gives you an idea how Lydia will be once she moves in here."

He scoffed. "You mean us, there."

"What?" He lost me. "You where?"

"We're moving up to that mansion once we get married. The girls, the dog, and me, we're all going to live where we were tonight."

I glanced quickly around the room. "You're leaving your home?"

He grimaced. "There are some bad memories here."

"Yeah, but," I began hesitantly, "there are some good

ones too." He was the one who'd told me about April looking at the chandelier when she was a baby. "I'm betting the good times outweigh the bad like three to one."

"It's not that simple."

I shrugged. "I think it is."

"She died here, Brann," he whispered.

"No, I know," I acknowledged, treading carefully. "But don't you think it would be better to focus on all the days she lived here instead?"

He nodded. "I do, but Lydia doesn't want to be here. It's too small, for one, and she doesn't want to try and mother my girls in Andrea's house."

"It can be her house too. I can't see your wife, here with all the things you guys loved so much, not wanting you to find that again—you and the girls."

His sigh was long, troubled, as he straightened and braced his arms at his sides, gripping the side of the table. "I wish you had been around to talk to Lydia before she made her decision. With all the interest she had in you this evening, you might have been able to get her to change her mind."

"Interest in me?" I asked as he stood and bent to pick up Olivia.

"Her and her maid of honor as well as Tricia, her other friend, another bridesmaid," he informed me, chuckling. "You should have heard them; it was like the sixth grade all over again," he mused, studying me.

"What?" He wasn't being clear, and as I stood up with April in my arms, I heard his breath catch. "I think I missed something."

"Between your heroics today and the way you look, you have all Lydia's friends ready and willing, to go out with you," he informed me with a grin. "I was told that you could start dating her maid of honor tomorrow."

I scoffed. "I think I'm gonna be a little too busy helping Livi figure out how to tie her gi."

He nodded, a faint smile curling his lips. "Yes. I suspect so."

We stood there, staring at each other, and then he cleared his throat softly and turned to take Olivia to bed. I went to April's room, took off her slippers and slid her in under the covers. Once she was tucked in, I was about to leave when she lifted her arms for me. I bent down, and she hugged me, then let me go and rolled over. I turned on her twinkle lights because she'd told me her mother had strung those for her right before she died, left the door open, and returned to the living room. Moments later, Emery walked back in as I was turning off the TV and the lights. When I reached where he was standing, under the square archway leading from the living room to the kitchen, I was going to ask him which lights stayed on at night, but the expression on his face, a bit sad, vulnerable, and gentle, made me still my movement.

After a moment, he sighed deeply, and I saw a faint tremor run through him even as he dropped his gaze to the floor. "It's really nice having you here."

"Your home is awesome. I'm happy to help for as long as you need me."

He crossed his arms, then lifted his head, eyes flicking to mine. "I forgot how nice it is to not be parenting alone."

I had no idea what to say.

"You're so very good with children," he said softly as he reached out and put a hand on my chest, staring into my eyes. "Did you know you would be?"

"I—no," I answered honestly, hearing the approval in his

voice and that ever-present kindness of his coupled now with deep and abiding affection.

"Well, you're exceptional with anticipating what they need and in showing them that you'll be both a confidant and a protector. I couldn't have asked for better."

There was a weight to it, to his words, a heaviness that told me he wasn't being charitable but that he meant precisely what he was saying.

"You'll make a wonderful father yourself someday," he said, almost sadly.

"I never gave it much thought," I replied, speaking low and quiet, not wanting to do anything to jar him because I didn't want him to move. I wanted him to stay where he was, staring into my eyes even as my heart stalled with the closeness and his touch.

"Well, you're a natural," he assured me, letting his hand slip off me. "Sleep well; I'll see you in the morning."

I watched him leave and knew, without question, that sleep would be impossible. I would be far too busy wondering what having the man's hands all over me would feel like.

NINE

I got up early to run, as I always tried to do, and was back, having done my cool down afterward, gulping water in the kitchen when first April woke up and then Olivia moments later.

"You didn't wake me up," Olivia accused me, hands on her hips. "You said we were gonna work out together and get me strong."

"I figured Sunday was your sleep-in day? Is it not?"

She considered that, I could tell from the tip of her head and the narrowing of her eyes. "Yeah, okay, maybe it is."

"Are you okay with me waking you up even earlier than the time you normally get up for school on weekdays?"

"It's just gonna be you and me, right?"

I nodded. "Yep, just you and me, unless April wants to wake up too," I ventured, turning to look at her sister. "You want in?"

"What are you guys doing?"

"Strength training," Olivia answered. "Brann said he'll make me strong."

"And fast," I amended, waggling my eyebrows for her.

April pursed her lips, eyeing me. "Will you be mad if I don't?"

I made a face at her. "As if. No worries."

She brightened instantly. "Okay then, I don't wanna. Maybe when winter's over, but not right now. I have enough trouble getting out of bed when I have to."

"I hear you," I said, smiling at her.

"It's winter," she said, sounding disgusted. "I hate being cold, and I really hate getting out of my warm bed. It makes me cranky."

Olivia's eyes got big. "She's not kidding, Brann. She's super mean. One time when Gramma was visiting, she said that April had her knickers in a knot."

I looked at April. "I guess that's bad."

She nodded.

"Where do your grandparents live?"

"In Nashville, Tennessee," she answered. "That's where Daddy's from too."

I had to wonder why he hadn't moved back there to be nearer to his parents after his wife died. It would have made sense to have family close by, and they probably would have helped him with the girls. I knew from reading the file that Andrea had no other family, but perhaps being on the board of Darrow Holdings required him to be close. Perhaps they wouldn't have let him get by with flying out once a month.

"Daddy says that he loves Gramma and Grampa so much because we live so far away from them."

I chuckled, having my answer.

"We're the only ones that don't live in Tennessee. All our cousins and aunts and uncles live there too."

"Well, that's good; at least your grandparents aren't lonely."

Both girls smiled up at me.

"I bet your grandparents miss you guys, though. I'll miss you when I go away."

April caught her breath and spun around, away from me. Olivia's eyes filled fast, and she started to cry.

"Shit," I muttered, grabbing Olivia's hand and walking around in front of April, taking hold of her arm so she couldn't turn away a second time. I gently shoved the two girls together and held them there as I went down on one knee. "I'm not leaving today, for crissakes. I'm not going anywhere until your dad marries Lydia."

Olivia was sniffling. "You swear?"

I held out my pinky for her.

April wiped her tears away fast, sucking in a breath. "What if we're bad?"

"I'm bad; you guys got nothing on me."

Olivia wrapped her little pinky around mine. "What if I barf on you? I heard you tell the person on the phone last night that if they started barfing, you would too, so maybe you don't like it when people do that."

"I have a thing—if I see you barf, I will too."

April stared at me in disbelief. "There's a kid in my class like that. He barfed when I brought Winston to school 'cause Winston threw up yellow chunks and then he ate it."

I put my head back and focused on breathing, taking in air though my nose.

"Are you gonna barf?" April almost cackled, sounding way too excited over the prospect.

"No, demon spawn, I won't. I just need some more water."

Olivia started giggling, and then April did too.

It only took seconds, and I tilted my head back and glared at them.

"I'm so glad you're not leaving," Olivia whispered, wriggling out of my grip to wrap her arms around my neck and squeeze.

"I'm all sweaty," I told her. "You're gonna be gross now too."

"It's okay," she murmured, her voice tiny. "I don't mind."

April leaned in and kissed my cheek. "I do. Don't hug me, okay. We can hug later."

"When I'm clean," I teased her. "Yeah. Super clean."

I pretended to grab her, and she shrieked and bolted across the kitchen. Scooping up Olivia, I ran after her, and in moments we had Winston chasing us, and it was a lot of noise, which brought Emery from his room, sleep-tousled and bleary, only one eye open.

"Really?" he snapped at me.

The man was definitely not a morning person.

I couldn't help but smile. He was adorable and needed a hug badly.

"You," he said, pointing at me, "start making breakfast, and you," he grumbled, pointing at April, "come give me a kiss."

"What about me?" Olivia asked, comfortable in my arms, her hand on my shoulder.

"You and Brann are both sweaty," he said, shivering like that was disgusting. "I don't want that on me."

"Oh no?" I dared him, playfully arching an eyebrow.

He put up a finger. "Now wait."

April squealed and bolted. "Daddy, run!"

His smile caught me off guard before he ran.

"Oh, they're both toast," I announced loudly.

"Toast?" Olivia asked me as we heard April's door slam shut.

"Yeah, it means they're—" I couldn't say dead. You didn't

say dead to a little girl whose mother had died, even in jest. "It means they're in big trouble."

"Are you gonna open up a can of whoop ass on 'em?"

I did a slow pan to her. "I'm sorry?"

"It's what Grampa says. He told me on the phone last week that he's gonna open up a can of whoop ass on the squirrels 'cause they eat the birdseed that's supposed to be for the finches and the cardinals and the chickadees."

"Ah," I said, walking toward April's room.

"I told Gramma that she shouldn't let Grampa hurt the squirrels, and she said, well, sugar—'cause that's what she calls me—cats have kittens."

I stopped moving to look at her. "And what does that mean?"

"Daddy said it means one thing follows the other."

"Which has what to do with your grandfather's war on the squirrels?"

She shrugged. "I'm not sure, but whenever we go see them, I have to ask him what a lot of things mean. Gramma always says we should visit more."

I grunted. "Hey, you don't have any Nerf guns, do you?"

Olivia's eyes lit up as she nodded enthusiastically.

We breached the room at oh-nine-hundred, but had failed to take into consideration the possibility that our enemy had also taken the time to arm themselves. The air was filled with blue Nerf bullets with orange tips. Others were green. Apparently those were the zombie ones.

April was screaming when I pretended to dive onto her bed.

"No! Brann! Don't you dare! You're gonna get sweat all over my Wonder Woman comforter, and that's—Olivia!"

Emery caught his youngest, mid-leap, and she wrapped her arms around his neck and tried to kiss him.

"No, no," he cried out, turning his head back-and-forth, "anything but that. I just woke up; I don't want sweat all over me!"

April apparently didn't care all that much as long as I stayed off her bed, because she stood up on it and leaped at me like a spider monkey.

"Ohmygod, you're so heavy," I yelled, dropping to the floor on my back. "You weigh a frickin' ton!"

She was laughing like crazy, and Emery was there, staggering around, and I moved faster than he noticed, and the room wasn't that big to start with, so he stepped between my knees. Instinctively, I jerked my thighs together to protect my groin, and he overbalanced to make sure he didn't fall, which of course, made him do just that. He ended up tossing Olivia onto the bed before he came down beside me.

I meant to roll to my feet, but April bumped me out of position, which would have put Emery on my chest, but since I was more coordinated than that, I caught him and protected his head, which would have hurt if he'd knocked it on the floor, even with it being carpeted. As Olivia ran from the room, shrieking with abandon, her sister hot on her heels, shooting, I was on my hands and knees hovering over Emery.

He was gorgeous.

Face flushed, laughing, gazing up at me like I was the second coming, it took all my will-power not to drop down and pin him under me. He was ready to be kissed, he needed to be kissed, but instead of listening to my instincts, I kept still. My hands were braced on either side of his head and my knees caged his hips.

"You realize," he said, his hands slipping around the back of my thighs, "that my girls will want to have a Nerf war every Sunday from now on."

His hands slipped just under the cuffs of my shorts, and I shivered with the contact, the excitement rippling over my skin, causing goose bumps. But while I was there, slowly coming undone, losing control with every passing second, thread by thread, his gaze was not full of heat but instead—awe. The appreciation was rolling off of him. Like he couldn't believe he was so lucky to have me there, with his family. He thought of me in one context only... as the nanny.

I groaned out my frustration, because all I wanted was for him to lift his legs and wrap them around my hips.

"Brann?" he said my name reverently, and I hated it. I would have preferred my name torn from his throat on an urgent moan. "What's wrong?"

"Daddy!" April squeaked, running back into the room with Olivia right behind her.

I lifted up off him in time to catch April as she flew into my arms. Olivia practically vaulted at her father, and he got up only to sit down hard on the bed.

We were all panting and smiling.

"You know," Emery said after a moment. "Technically Olivia only has sweat on her robe, not on anything underneath.

"Oh, yeah, huh," April agreed with him. "She's not gross, only Brann."

I sighed deeply.

"Brann's not gross either, I promise you."

Standing, I put April down, and then walked from the room, suddenly tired, needing to eat and drink water.

"Brann, I'm making breakfast," Emery called out to me as I reached the door to my room.

"Thank you," I called back. "I'm just gonna take a quick shower."

I didn't wait to hear if he said anything more.

Under the water, I stroked myself and thought of him and came hard, spurting onto the tiled wall. When I came out, it was as though nothing ever happened. I suggested we go shopping, and both the girls made faces at me like I was nuts.

"We hafta go to church," Olivia informed me. "You need to put on church clothes."

I smiled at her. "Not on your life."

April whirled around to face her father, eyes pleading, biting her bottom lip. I would have had to be blind to miss that I was in the middle of an ongoing issue.

"No," he said firmly. "Brann is a grown-up, so he's allowed to make his own choices about his faith. You don't have that luxury until you're eighteen."

April stared piteously up at me, slipping her hand into mine.

"Don't give me this solidarity crap," I said, squeezing her hand before I let it go. "You're on your own, kid."

She scowled and crossed her arms.

"We normally have brunch with Lydia afterward," Emery informed me. "You could meet us at—"

"That's all right," I said quickly. "I don't wanna interrupt your family time. I can walk around and get better acquainted with the town."

"No," Olivia whined, walking over and wrapping her arms around my waist. "I don't want you to be by yourself."

"I'll be fine, love."

But she didn't appear convinced.

Emery made ham and cheese omelets for breakfast, and listening to him explain about the sanctity of the omelet pan to me while Olivia shook her head and April rolled her eyes was fun. He made ours with avocado and salsa as well, and made hash browns from scratch, and finished it off with slices of cantaloupe on the side. I offered to clean up so they could all get ready for church.

"Are you sure you don't want to meet us for brunch?"

"I'm sure, thank you."

But he didn't move.

"What?"

"Yesterday you said that you didn't know if you'd make a good nanny because you yourself were never truly able to be a child."

"Oh, that's noth—"

"Please, Brann," he soothed me, hand on my bicep, squeezing gently. "Please trust me with something personal. You know practically everything about me."

I knew too much, that was the problem. "My mother died when I was really young, like not even two, and my father wasn't really parent material."

"So you said," he replied softly, giving me all his attention, his thumb sliding back-and-forth over the same spot.

"He drank," I explained, not wanting to get into the part about how he took me to the bars with him and let me watch him shoot pool, and if he won, I got treated to hot dogs on the good days. "He drank a lot. And when he did, he banged me up a little bit."

Emery took a breath. "Just a little bit?"

I nodded. "It wasn't like—you know. That."

"I do know. I'm a teacher, after all," he said, hand cupping the side of my neck as he stepped in closer, checking on me, his gaze locked with mine.

"Yeah, so... you understand."

"And where is your father now?"

"The drinking finally took him."

"Oh, Brann, I'm so sorry."

I shrugged, because it was a long time ago, but I could

still remember what life with Raymond Calder had been like on the bad days. If I could make it to school, there was lunch there, and that was it for the day. When I got on the breakfast program as well, I made sure I was there even if my old man had knocked me around the night before and I was still sore.

Weekends were rough but if I was lucky, I got invited over to a friend's house and camped out both days, not leaving until Sunday night. All my friends' parents liked me —I washed dishes and mowed lawns, made sure I was super helpful so they had no problem with me. By high school, I had my own job as a barback because the club owner wanted to get in my pants even though I was only sixteen. I made great tips as a runner, because my jeans were tight and I flirted hard. I actually had to give a blow job now and then or get a reputation as a cocktease, but it had been a reasonable trade-off to be able to eat regularly.

My father signed my enlistment papers when I was seventeen because, what the hell did he care, and a year later, as soon as I graduated from high school, I was gone. I left San Diego behind, with everything I had in the world packed into one large backpack. A year later I got the news that he'd remarried. Three years after that, he died of cirrhosis of the liver. Apparently he hadn't stopped drinking in time. His new wife—I didn't remember her name—sent paperwork for me to sign because he had life insurance money that he'd left to me. I signed it over to her instead. I got a note six months later, thanking me and saying that if I was ever in Santa Monica, to please visit.

It was the last I heard from her.

"Brann?"

"Sorry," I said quickly, smiling for him. "You should go shower. I'll see you guys later."

His face broadcast his concern. "I don't feel right leaving you."

"I'm good," I assured him. "And thank you for asking about me—about my life. It means something to me."

The furrow of his brows, the way he hesitated instead of leaving the room, I could tell he was uneasy.

"I promise you, I'm fine."

They were all stunning when they left, the girls in chunky sweaters and leggings and boots, swaddled in their long puffer coats, and Emery in a navy Hugo Boss suit that fit him like a glove. The black cashmere trench he put on over it completed the look of style and sophistication. I felt strange, left out, and it made no sense, because I'd been invited to go, but I realized there was no suit in my duffel, and the nicest thing I owned was my Navy dress uniform back in Chicago.

As I stood on the porch, watching Emery navigate down the driveway from the garage around the back of the house, I waved, standing in the doorway, dish towel in my hand, Winston sitting like a statue beside me.

Emery stopped the car suddenly, and the back door popped open, and Olivia bolted out, running toward me, legs churning under her, tearing up the ground between us.

I knelt and she flew into my arms, wrapping her arms around my neck, which was hard to do, considering her coat was so thick.

"What's wrong, Livi?"

"Don't leave, okay? Stay here and don't leave."

I patted her back. "Listen, even if I'm not here when you get home, I'll be back tonight. We're gonna have dinner together."

"Promise?"

"I promise."

She nodded against my cheek and then pulled back and smiled at me. I was surprised that when she turned for the car, April was there in front of me.

"Oh, come on," I griped at her. "You know I'm gonna be here."

She didn't appear convinced.

"You think I'd ditch you already? You were a B to me yesterday, but we got over it."

Her eyes got huge. "You thought I was a B?"

I grunted.

She laughed like that was the best thing she ever heard, before leaning in and kissing my cheek, then pivoting and running back toward the car. Rising, I waved to Emery, who seemed undecided for a moment, just sitting there, waiting, but then smiled, waved, and drove the car the rest of the way out of the driveway.

I watched the car disappear down the street only to be surprised as a patrol car moved from where it had been parked across the street to idling beside the curb.

Ordering Winston inside, I closed the door, took the steps fast, then jogged down the path that led to the front gate. Deputy David Reed was there in his Ursa Sheriff's Department jacket, coming off as uncomfortable and awkward as I'd ever seen anyone.

"Deputy," I greeted him, arms crossed as I stood on my side of the gate, not opening it, not inviting him inside.

He walked up to the gate but stopped a few feet away. "Sheriff Thomas suggested I drive over here and have a talk with you."

Suggested, my ass. His boss had ordered him to come see me for whatever reason. "About?"

"The sheriff received several dozen complaints about how I treated Emery Dodd at yesterday's soccer game."

Interesting. "Emery wasn't one of them who complained," I told him, bristling, bracing for whatever he had to say.

"No, I know that," he said, his voice faltering as he glanced away and then back to me. "And just so you know, he received even more calls about you and how you handled yourself. Apparently having you there made everyone feel safe, and that things wouldn't escalate to a place they normally do with Mr. Barr," he said solemnly.

"The man is a menace, and he should be banned," I stated, implacable as I stared at him.

"It's hard to do that in a small town."

"I would think it would be the opposite," I pointed out.

He was quiet a moment, and I was guessing, collecting his thoughts. "So about me and Emery yesterday... that stems from his relationship with Lydia Cahill."

I stayed quiet instead of saying *Oh* at the top of my voice or drawing the word out like a child. Already being around kids was making me act less like one in my personal communication. It had been something written down in all evaluations, stated to me in person by whomever was my acting CO at the time, and now, on more than one occasion, by Jared Colter. I had a terrible tendency to either have no filter or make someone feel stupid by stating the obvious. But realizing that, compared to Olivia and April, I was the grown-up, I had my first lesson in shutting up.

He uncrossed his arms and shoved his hands into the pockets of his jacket. "You see, I thought that when we both came back here after college, we could pick up where we left off in high school."

"You dated?"

"We were a couple," he corrected me, giving me a trace of a smile. "All four years, freshman to senior. I played foot-ball, and she was the head cheerleader and prom queen," he explained and then looked at me like I should have had some comment.

"And you thought, what? That it was fate?"

"Something like that, especially after I went to work for her father."

His argument for reunification seemed valid. "You work for Cahill Lumber?"

"I do, yes. I'm the logistics manager at the plant."

"So you're not a full-time deputy?"

He shook his head. "Oh no. The city of Ursa pays forty-thousand dollars a year for the sheriff and thirty-two for the deputy, which is a huge bump up from the twenty-eight it was three years ago."

"How much do you actually need to live well in this town?"

His shrug told me that he agreed, but his grimace said caveat, and I was pretty sure I knew what it was.

"Lydia is a Cahill, and they have a different quality of life than the rest of us."

"Sure," I agreed.

"And Emery, he has Darrow Holdings, and that's what her father is interested in, and I know she still has feelings for me, but she's also going to do what her father wants, but also, let's face it, with the merger of the two companies, she won't have to change her lifestyle in any way." He finished in a rush, trying to meet my gaze but having trouble. It had to be really awkward for him, discussing this with me, of all people. I was a stranger and I worked for the guy who had stolen his girl.

"Have you spoken to Lydia about your feelings about the wedding?"

"No, I... it's inappropriate."

I winced, feeling a pang of sympathy for the man. "Don't you think you should maybe say something to her?"

"I don't. She's very invested in her father's company, and soon she'll be taking over the day-to-day management of the company, so even if we were together, I would have to find another job, and there simply aren't many of those in Ursa."

"So you're gonna do what?"

"Well, Mr. Cahill is backing me for sheriff. There's an election coming up. I don't know if you knew that."

"I didn't, no. Is Sheriff Thomas retiring?"

He nodded. "He is, and it seems like a logical transition from him to me."

If Reed would make a decent law enforcement officer, then yes, but as it was, I had no trust in his ability at all. And as far as I could tell, from the few things people had said, no one else did either.

"Are you quitting the logistics job, then?"

"If I get the job as sheriff, yes," he informed me, like it made all the sense in the world to have his plan B for his life be nothing remotely similar to his first choice.

"You know, I'm not trying to be a buzzkill here, but it seems to me that you should want to serve the people of Ursa, and if you can't be sheriff, that you would want to remain as deputy."

"Yes, but the new sheriff would certainly replace me. The deputy is the sheriff's choice."

I refused to stand there and argue with him over something he should have felt in his gut. The fact that he didn't, did nothing to fill me with confidence in his ability.

"But anyway," he rushed on, "I wanted you to know that whatever happens with me getting the top cop spot in town, or not, I won't treat Emery again how I did yesterday. It was the first time I'd been around him since the wedding was announced, and I think I was perhaps more distraught than I realized."

A dozen quips came to mind because, clearly, it was the understatement of the year, Lydia being the love of his life and all, but I plastered a smile on my face. "Well, as long as you treat Emery well going forward, you and I won't have any trouble."

"Great," he said, returning my smile and making like he was going to turn and leave.

"But you should make time to apologize to the man himself," I suggested with a shrug. "You wouldn't want your constituents to think you weren't a good guy."

"No," he conceded. "I don't, and I want Lydia to see that I bear Emery no ill will as well."

"Well, they're all having brunch after church, so maybe you could see them there or even in the parking lot once the service concludes."

"Excellent idea," he said cheerfully. "Thank you. I appreciate your candor and your advice, Calder."

I had a terrible urge to punch him just to see what he would do, but I squashed it down, gave him a nod instead, and watched as he walked away.

"God help this town if he becomes sheriff," I muttered under my breath, turning and heading back to the house.

Ursa really needed another candidate.

TEN

I called Huck on my way over to the sheriff's station to see if he'd found anything new. He hadn't, but he was more on board with coming to see me. He didn't like me being all alone in town, and even though I explained I had Emery and the girls, he wasn't convinced.

"You need someone who can actually put himself between you and danger," he explained. "And that's not your sweet English teacher client; that's another SEAL."

I couldn't very well argue. He made a lot of sense.

At the sheriff's station, I sat with Thomas in his office until it was time for him to go out on a call. He insisted I go with him, and that part was fun, meeting new people, in need, like Mrs. Velasquez who had locked the punk kid trying to steal her car into her tool shed. He was screaming about black widow spiders when we got there.

"Spiders hibernate just like bears," Thomas told him through the cracks in the door as I took the key Mrs. Velazquez gave me and opened it up.

He couldn't have been more than sixteen.

I turned to look at Thomas. "I thought black widows

went into hyper-toxic mode during the winter and spit blood. Are you sure they hibernate?" I asked him seriously, brows furrowed, really playing up the confusion for the kid's benefit.

The kid ran screaming from the yard, and Mrs. Velazquez gave me a big smile. "Spitting blood?"

"He had no idea."

She snickered, her lovely face infused with mirth. "No, he didn't."

"You call us—I mean, Sheriff Thomas here—if he comes back, all right?"

"I certainly will," she said, beaming at me. "Can I get your number?"

"Mrs. Velazquez," I said, winking back at her, "you gonna call me day and night?"

"Mostly night," she told me with a leer.

"Anytime you call, I'll get right over here."

"Do you like pumpkin cheesecake?"

"I certainly do." I sighed, unable to stop smiling at the adorable, and incorrigible, flirt of an older woman. She had to be eighty if she was a day.

Back in the sheriff's cruiser, I looked over at him when he didn't immediately start the car up. "Are you all right? Did you forget where we were going? Did you have a stroke?" His scowl made me snort out a laugh.

"How old do you think I am, Calder?"

Turned out he was just as funny as Mrs. Velazquez.

We drove around together for a couple of hours, talked about the town and Mr. Cahill and about Peter Bannon, the man who'd been killed.

"So you don't think there are actually any rare earth elements on Emery Dodd's land?"

He shook his head. "No, I don't. I think if there were any

of that up here it would have been found years ago or, as Mr. Cahill said, whatever's there is too small to support the cost of the drilling."

"Then why do you think Bannon was killed?"

"I don't know, but I think it's something I'm not seeing; though lately, that's not too hard to imagine."

"Why would you say that?"

He sighed deeply. "I allowed Cahill to saddle me with a part-time deputy who we pay as a full-time one because I wanted to make the pillar of our community happy."

I shrugged. "There's an election coming up. There's no certainty Reed will win. How many other candidates are there at the moment?"

"None, and that's the problem. I want to retire, but I don't think I can. I refuse to leave this town in Reed's hands."

I couldn't very well blame him.

We stopped for Mexican food for lunch, and I was surprised at how good it was. I'd grown up in San Diego, so I knew what I was talking about. Afterward, Thomas had to go pick up his wife and run her over to her book club before he went to check on a pet adoption event at the park. He dropped me at Jenny Rubio's house on the way.

She had a whole group of neighbors helping her clean up, hang her new front door, and do some spackling and painting around the house. I got right to work after she hugged and kissed me, followed by her daughter doing the same. She told me she had started seeing a therapist and I told her how thrilled I was to hear it. Her mother, who lived in Helena, was moving in with them, and it was great to meet her. She squeezed my face really tight when she thanked me for saving her daughter and granddaughter from her monster of an ex-son-in-law.

"What if he comes back once he gets out?" Jenny asked me.

"Then you'll call me," I told her, reciting my number so she could put it in her phone.

I saw her exhale all her fear, utterly certain I would protect her, and I had my own stab of worry about how I would go about doing that once I went home, but the director of the Ursa Women's Shelter, Megan Farraday, who was on Emery's board of directors at Darrow, was there helping out, and she and I had a nice talk about her excellent relationship with the Whitefish Police Department.

"They'll come running if you're not here," she assured me.

I didn't like the idea of the delay. "Well, I'm here now, and I run twice a day, so I'll check on her when I do."

She was smiling at me. "And who knows, Mr. Calder, you just might end up staying. I'd love to have our group endorse you for sheriff."

I squinted at her. "Ma'am, I live in Chicago."

"For now."

For now? They were all nuts. "I'm sure you'll find a wonderful candidate for sheriff."

Her eyes were locked on me. "Yes, Mr. Calder, I'm sure we will."

All of them were seriously insane.

OLIVIA CALLED me when I was on my way home, having left Jenny Rubio with more people than she actually needed, and asked me to please come to the craft fair and pick her up because she wanted to go home but her father was stuck there and couldn't leave.

"It's all junk, Brann. I wanna come home and play with you."

"Does your father know you're calling me?"

"Yeah," she said like I was an idiot. "'Course. I'm using his phone."

"And where is he?"

"He's looking at metal suns with Lydia."

"I have no idea what that is."

"Well, come see, then. It's really lame."

"You're supposed to be spending time with your father and Lydia and your sister. I don't want to interrupt family time."

"It's not family time if you're not here; don't be dumb."

Her telling me I was part of her family only gave me a small heart attack. It didn't kill me outright like I thought it would. Stupid kid making me have stupid feelings about things I couldn't have. It was annoying as hell.

"Don't you have to paint the flag of Argentina?" I reminded her.

"Oh, yeah," she said, less than thrilled. "I forgot I told you about that."

I chuckled because I could just imagine her little scrunched-up face. "I'll see you guys at home later."

"No," she whined. "Come now."

"I don't—"

"Daddy!" she yelled into the phone, which nearly took out my right eardrum. "Talk to Brann and tell him to come get me."

I was going to reiterate that I would see her back at the house, but then there was his voice, all silvery and rumbling on the other end of the line.

"Brann?"

"Hey, sorry about her calling me. You shouldn't have let her have the—"

"Are you done visiting with the sheriff?"

"How did you know I was—"

"I saw you drive by in the patrol car a little while ago. I waved, but you didn't see me."

"I'm sorry. I was probably still reeling from having Mrs. Velazquez hit on me."

He laughed and it rolled through me, warming me up all over and especially in places that were not helping me want to go back to Chicago anytime soon. Thinking sinful thoughts about a man who was about to get married was ten kinds of stupid.

"Every time she sees me, she tells me to leave Lydia," he said, chuckling. "And her pumpkin cheesecake is amazing. I think she uses it as bait."

"Yeah, I got offered the same thing."

"Well, of course you did. I'd offer you pie myself."

I would take whatever he offered in a heartbeat. "So," I said, gulping around my rapidly closing throat, my voice a raspy whisper, "where are you?"

"We're looking at metal sculptures toward the back. Olivia's about to go catatonic, and April is walking around with her friend Lucy and her mother and a couple of other girls."

"Okay then, is it all right if I come and get my girl, because she does actually need to color the map of Argentina and explain to her class about one great export, besides Lionel Messi, that the country has."

"We're almost done here; we can all go home together. Take a walk over here so we can ride home and stop at the store."

It sounded so settled and domestic, and the longing that

surged through me was a surprise. Because yes, I knew I wanted him, but to think there was even more I wanted—family, home—was not something I had given much thought to before.

"Don't you have things to do with Lydia? I don't want to—"

"Stop trying to get rid of me," he teased. "I like spending time with my family too, you know. And Lydia has a lot to do, and now she has friends in town."

"Oh, I didn't mean to imply that you didn't want to spend time with your girls or—"

"Not only the girls," he murmured. "You just arrived, and you're sort of interesting."

My heart squeezed with words that seemed simply kind and generous on the surface but struck a chord in me much deeper.

"Walk faster, Calder," he ordered and then hung up.

The man would be the death of me, I could tell.

I THOUGHT when Emery said metal sculptures that he meant small pieces that would go on an end table or something. That wasn't what it was. These were ginormous, "fill up a wall in your house" sized installation works.

Olivia saw me and bolted over, grabbed hold of my hand, and squeezed tight.

"What?"

"Dying… of… boredom," she choked out, pretending to faint.

I picked her up, and she draped herself over my shoulder. "Are you gonna make it?"

"Need… ice cream… hurry," she said, her face muffled in the side of my neck.

"You're layin' it on a bit thick, don't ya think?"

She coughed for emphasis as I felt a hand on the small of my back. Turning my head, I found Emery there beside me, close.

"Hey," I greeted him, holding his reclining daughter. "I think Ophelia and I are gonna head home."

"O-liv-vee-ah," she said, enunciating the syllables for me. "Geez, how old are you?"

I started laughing, and so did she, and I couldn't miss the way Emery was looking at me. He liked me as much as his kid did, or I was getting really bad at reading people.

Lydia joined us then, along with her friends from the night before, and I said how nice it was to see them again as Emery stepped around me, bumping my side, my shoulder, my back and then drifting over to the other side as I shivered, not at all from cold.

"That jacket isn't going to cut it too much longer," he said, tucking a long strand of hair behind my ear. "We need to get you a heavy scarf too."

"And a beanie," Olivia said, putting her arm around my shoulder before pointing. "Lookit, April wants us."

I followed where she was pointing. "Yeah, she does. Excuse us," I said, tipping my head to Emery, including him, not wanting to leave him with Lydia.

"We'll return shortly," he said with a smile at his fiancée, hand again at the small of my back, easing me forward.

April looked sad as we joined her and her friends and a woman—had to be Lucy's mom—who appeared uncomfortable as we reached them.

"Donna," Emery greeted her, his hand between my shoulder blades. "I'd like you to meet Brann Calder. Brann, this is Donna Bailey, Lucy's mom."

We shook hands, and then I met Lucy herself and another girl named Kate.

"What's wrong?" Emery asked April.

Before she could answer her father, Donna chimed in.

"She wanted to go to the Wiccan tent, but it's Sunday, Emery, so I didn't think you'd want her there on the Lord's Day," she said indulgently, nodding. "I mean, I would never let my kids go anywhere near anything with devil worship, but—"

"Wicca's not devil worship," Emery replied smoothly, his tone indulgent but firm as April moved forward, leaning into his side. "I taught a whole unit on it last year before Halloween. We had a great speaker from the university come out and talk with my class, and a couple of my kids are doing projects with that same professor, with an emphasis on pagan studies."

Donna stood there in front of him, mouth open, utterly floored.

His smile was warm when it curled those lush lips of his. "I mean, really, when Christmas originated as Yule, we have to keep an open mind, don't we?"

She nodded.

"It's important for us to model tolerance," he professed before turning to his daughter and taking her chin in his hand, lifting her gaze to his. "You know, at the farmer's market where your mother and I used to live in New York, there was this amazing Wiccan booth that sold essential oils and a really great organic beeswax lip balm."

April smiled tentatively up at him.

"What did you see at the booth you found?"

"I didn't get to look around," she told him, glancing at Mrs. Bailey and then back up at her father.

"Maybe we should go check it out," he offered, grinning at her.

Her whole face lit up. "That'd be awesome."

He turned to me. "Sound good?"

"Absolutely," I assured him. "I could use some stuff."

April leaned around her father so she could see me. "You wanna go?"

"Yeah, I wanna go," I said, noticing that the smile I was getting from Emery warmed his rich brown eyes. I put Olivia down and then took her hand. "Show us where the booth is, kid."

"Are you certain you should—"

"You don't have to come, Donna," Emery said over his shoulder, letting April lead us.

"Well, if you're going, we should all stay together," Donna said quickly, she and Lucy and an excited Kate trailing after us.

At the deserted booth, there was a tall, willowy woman with long, golden-blonde dreadlocks piled up on the top of her head, and a lean muscled man with straight black hair that fell to his shoulders, pulled back from his face with a leather cord. They looked like college students to me, and from their expressions, were happily surprised to see us.

"Afternoon," I greeted them both.

"Hello, welcome to Kitchen Witchery," she said brightly. "I'm Miranda and this is Ben, and we're so happy to see you all." Even as she spoke, she offered all four girls a small red velvet drawstring bag. "Go ahead and pick out five stones to put inside your mojo bag."

"Oh, that's so nice of you," Emery said quickly before he turned to the kids. "What do you think, guys?"

There was a chorus of quick thank-yous, but none of the girls moved.

"Hey, look," I said, pointing to one of the baskets full of rocks. "Do you guys know what this is?"

It was cute how all four girls shook their heads at the same time.

"This is tigereye. A buddy of mine had a bracelet made of this that he wore the entire time we were deployed. He always said he felt safer with it on."

All four girls grabbed one as Ben gave me a wide smile before explaining to the girls about hag stones and then the geodes and the raw amethyst.

I drifted away, looking around until I found some eucalyptus oil as well as peppermint.

"Do you have a cough?" Miranda asked me.

"Not right now, but you never know, and I hate taking medicine, so it's better to just diffuse it."

"It is, yes," she said, grinning at me as other people started hovering around.

"Good afternoon, Mr. Calder," Mrs. Whitley, the woman I'd met the day before outside Jenny Rubio's house, greeted me.

"Brann, please, and how're you, Mrs. Whitley?"

"I'm better since you took care of things for Jenny yesterday."

"It was nothing."

"No, no," she corrected me, smiling, moving closer. "It was a huge deal actually, the biggest and bravest, and please, call me Susan."

"You know," I told her, ignoring the compliment, "we should probably grab some white sage for Jenny and some palo santo wood so she can smudge her house and get any residual bad juju outta there."

"Do what now?" She chuckled, reaching for me.

I snorted as she took my arm, and I led her over to

where the sage bundles were and explained how even if you didn't believe in it, the process of doing it was helpful.

"You see, I think sometimes there's this bad, sticky energy that lingers in a place, you know? Sometimes you gotta get it out so you can breathe easy."

"I think I need some of that for my house too."

"Keep in mind that not everyone loves the smell, but it dissipates pretty quickly."

"Well, that's what open windows are for," Mrs. Whitley offered cheerfully.

"That's exactly right," I said, handing her off to Ben, who started explaining what different kinds of smudging sticks were used for.

"Do you have any tea tree oil?" I asked Miranda.

"I do, yes. And since you asked for the eucalyptus oil, I have some dried eucalyptus if you want some for the shower."

"Oh, that'd be great, thank you."

Donna Bailey was hovering close to me, and I passed her the peppermint oil, which she took without thinking.

"If you put that in water and spray it around the house, it'll get rid of a lot of bugs. Spiders for sure—they don't like the smell," I explained to her.

"Really?"

I nodded. "We used to put it in our water so it tasted better, makes you wake up a little, and bonus, helps with your breath."

"Oh," she said, looking at the small bottle in her hand. "I had no idea that they would have things like this here. I mean, I usually have to drive to Helena to pick up my oils or order them online."

"One of my buddies, in the spring and summer, his wife

sprays her curtains with sandalwood so that when the breeze hits them, the whole place smells awesome."

Her slow smile was good to see. "That sounds lovely."

I turned back to Miranda. "Do you guys have any beeswax lip balm or those wrapped candles?"

Miranda nodded like she was in a daze, staring at me.

"Could you show Donna where that is?"

"Yes," she said sweetly, waiting on Lucy's mother. "They're right over here."

"Thank you," Donna said, stepping around me to follow Miranda.

Moving off to the side, I squatted down so the girls could show me what stones they picked out. Lucy and Kate wanted me to see too. I didn't miss that the booth was now swamped with people, and Ben was quickly working the Square Reader attached to his iPad.

"Do you get a cut of the action?" Emery teased, his hand on my shoulder as I stood up beside him. "Because your interest in those things certainly sold them to others."

Half of me wanted to say, *you touch me a lot and it's doing weird things to my breathing, so knock it off*. The other half didn't care. Standing there, staring at him, brain addled, my focus not what it should have been, I wasn't sure *what* to say.

"How do you know about all this stuff?"

"Well, whenever my unit wasn't deployed, I stayed with my buddy Huck Riley, and he's 'that guy'—the all-natural, 'God keep us from prescription medication' type. He tries to never put anything chemical into his body, which was impressive when we were in SEAL training together, because you fu—" I noticed Olivia close to me. "—you hurt all the time. I don't care what kinda shape you're in. So the fact that he wasn't popping eight hundred milligrams of Ibuprofen every few minutes was a surprise."

"I'll bet," he said, drawing me forward, out of the way of some more people trying to get into the booth. "Who got your friend interested in his pursuit?"

"His grandmother," I answered, passing the oils I had to Ben, ready to pay for them. "And he explained it to me as certain things have been around a long time. I remember being in Thailand, and there was stuff there I'd never seen and really didn't even wanna try, but Huck insisted, and he's right—sometimes a good cup of tea can cure what ails you."

"Along with good company, I would agree."

"I saw you gave away your peppermint oil," Ben reminded me. "You want me to grab you another one?"

"And some kind of orange, if you have it. Please."

His gaze met mine, lingering, softening, and then one eyebrow lifted. "I have that. Is there anything else?"

Handsome man, with his dark blue eyes, long lashes, and fair skin. Normally I would have actively noticed, like seen him and flirted and checked to see what he was into or up for. But standing there, with Emery at my side, his gloved hand loosely gripping my bicep, showing, whether he realized it or not, possessiveness, made me impervious to the charms of other men. I still noticed the beauty around me; I just didn't care.

"You have any lavender?" I asked Ben.

"Oh." He was surprised I was still shopping, I could tell from the almost audible pop of the spell breaking. He'd been staring at me, which I got a lot, and me talking had rattled him. "Yeah, lemme—hold on."

He stepped away, and I turned to find Emery scowling, gaze on Ben.

"Hey."

His attention returned to me.

"What's wrong with you?"

"Does that always happen? People hit on you wherever you go?"

"Oh, yeah, are you kidding? All the time, just throwing themselves at me right and left."

He chuckled, shaking his head. "Why the lavender?"

"I need it for Livi. I think if I grab a diffuser for her and run it in her room with some lavender, she'll sleep better, between the smell and the sound the machine makes."

"How do you know she's not sleeping well?"

"Because she was up and down a lot last night, and she even came in to see if I was sleeping a few times."

"I'm sorry she woke you."

"I don't sleep hard, so it was no problem. But it's no good for her, especially on school nights, so with your permission, I—"

"It's fine, Brann. You don't need to check with me about the girls. I think we covered that yesterday. We're on the same page."

"Oh yeah? You trust me?"

"I do, yes."

It was better to hear than I would have thought.

ELEVEN

When we got back to Lydia and her friends, she was overwhelmed, I could tell, when Olivia passed her a mojo bag with stones inside that both she and her sister had picked out for her. She opened it and put them in her hand as they explained to her what they got. She was further touched when April took her hand and led her a little away from the rest of us so she could talk to her.

"Oh, Brann," Shelby said, leaning into me and giving me a quick hug. "You're such a good influence on the girls."

I squinted at her. "Those girls have big kind hearts, and I can assure you that it's their father's influence on his children and nothing to do with me."

"And yet," she said, rounding on me, "you being here seems to have made them warm-up to Lydia."

"It's not me."

"She's been dying for those girls to like her."

"They will; they just need time."

Emery stayed quiet, even though I was sure he could

hear us from the short distance away, speaking to Lydia's other friends.

Olivia walked over to slip her hand into mine. "It's cold. I wanna go home."

April and Lydia walked back over to us, and as soon as April reached me, she leaned into my side, wrapping her arms around my waist.

"What's wrong?" I asked, petting her hair.

"Can we go?"

It did not escape my notice that both of them were clinging to me like I was a life raft in the middle of the ocean.

"Come on, let's go," Emery announced, coming up beside me. "There's grocery shopping and homework—we've got things to do."

Emery gave Lydia a peck on the cheek, and then with a move he'd been perfecting all day, had his hand on my back as he steered me forward, shepherding all of us, me and the girls, toward the parking lot.

I had a perfect day once we got home. Everyone pitched in putting away groceries. Then I helped Olivia with her homework, Emery helped April with hers, and the girls called their grandparents while I made a report to my boss. It went on from there, a day filled with talking and cooking and getting ready for the coming week. I felt like I was part of a family, and even though I knew loving it and wanting it was inherently dangerous to my heart, I couldn't help falling for the man and his girls. I put thoughts of leaving out of my head.

MONDAY MORNING, Emery had to leave early for an English department meeting, which worked out great because I had to accompany April to school so I could speak with Mrs. Dabney. What was great was that Emery had the foresight to put me on the list at the school as a guardian before I arrived. It meant I was able to go to the office and receive a pass to walk around for a specific amount of time. Apparently, he had also given them a copy of my immunization record and background check. The man was definitely thorough. I had to hand it to him, as his diligence allowed me access to the building after showing the clerk my ID.

"Maybe this isn't such a good idea," April said, clinging to my hand after I hugged and kissed Olivia goodbye.

"Come see me before you leave," Olivia prodded me.

"I'm not supposed to bother you in class," I told her.

Her smile was blinding. "You won't bother me."

"Of course it won't bother you, dork, but it'll bother your teacher."

She made a face, and I made one back and then promised I'd stop in before I left.

At the library, Mrs. Dabney came to the counter when she was told by the assistant librarian that I was there to talk to her.

"Why did you bring her flowers?" April grumbled beside me.

"Because I'm gonna try talkin' to her man-to-man before I do anything else."

"Man-to-man?" she said like I was nuts.

"Shuddup."

She giggled but got serious once the older woman stepped up to the counter.

I passed her the roses and lilies before she could say a word. She was surprised the flowers were for her, as evidenced by her mouth falling open and her wide eyes.

"I'm sorry about Saturday," I rushed out, meeting her

gaze. "I get loud when I'm surprised, and if you were shooting at me, I could handle that, but this whole regular one-on-one human interaction is not my strong suit."

"Oh," she said, huffing out a breath, her hands moving to the sides of the large vase. "Yes, well—I, too, wasn't at my best."

I nodded. "Here's the thing," I said, putting my hand on April's shoulder, "she's been drawing stuff in her book because she's had a lot of questions about how her mother died and nobody had been answering them. But instead of bottling that all up, she's been getting that out creatively so she doesn't explode."

Quick glance at April before her attention returned to me.

"But this past weekend, she talked to a doctor and got a lot of her questions answered, so I suspect that the art inside the book will change somewhat. Now, she's not all fixed-up and she's still sad, and she's still gonna have good days and bad days, so you still might notice a picture you don't love now and again, but that's okay, isn't it?"

"It is," she agreed, taking a breath, smiling now.

"So since you're a librarian and you're all about books, and since April loves to read and she's all about the books as well... do you think we can fix this thing?"

"Yes, I do," she informed me, her eyes never leaving my face.

"Then would it be all right if April comes back to the library and checks out books?"

"Yes," she said softly, her eyes back on April. "I'm sorry I kept you from reading, young lady, and I'm very sorry about your mother, as you know. She was a lovely person who we all adored. I miss her too."

April nodded, tears welling up in her eyes.

Mrs. Dabney followed suit.

I had to sit them both down at a table and go on the hunt for Kleenex, which thankfully, the assistant librarian had in her desk.

"I don't have the whole nanny thing wired yet," I confessed to Mrs. Dabney, "but I'm working on it."

She took my hand in hers. "You're doing better than you think, Mr. Calder."

I told her to call me Brann. It was a hell of a morning.

On the way out, I poked my head into Olivia's room to say goodbye, and she came tearing over to me, hurling herself into my arms.

"What's wrong, Livi?"

"We can't go on our hike 'cause Mr. Daniels can't come."

I glanced up as Olivia's very pregnant teacher, Mrs. Nakama, walked over to join us. I of course had been regaled with stories about the epicness of Mrs. Nakama on the ride to school, so I knew all about her. "And who is this, Olivia?"

"This is my nanny, Brann."

"This is your nanny?" Mrs. Nakama said, the surprise clear in her voice.

"Yeah, I'm the nanny," I advised her as I stood up from my crouch.

She looked me up and down.

"Can we still go if Brann comes with us?"

"Oh, honey, he's not even allowed to be––"

"I got a pass," I told her, flashing the sticker that was on my hoodie underneath the open flap of my jacket. "I'm legal."

"See," Olivia said, jumping on the bandwagon, "he's legal."

Mrs. Nakama gave her an indulgent smile. "Yes dear, I

see he does, but he would have to have a background check and—"

"The sheriff will vouch for me," I told her. "Will that work?"

"Well, yes, I think that, uhm—yes probably, but we were having a forest ranger come with the kids today, Mr.... uhm..."

"You can call me Brann."

She coughed as her cheeks turned pink. "Oh, yes, Brann. That's nice. But, uhm, we were having a forest ranger come to go with the... the—"

"Kids?"

"Yes. The kids. We were having a ranger come and—do you have any survival skills, Mr.—I mean—Brann?"

"Does retired Navy SEAL count?"

She squeaked. It was cute. "SEAL." She sighed and put her hand on her chest.

Olivia tugged on my hand, and I gave her my attention.

"What?"

"How come people care that you worked with seals? Dolphins would be better."

"I one hundred percent agree."

A quick call later to the sheriff, and I was cleared to go on the field trip.

On the trail, I turned to Olivia, feeling like crap. "Aww, dude, I forgot about Winston. Is he going to pee in the house?"

She giggled. "That's what the doggie door is for, Brann. Duh."

I scowled at her, which sent her into peals of laughter. "You're a real smartass, you know."

She waggled her eyebrows at me. "Yeah, I know. Can you show us all what not to eat now?"

I could do that.

EMERY WASN'T there when we all got home that afternoon, and after April fed Winston, and Olivia gave him fresh water, we took him with us when we walked first to the dojo and then down three more doors to where April had fencing practice.

"You can sword fight?" I asked April, excited over the news.

"Yeah," she said, beaming up at me. "You want me to teach you?"

"Shit yeah."

She laughed at me as Olivia told me to not use the word *shit*. It was naughty.

I went back-and-forth between the two girls for the next hour, checking on both, Winston trotting along dutifully beside me, and I was at the halfway point when they came running out to find me.

That night, we all caught Emery up with the events of our day.

"I think Mrs. Nakama liked Brann a lot," Olivia reported to her father. "She turned pink when he held her hand to make sure she didn't fall."

Emery grinned at me. "You're like a knight in shining armor, aren't you?"

"Not quite," I teased him, passing him the steamed broccoli.

"I think you're being modest," he assured me. "And that too is a lovely quality."

During the rest of the rehash, I left out April's and my chat with Mrs. Dabney, because he'd told me I didn't have to check in with him on everything, and since it was all fixed, repeating what had gone on, and the resolution, seemed useless. Besides, I was doing what I was supposed to—removing obstacles for his girls and taking care of them when he wasn't around. As it was, he had more than enough to respond to between April talking to him about the bombing of Pearl Harbor and listening to Olivia dramatically explain the horror she felt deep in her heart when no one in her class besides the girls on her soccer team knew who Lionel Messi was.

"It was just so awful," she told her father as I pretended to cough so I wouldn't laugh.

After having fun doing the dishes together and talking some more, when the girls went to shower, I took Winston for a walk, checking in on Jenny Rubio's house in the process, while Emery graded papers. When I got back, he was lying on the floor in the living room, arms and legs flung out, eyes closed as Olivia and April sat close and giggled.

"What happened?" I asked after locking the door behind me.

"Dad is giving up on teaching because some of his students are so stupid."

"Oh, come on, that's mean."

Without opening his eyes, Emery pointed at the coffee table. Crossing the room, I picked up a paper that appeared to be bleeding with how much red pen he'd used.

"Before the Industrial War," I read and then glanced at the man lying prone, all rumpled and sexy in his sweats, a long-sleeved t-shirt, and crew socks. "Did I miss something?" He shook his head. "When, uhm, did the Industrial War occur?"

"After the Industrial Revolution, of course," he said dramatically.

I laughed all the way to the kitchen for water, and he stayed there, on the floor, until his girls attacked him and he chased them around the house.

It would be so easy to get used to this.

That night, after the girls headed to bed, I went in and kissed them both goodnight. When Emery followed me, I thought maybe we'd have time, just the two of us, to talk. But he got a call from Lydia and went to take it in his bedroom. I was reminded then that the man did not belong to me, and it hurt more than I was ready for it to.

Later as I was lying in bed, texting Huck on my phone, I heard the creaking of the floorboards right outside my door, like he was standing there, then nothing for several seconds before there was the same sound again, as though he'd walked away.

I thought a long time about that.

I DECIDED, during the second week, that even though I loved being in the house, putting some distance between myself and Emery was the smart thing to do. I was so attached already, and when I talked to Huck at night, he was all over me about taking a night off from being the nanny to drive somewhere and get laid.

"Just find a bar, pick somebody up, and fuck 'em in a bathroom stall."

"Oh, you romantic you."

"You know what I mean, Brann. You're not gonna be any use to this guy if you're living in a fuckin' fairy tale. Don't be an idiot. He's straight and he's getting married and just because you're there helping him with his kids, that doesn't make you his husband or their parent."

He was always the voice of reason when I didn't want

him to be. "I know that, all right?" I snapped at him because he was right and I was there, in the man's house, eating my heart out.

"Then fuckin' act like it."

He was right, and I knew that, but going to the movies with Emery and the girls, eating dinner, sitting around talking in front of the fire, taking care of Olivia when she got a stomach bug and had to stay home with me, or going on a field trip with April made it really hard to separate me from them.

The way Emery treated me didn't help.

He called me during the day. He bought me a parka and a scarf and a ridiculous neon orange beanie.

There was a school song contest on a Saturday, and after the third hour, I did a slow pan to him, and my expression must have been grim, because he turned and spit out his water. It was lucky we were at the end of the bleachers, or he would have done his dolphin impression all over some unlucky people.

"Seriously," I whined without meaning to. "Every grade level in the whole school sings?"

He nodded, wiping his mouth, chuckling.

"Like the whole elementary school?"

"You need to wrap your brain around this," he teased me.

"But... we could die here."

More nodding and he cackled that time. "It's like a high school graduation," he explained cheerfully. "And I'm speaking from experience."

"Oh," I said soberly, feeling for him. "You gotta sit through that every year, huh?"

He waggled his eyebrows at me.

The horror.

EMERY FOUND April a new therapist in Whitefish. Even though she didn't want to go at first, we both insisted, because united front and all, so she relented. She had to go, it was that simple, because even though she'd turned a corner after talking with my buddy, I knew from experience with others, Huck included, that there was no magic cure for grief. Children were resilient, more so than people often gave them credit for, but she was going to have residual periods of mourning. She was going to lapse. She was going to make progress, but there would be days, triggering events and memories that would cause her to backslide.

Wonder of wonders, it turned out she liked Dr. Haggerty quite a bit. He was funny and down-to-earth, and it was like he said, the thing that hit home for us, three years in the life of a child so young was an eternity. Closure and progress didn't happen in a day. He was thrilled that both Emery and I were on board with an ongoing treatment effort.

His only concern was with me.

"April is quite attached to you," he told me after one of her appointments, having invited me into his office while she sat in the lobby. "I'm not convinced that your leaving is in her best interest."

I had no control over that. "Maybe Lydia—that's Emery's fiancée—should start coming with her instead of me. What do you think?"

He nearly choked on the Earl Grey he was sipping. "I— uhm, no. No. That's not—April's not all that fond of Miss Cahill. I think we'd be moving in the opposite direction of progress."

I nodded. "Then I should do what?"

He didn't have an answer.

When I walked into the lobby, April got up and put her hand in mine. Outside, on the sidewalk, walking toward my Toyota, I asked her if she thought, maybe, since Lydia and her father were getting married, she should start coming to talk to Dr. Haggerty with her sometimes.

"I'd rather go on poop patrol every day than have Lydia come with me," she replied succinctly, capping off her statement with a quick nod.

Poop patrol was what Emery called picking up Winston droppings in the backyard with colorful orange baggies. It was the least favorite chore of both his daughters.

The message was crystal clear; Lydia was not about to be invited into April's therapy.

ONE FRIDAY, I had a beer with dinner, and when I glanced up, he was looking at the bottle like it was the Holy Grail.

"Hey," I said, and his gaze met mine. "Would you like a beer?"

The whine was really cute. "Yes, please."

I opened it for him, set it down in front of him, and he savored it like he hadn't had one in years. "Maybe I'll get some good stuff and put some mugs in the freezer," I suggested.

"I think that sounds perfect," he murmured, and how he leaned his chin on his palm, smiling at me, made me wish I'd thought of it weeks ago. Seeing the man happy was something I found myself craving. It was the same with the girls.

I had no idea that playing board games would be more fun than going out to a club and picking somebody up.

The following Wednesday night I was going with Emery to the Fall Open House at school. When I strode into the kitchen in jeans and a sports coat, he turned and walked into the stove, bumping his head on the range hood.

"You all right?"

He nodded but I heard him take a gulp of air, and the glazed look in his eyes was very satisfying.

"Is this okay?" I fished, opening the jacket, letting him see the navy dress shirt underneath and how it clung to my chest and abdomen. "Or should I go change?"

"No, you—no. Brann. You look great. You look... really great."

"Are you sure? It's not too casual?"

"No. You'll fit right in with me and the other parents."

Other parents was nice to hear.

It was not lost on me that during our walk through the school, as so many people stopped to talk to not only him, but me as well, that he never once left my side. And I'd have had an easier time counting the number of times he didn't have a hand on me, than the times he did.

But that Friday, he left to spend the weekend with Lydia and her friends in Helena, and it hurt to watch him drive away, to see him get into the car and kiss his fiancée and laugh with the others. Clearly, when all was said and done, I was the help, nothing more. Whatever I thought, and hoped, was idiotic.

When he came home late Saturday night, it shocked the hell out of me. I was on the couch, reading, and the girls were in bed already, when Winston's head lifted up off my thigh and he focused on the door.

I heard the jingle of keys, and then the door opened and Emery came in.

"Hey," I greeted him, smiling wide, my heart clutching at

the sight of him, as was most often the case. "You're home early."

"Yeah I—I just wasn't comfortable, and I had this feeling like I was supposed to be here. Home. And I couldn't get it out of my head."

I nodded. "Well, I always go with my gut."

"Me too," he replied, his gaze all over me before landing, like a fluttering bird, back on my eyes. "Is there anything to eat, because I skipped dinner to fly home."

He'd flown. He'd taken the Darrow Holdings jet that was only supposed to be for emergencies, because he felt like home was where he needed to be.

"Yeah, I made chili and cornbread."

"My girls ate chili?"

I grinned at him. "Every time they eat something I make, you always say that, like it's a big surprise when they don't complain about salad or vegetables."

"I think it's the homemade part they like," he informed me, staring, moving closer, his hands on the back of the couch. "I know I do."

"Well, come on," I said, as I got up and went to the kitchen, glad I'd cooked instead of waiting for the next day, having hoped he'd be home for Sunday dinner. "I'll heat it up for you, and you can tell me all about your wild time in Helena."

"Not that much to tell," he said, standing there, watching me as I pulled out Tupperware and got out a bowl and a spoon for him. "We had dinner, drinks last night; there was some dancing and more drinking."

I turned to look at him. "You dance?"

"You didn't have to ask it like that," he said sourly.

My chuckle was not subtle, even trying to stifle it down. "I just—do English teachers dance? Is that a thing?"

"I'll have you know I'm a very good dancer."

"Huh."

His grin was warm and unguarded, and he stood there and breathed, like simply being there, sharing space with me was so much more than good.

That might have been why I did it, but really, I wasn't sure.

Maybe it was because of the house. Being in the warm, cozy place with him and his girls felt like the home I never had.

Maybe it was how much I was clearly needed in the town and the good I'd done in mere weeks. I was as needed as I'd been in the Navy, and that was a surprise.

Maybe it was because I was afraid for him and for the changes that were going to happen in his life.

I had no idea what the impetus was, and possibly I was overthinking it all and it was just him, just Emery Dodd and how drawn to him I was and how much I simply wanted. In the end, there was no telling, but in that instant, there was only him and me in the kitchen, illuminated by the soft reflected glow of the chandelier, the sparkle of light glittering in his big brown eyes.

He was supposed to be mine.

It was why he came home. He knew that he was supposed to be home with me and his girls. Me and his girls. Not Lydia and the girls. Me and the girls.

And suddenly all I could do was show him.

Show him where he belonged... and to whom.

I stepped into his space, took his face in my hands, and kissed him.

His lips were soft, and I parted them with my tongue, wanting to taste him, needing him to realize something important... that I was there for the long run. He tasted so good, like brandy and chocolate, and I kissed him hard and deep, taking what I wanted, but even more than that, needing him to know I was serious and solid and I could be his foundation. I could be what he built the rest of his life on.

It took longer than it should have for me to realize he wasn't kissing me back.

In the rush of adrenaline and heat and lust, I missed that I'd knocked him up against the wall and held him there while I mauled his mouth. When I finally registered him pushing me away instead of pulling me in, I stepped back as he scrambled off the wall.

"What the hell are you doing?" he rasped angrily, his face a riot of emotion—shame and anger were what I saw first, and what seared into my brain.

Oh God no.

"Why would you—how could you—what are you doing?" he yelled, and I heard the revulsion, saw the disgust on his twisted features.

"Fuck me," I barely got out, horrified I'd pushed myself on him, forgetting my own strength. "I'm so sorry. I didn't mean to force—"

"I'm not—how could you think I—"

"I'll get outta here, and Torus can send—"

"The girls," he whispered harshly, and then darted from the room. I heard the door to his bedroom bang shut seconds later.

His words were crystal clear.

He certainly didn't want me, was appalled over what I'd done, but for his daughters... I could stay. He'd suffer with my continued presence for them. They couldn't have even one more change, one more disruption, or one more good-bye. He wouldn't allow that.

Rushing to my room, I went in, closed the door behind me, and climbed onto the bed. And though I was exhausted, I couldn't sleep at all.

TWELVE

I waited as long as I could before I got up the next morning. It was still just after seven when I woke up Olivia and asked her to help me make breakfast.

"You never get up this early on Sunday," she said, smiling sleepily, rubbing her eyes. "Where's the fire?" she asked, using an expression she'd picked up from me.

I didn't explain to her that it was because, when I'd finally drifted off from exhaustion, I'd still woken up several times in the early hours of the morning, my brain running through everything I'd done, over and over again.

The look on Emery's face, his horror and humiliation, wouldn't get out of my head. Every instinct I had said to run, but what kept me there, rooted, planted in the house even though I was filled with shame... was the girls.

The girls needed me.

The girls were counting on me.

The girls trusted me to remain.

If I focused every drop of my attention on them and then left clean, cutting the cord the moment the wedding was over, I could still be of service to Emery. I'd irreparably damaged our—whatever it was, not relationship—but the girls were another story.

All I wanted was to erase what I'd done, and if I was there, steady, strong, an absolute rock of dependability, then perhaps he'd stop seeing me as someone who'd disappointed him, or worse, accosted him.

When he finally stumbled into the kitchen an hour later and saw both girls eating biscuits and gravy, he came around the table and stood beside me after pouring himself a cup of coffee.

I couldn't look him in the eye.

"Brann," he said, his voice low, rusty, as though he hadn't spoken in years. "We need to talk about—"

"It's okay," I assured him, sad but resigned, knowing it was actually for the best. "I figured you'd change your mind and you'd want me out this morn—"

"No," he snapped under his breath, taking the last step forward, into my space, so we were shoulder to shoulder. "I don't want you to go anywhere."

I had no idea what I was supposed to say.

"Last night," he began under his breath. "That wasn't what you—"

"I didn't mean to force my—"

"*You didn't,*" he made clear, the stress on his words, in his tone, changing things for me in an instant. "You're not like that, and that's not what happened."

I finally turned my head and met his chocolate-brown gaze. His eyes were so soft and deep, and every instinct I had said to claim him, to turn and kiss him again because he was supposed to be mine. And that made zero sense, as what he wanted had been made abundantly clear—it was, decidedly, not me. So instead of saying another word, I clenched my jaw tight so nothing stupid came out of my mouth.

"You surprised me, and—"

"No," I said fast, shaking my head, unable, it seemed, to remain silent. "I freaked you out and made you uncomfortable, and it was not—"

"I wasn't freaked out, Brann, and you're not the first—"

"I don't think sometimes—a lot of times—and it's gotten me into a ton of trouble in my life, and now I messed this up, and—"

"You're not," he growled, sounding frustrated, his right hand clenching into a fist on the counter, "listening to me, and if we could—"

"It's only been a month, so really, I could still go and—"

"No!" he yelled, and the room went silent.

I turned to the table, and both girls were staring at us. "I don't know why your dad got so upset, but he's taking a hard pass on chicken livers for dinner tonight, even though I said you guys would totally love them."

Both girls looked horrified.

"Tell your dad thank you."

"Thank you, Daddy!" Olivia yelled.

"Ohmygod, thanks, Dad," April echoed, squinting at me like I was insane.

He took a breath, smiled at them, and then turned back to me. "Would you please come into the other room with—"

"I don't want you to think I would ever do anything to—"

"Brann," he said huskily, taking a step away from me, "would you please walk into the hall so we can talk about—"

"I swear I won't ever touch—"

"I'm not worried about that," he insisted, clipping his words, glaring at me, reaching for my bicep. "Please come here."

Rushing by him, I walked under the arch that marked

the division between the kitchen and the hallway and then rounded to wait for him, only to realize that he was right there, nearly plowing into me.

I scrambled back, not wanting to touch him, afraid of what he'd think.

"Shit," he groaned. He'd been ready to reach for me, I felt it in a way I'd come to think of as instinctive, but he caught himself and let his hand fall to his side instead. "Brann, I need to explain what—"

"I never meant to scare you or disgust you, and I'm sick about it, and if I could take—"

"Oh, for the love of God, Brann, you didn't scare me or force me or anything else," he almost yelled. "You surprised me, and that's it."

I heard him that time, and my relief was staggering.

As long as I hadn't *made* him stand there while I kissed him, the incident was forgivable. If he hadn't been able to get away, if I'd cornered and caged him, made him feel defenseless and demeaned, then absolving myself was out of the question. But he wasn't saying that. He was telling me things hadn't happened that way.

"If we could—"

"I am really so very sorry," I said quickly, hoping he could hear the sincerity and pain there and know I meant it. Heart and soul meant it.

He shook his head. "No. You don't have anything to apologize for."

"I do."

His gaze was locked on my face. "Brann, you—"

"Please tell me, are we okay?"

His brows furrowed, and his face scrunched-up like he was in pain. "Of course we're okay, but I think we need to—"

"Forget it," I rushed out, feeling the weight of shame and

fear evaporate and leaving me so very thankful for the do-over. "We need to just forget it. You were clear, and I absolutely heard you, I swear to God."

"Brann—"

"No, Emery, really," I said, exhaling a deep breath as I pivoted around him, then looked back over my shoulder for only a moment. "I so appreciate you giving me another chance."

"Could you please—"

"Hey, is there a pumpkin patch or someplace for us to go?" I asked the girls as I rushed away from him and back into the kitchen, then stopped beside the table to look at them. "Because it's almost Halloween, and you guys are seriously lacking in orange around here."

The shouts for pumpkin patch were loud.

Emery couldn't go. It turned out Lydia and the others had returned as well, so now he had to be at a wedding planning session. He went on to explain that he had friends of his from college who would be in Helena for a conference until Wednesday night.

"But Wednesday is Halloween, and I usually—"

"You don't have to worry about taking us now," April said excitedly, like she was problem-solving his life. "Now Brann can take us, and you can be with your friends!"

"Honey, I—"

"Daddy was worried about how he was going to be in two places at one time," April informed me. "He was gonna have to take us trick-or-treating early and then leave us with my friend Nicki and her mom."

"Oh, then this works out great," I said to Emery. "I'll take them, and you can go."

"That's not—"

"What should I be?" I asked the girls. "Maybe we could go get me something and then hit the pumpkin patch after."

There was so much squealing it sounded like there were ten more kids in the kitchen.

"Let's clean up the kitchen, people," I announced. "Then we wash faces, brush teeth, and meet in my room. I gotta make a quick call and then we're vapor."

They both looked up at me.

"We're air," I explained. "Like we're moving so fast we leave nothing behind."

They both said *oh* at the same time, in a very indulgent way that was not lost on me.

"You guys are making me feel really damn old."

Lots of giggling over that, and I growled at them before I started clearing the table.

"I can clean up," Emery offered, and when I turned to him, I could have sworn he looked and sounded almost dejected, but I was probably reading him wrong. He had to be as relieved as I was.

We had everything straightened out. I apologized, and he said it was okay, which basically meant he forgave me, so... we were good. "No, we got it," I assured him. "You go do your thing with Lydia. Will we see you for dinner?"

"The girls and I were supposed to eat with her."

"Or... you guys could have date night instead, and the girls and me'll hang out and get ready for school tomorrow like usual."

Both the girls cheered because skipping dinner etiquette on a lazy Sunday sounded like heaven to them.

"No dinner! No dinner! No dinner!" they both chanted.

Emery gave us a slight smile and then kissed his girls.

I turned to the sink before he could say anything more,

because it hit me then, as I'd made plans for the day, what the best thing was that I could do for him.

I needed to make myself invisible.

If I was there for the girls but Emery didn't have to deal with me... how great would that be? He'd have the best of both worlds—a nanny there to care for his kids and a person he never had to have any interaction with. It was a win-win situation. I would work really hard to make up for what I'd done so the kiss wouldn't only be forgiven but forgotten as well.

I felt so relieved at having a plan.

APRIL WANTED me to be a cowboy, and Olivia was certain I'd make a better pirate, so they compromised and I was a musketeer, which worked out great since April was going as a princess and Olivia as a queen. I'd be their protector and dress the part as well.

Looking for pumpkins was insane, and we got way too many as well as some different-colored gourds, because apparently their mother had liked those and the Cinderella ones to put on the front steps of the house. We also bought small hay bales and decorations for the front door and fake spiderwebs to put all over the shrubs.

Emery was gone all day and night, and the girls were in bed when he got home. When I heard his car driving along the side of the house, headed for the garage around back, I changed into my running clothes and was on my way out as he was on his way in.

"The girls are down," I told him as I walked by. "I'll be quiet when I come in."

I didn't give him a chance to say anything more.

· · ·

HALLOWEEN WAS GREAT. I'd forgotten how much fun it was to go trick-or-treating. Dressing up and walking the girls around was amazing, and I met what felt like a hundred people. I couldn't remember ever shaking that many hands in my life. I felt like I was running for office.

I took video for Emery, and April made a great tour guide, narrating everything we saw—the decorations, the costumes, telling people to say hello to her dad, and having them all wave back. The girls didn't want to walk around for long, as they apparently loved handing out candy as well, so we got home so they could. I enjoyed watching them, so I left the front door open. We had a fire going, and kids came up on the front porch to get treats and show off their costumes as Winston sat beside me, dressed like a butterfly, complete with antennae.

Once it got quiet, I sorted through the candy with them, and we put it in Tupperware to take to school the following day. We watched *The Nightmare Before Christmas*, which I'd never seen, but I put the kibosh on watching *Sleepy Hollow* and didn't believe for a second that their father said it was okay. I didn't even have to call him to check. I wouldn't call him to check, because that would defeat my decision to be as invisible to him as possible. I was adamant, even if it killed me to keep my distance, that he would be comfortable again in his own home.

Things changed drastically in the weeks that followed.

Instead of being open and comfortable with him, I steeled myself to speak in bullet points of information. We didn't talk anymore; I reported to him. I gave him updates, and that was all. The girls were an amazing buffer. I was betting that was how people who had kids but weren't happy in their marriage ended up staying together. The house revolved around the children, and there was barely time to breathe.

By the end of the second week, I had my routine down cold.

I woke up with the girls, we'd do morning stretches, and then Olivia and I would work on her karate, and April practiced her new ballet steps. She had always wanted to learn, as her mother had studied ballet as well, and over text message, Emery had given me his blessing to get her enrolled.

After that, we had breakfast, and then I took them to school. When I got home, I went for my morning run and afterward took Winston for a walk for my cool down and his morning constitutional. Most days I walked with Mrs. Everman and Mrs. Patel and their dogs once around the huge dog park before we went to get a cup of coffee.

Once home, I showered, changed, and then went to see Sheriff Thomas at his office, which also served as the seat of the county clerk of Ursa as well as the detention center, which sounded nicer than saying jail. I enjoyed going on patrol with him, as it broke up my days. I would have gone stir-crazy otherwise, as I wasn't used to doing nothing. I got to where, after the first couple of weeks, I knew some of the "frequent flyers," as the sheriff called them, and many responded to me even better than they did him, because, let's face it, they couldn't outrun me. It was heartwarming too, that so many people stopped to say hello and ask after the kids and Emery when they saw me on the street.

During my rounds with Sheriff Thomas, I met Malachi Jezic, owner of Ursa Customs, one of the places in town that made no sense because he was one of the top custom motorcycle manufacturers in the country and his shop was in rural

Montana. I liked him the moment Sheriff Thomas introduced us, and though he had an icy rapport with both Thomas and Reed—they'd thought he was a homeless drifter when he first hit town, very *First Blood*—with me it had been warm from day one. I'd seen the Marine Corps tat on his forearm and grimaced.

"We're first in," he growled, defending his branch of the service, advancing on me as the sheriff took several steps back.

Standing my ground, I grinned wide. "Do you have any idea how many times we had to save your asses?"

He shook his head. "The hell you say."

I arched an eyebrow as I studied the big man, the massive shoulders, tree-trunk-sized biceps, and his towering height. "We're in and out, man, gotta provide you some cover."

He rolled his eyes, clearly I was ridiculous, but he offered me his hand, and I grabbed it tight. When he invited me to box with him, I was careful to steer clear of his hammer of a right hook. He always bought breakfast afterward.

Once I was done spending time with the sheriff, I would walk by the Ursa Women's Shelter on Boulder Lane, and if there were any men *outside*, ready to hassle the women *inside*, I explained that I was there, and if anyone had a problem, they should feel free to discuss it with me. And it wasn't that I thought the women there couldn't handle themselves, but everyone deserved to have their sanctuary actually be one. I'd visited lots of guys I knew in halfway houses after they came back from a deployment and had trouble transitioning back into society. Sometimes people got obnoxious with returning military as well. I would have been just as vigilant in that case. But there was never any trouble. Talk of

Jenny Rubio's husband had gone a long way to helping that along.

LUNCH for me was usually spent at the Little Dipper, where Nadia Woods served huge deli sandwiches and amazing soups and salads. I sat at the counter and talked to whoever sat down beside me, as well as talking to Nadia's husband, Homer, who would come out of the kitchen most days and visit. Nadia always appreciated me spending time with Homer and never hurrying off. He was a nice man who had been shot in the head during a robbery before they moved to Ursa. The brain damage he suffered had changed their lives. They went from her being a stay-at-home mom with a CFO husband, to her running a sandwich shop and her husband carving pastrami. At times, his thoughts got jumbled together. She said a lot of people didn't have the patience for him. I had nothing but. The three of us, plus her three teenagers, got along great.

After school, I picked up the girls every day with Winston, which was a big hit with all the other kids as well as for the attention whore of a dog. We'd have a snack on the way to whatever was on the agenda that day—soccer or karate for Olivia, fencing or ballet for April. Winston and I hung out, and I checked in with Huck about his ETA for visiting Ursa and if anything was up with Cahill. Once the girls and I got home, there was homework, though April had to assist Olivia with her math, because I had no clue what was up with the fancy new way it was supposed to be done, Common Core something or other, and then they helped me make dinner.

Sometimes, Emery joined us, and I stayed quiet as the girls told him about the events of their days. He had given me a credit card for groceries and other things the girls needed. And even though he seemed sad that he missed our trip to the soup kitchen and delivering blankets to the homeless shelter, he was honestly far too busy to ever join us. I had no idea how he'd done everything he had to do before I got there. I'd never really given being a single parent a lot of thought before, but seeing what he was up against, I wondered how people without money to hire someone coped. I had a new respect for mothers and fathers who parented alone.

MID-NOVEMBER, on a Friday, I had to take April and Olivia to a fitting for their flower girl dresses for the early December wedding, and when I saw them walk out of the back to stand on the little dais in front of the wall of mirrors, I nearly fell off the bench I was sitting on. I hadn't laughed that hard in years.

"It's not funny!" April railed at me, trying not to smile as Olivia ran around pretending she was an abominable snowman.

"C'mere." I snickered, touching all the layers of white satin and the fur cloak and chiffon that she was wearing, trying to pat it all down to find her head. "Dude, you look like you're covered in frosting!"

Olivia attacked me, climbing up into my lap and hugging me so very tight as April put the cape over her face and stood in front of me with her arms out.

"Let's get googly eyes and glue them to this," April suggested, muffled under the cape.

"You guys need ears 'cause you look like polar bears in dresses."

Olivia snarled and growled into the side of my neck, and

it was April's turn to run around like a crazed yeti until both her sister and I were gasping for air.

"I can't even with these dresses," I said, wiping my eyes as the three of us lay there, side by side on the little stage, breathing hard. They probably weren't supposed to lie down in all the finery, but I couldn't muster enough feeling to care.

"I don't want Daddy to marry Lydia," April said suddenly, and Olivia grew still on my left before taking a breath.

"I don't wanna leave my room," Olivia confessed. "Mommy painted the clouds on my ceiling and walls, and what if, when we move, the next people paint over it?"

"Lydia's house is so big," April echoed, sitting up and crossing her legs, which looked strange in the dress. "And her dad lives there, and he always tells us not to put our feet on the furniture, and he said that Winston won't be able to go in all the rooms."

"Well, Winston's pretty cute," I reminded them. "So maybe you need to show Mr. Cahill how great he is."

Both of them were making faces like I was nuts.

I gestured at April's dress. "I mean, clearly Lydia likes white, and Winston is white, so... maybe you guys should brush him more and make him super fluffy, and then if she likes him, her father will too, and it'll be all win-win."

Olivia sat up then, and so did I. We were there, quiet being still together. I didn't know what to do to get their minds off things, so I did the only thing I could think of, and punted.

"You don't think these capes are real fur from, like, an animal somebody killed, do you?"

Their eyes got really big, and April pulled hers off and checked the tag.

"There's only a name on it," she told me. "Let's ask the lady."

It turned out that for the winter wonderland wedding Lydia wanted, she was wearing white mink, her maid of honor and bridesmaids were wearing fox, and the girls were wearing Angora rabbit. I informed the nice lady in charge of the fitting that if the girls ever saw those capes again, they would vomit all over them.

We *definitely* made an impression.

It was my fault, but they weren't sad thinking about moving after that. They were, instead, sad about the bunnies. I took them for ice cream before dinner, even though it was thirty-two degrees outside, which was apparently normal for the second full week in November in Ursa. Bundled all up, hats and boots and gloves and scarves, they looked like polar bears all over again, except this time they were red and purple.

We had to stop at the store to get dinner, but we were all tired, so we got stuff to make burritos and headed for home. That night after we ate and cleaned up, did homework and they took showers, instead of me changing into my running clothes and the girls going to their bedrooms to read before bed, we all convened in my room. They both got under the covers, and I lay on top with just a quilt that their grandmother, Emery's mother, had made. I was reading them *Harry Potter*, since I had all the books on my Kindle, and as we vegged, Olivia did her favorite thing and put her fingers in my hair, which I really needed to cut.

"You used to do that––" April yawned, then continued talking to her sister, "––to Mom."

"I know. Brann's hair is soft too, and look at all the pretty colors."

"Yeah, it is pretty. I want blond hair."

"Brown is better," I assured her. "Like your dad."

She yawned again. "Brann."

"Yeah?"

"Are you gonna leave the day of the wedding or right before?"

"I dunno," I said, not really having given it much thought. "Probably before, I would think."

"You're not coming to the wedding?"

"I don't think I'm invited."

"But once Dad marries Lydia, he'll have to do even more stuff with her, so who'll take care of us?"

"Lydia probably has that figured out, don't'cha think?"

They were quiet.

"Maybe I can go live with you," Olivia told me. "'Cause maybe Daddy's gonna have a new baby with Lydia."

I scoffed, and they both looked at me. "Don't be stupid. Your dad loves you guys more than anything. He would fight anybody to keep you guys with him."

"You think so?"

"I know so."

"Okay," Olivia agreed and then put her head next to mine on the pillow.

I wasn't sure when I stopped reading, but when I woke up a bit later, Winston was asleep on the end of my bed, Olivia had her arm thrown around my neck on the left, and April was snoring away on my right.

I should have gotten up and carried everyone to bed, but I was too tired. There was a storm outside, I could hear the rain pelting the windows, but I was warm and safe inside, and quite content to be the protector of two little girls and a Westie.

THIRTEEN

Saturday morning I was crippled from sleeping like a contortionist in my own bed. All because I didn't want to disturb either kid or the stupid dog. It was like real-life Tetris, fitting us all together, and my back was not a fan.

Crawling over April, I got up, one eye open, and nearly killed myself on the dismount. The second I overbalanced and bumped the wall, Winston lifted his head, jumped down off my bed, and was there, beside me, staring up like I was nuts.

"If you were getting up anyway, you could've moved then, ya dick."

He appeared very smug. *Annoying dog.*

As I staggered to the kitchen, Winston darted ahead of me to greet Emery, which was a surprise. Not that the dog went to him, but that the head of the house was up already at—I had to check the rooster clock on the wall—a quarter to nine. At first I had dreaded the weekends, because it was always awkward with him being home, but lately he'd been gone before any of us got up.

"G'morning," I greeted him, watching him pet his dog for a moment before making my way to the coffeepot. "Thank you for making this."

Nothing. No response at all.

That was new. Normally we were at least civil in passing. I'd worked so hard to stay out of his way, walking out of a room when he came in, always on my way somewhere unless we were stuck having a meal together, me quiet as he talked to his girls, and getting up and starting the dishes as soon as possible.

"You going somewhere?" I asked, trying again to make conversation, noticing how he was dressed—the jeans and the tweed blazer with the matching waistcoat and brogues a bit much for an early Saturday morning.

He ignored my question. "Lydia is livid with you."

I stopped admiring the cut of the jacket on his shoulders, the swell of his chest, how long his legs were, and how the collar of the crisp white shirt looked against his tan skin, which I'd come to realize was his natural color. "And why's that?" I asked, even though all I could think was... *Livid Lydia*. It sounded like a children's book where the main character had anger-management issues.

"The fur capes the girls were supposed to wear."

"Lydia likes to be livid," I responded, going for overly cheerful.

"What?"

I waved him off.

"She was furious about the girls not wanting to wear the capes. It meant a lot to her that there would be a specific look to the ceremony."

"Okay," I said as I walked to the doggy door with Winston and slid the metal piece up that opened it for the day. Last one to bed slid the guard down at night, which lately had been all Emery. He was the one coming in at all hours.

"Okay?" he said sarcastically. "Is that all you have to say?"

"What?" I wasn't even following him, having been barely listening.

"Did you hear me?"

Why was he giving me crap so early? If he wanted to yell at me, he really needed to wait until I had more coffee. "Sorry 'bout that, the cape thing I mean, but if you'd heard the alternative, then—"

"But I didn't, Brann," he snapped at me from where he was, leaning against the counter by the refrigerator. "I don't hear anything from the girls because they've already told you. They've already confided in you, and they don't care about talking to their father anymore."

I was going to blast him and tell him that was total crap, but I had no right, and more importantly, I didn't want him to throw me out of his house and cut me off from his kids before I had to be. So instead of ripping him apart, I turned to leave instead. I could change and go for a run and get coffee while I was out. He made crappy coffee, anyway; it was weak and—

Emery caught my wrist before I could charge by him, and his strength was startling as he held me in place, as well as the fact that he'd moved really fast to intercept me.

When I turned to look at him, to figure out what was wrong, I was surprised to find him staring at me. There was all that gorgeous, melting chocolate brown, and he kept me there, locked in his gaze, as he closed the distance between us down to nothing.

"Stop running away from me," he said tightly, plaintive and demanding at the same time.

My mind went blank. I forgot to breathe as my mouth went dry. The lump in my throat would have made it impossible to speak, so it was fortunate I didn't have to, because again, him touching me had shorted out my brain.

"I know what's going on. I'm not stupid."

"What do you—when did I ever say you were stupid?"

"I walk into a room and you walk out, and I'm... I'm sick of it."

I had no idea what to say.

"And then last night... I came home, absolutely drenched from the rain, and all of you were in your room snuggled up in your bed."

I waited, marveling at him, watching as he lifted his hand to my cheek, and I felt each brush of his fingertips like a tiny brand on my skin.

"At first I was furious," he confessed, and I felt my face heat as he held my gaze. "Or, more truthfully, I was angry again because lately I'm mad at you all the time."

"Me?" I ground out, barely, the sound more like a croak than an actual word.

He nodded as he slid his thumb across my bottom lip, slowly, decadently, and I realized that his entire focus was there—on my mouth. "I feel like you're taking my place with the girls. I've felt that way for a while now, but then I heard what you said, and you told them the absolute truth... that I love them more than anything."

He spoke the words haltingly, roughly, like they were being dragged out of his throat, and I wanted to help him, soothe him, make him feel better, but he was still holding on to my wrist and the pressure there, how tight his grip was, made it hard to think about anything else. The man was holding me still, keeping me close, and I had no idea how to react or what to say.

"I'm so sorry, Brann," he said gruffly, and I heard the need in the low, aching sound. "I was such a coward that night, and I should have stayed and talked to you, and—"

"No," I choked out, shaking my head, taking a step back. "I wasn't thinking, and—"

"Stop," he pleaded, following me, reaching for my face, even as I turned my head away. "I need you to—"

"Emery—"

"Hello!" Lydia called out as she walked in. Apparently Emery had left the front door unlocked when he came in the night before. "I'm using my key, so I hope everybody's awake!"

Key. Of course.

We stepped apart, didn't rush, neither of us, as people walked in the front door—Lydia first, followed closely by two women, one of them Shelby, and then three men after that, who were talking together, in mid-discussion about something.

Winston darted over, barking and greeting everyone. Lydia wasn't a fan of his, of dogs in general, Olivia had explained to me, and only one of the men bent to pet the Westie.

"Good morning," Lydia greeted Emery, smiling warmly, swaddled in a heavy, oversized turtleneck sweater, leggings, and knee-high boots. Her friends were similarly outfitted, and the men were all in sweaters and sports coats and dress shoes. The whole group together reminded me of a beer commercial—pretty people spending quality time together.

What was interesting was that Lydia didn't cross the room to Emery, and he didn't go to her. Instead he forced a smile, and having spent this much time with him, I knew what I was talking about. There was a discernable difference in the man when he was truly happy, a relaxation that came over him when he was sitting at the other end of the couch from me or across the dinner table, or on a stool in the kitchen like the last time I'd made grilled cheese sandwiches. I had been ready to leave, finished cooking, when he said he wanted one as well and would I please make it since everybody knew food made by someone else was always better. I'd agreed and I got a smile, his smile, the real one that was completely lacking at the moment.

I was halfway out of the room, leaving to wake the girls to start our day—soccer for Olivia was canceled due to the flu—when there was another knock. I kept going, assuming Emery had more company, but then I heard him say good morning, and there was a familiar rumble in return.

Stopping, I glanced toward the door, and outside on the porch was my buddy, Malachi Jezic.

"Mal," Emery greeted him as the big man stood there filling the doorway. "Would you like to come in?"

"No." He sighed after studying Emery for a second. "I just need Brann."

"Are you sure?"

Mal seemed out of sorts, uncertain, almost sad, and Emery's face was all scrunched-up like he was upset as well.

"Yeah," Mal muttered, looking over at me.

Winston ran to Mal then, and the big man bent and picked up the dog like it was the most natural thing in the world. I watched Winston wiggle and then lick his chin as Mal pet him and told him what a good boy he was.

Since when did Mal know Winston? What was I missing?

Darting across the room, I took hold of the door as Emery took Winston from Mal before returning to the others, bumping me gently as he moved by. Mal walked out onto the porch, and I followed him and closed the door behind me.

"Morning," I greeted him, pointing back over my shoulder. "What was that in there? What's with you and Emery?"

"Nothing."

Clearly that wasn't true, but I didn't want to pry. "Did we have plans I spaced?"

He looked like he was in pain. Or constipated. It was hard to tell which.

"Mal?"

He cleared his throat. "Have you, uh, seen the ads around town?"

Oh man, it was a shitty time not to have any caffeine in me yet. "Ads?" I said lamely, having no clue what was going on. "The handbills you mean, for the upcoming election?"

"Yes, for sheriff. Those along with the yard signs and the signs along the side of the road," he replied like he was making perfect sense.

"Probably," I conceded, sounding unsure, my voice still gravelly because I hadn't been awake that long and, again, there had been no coffee. "There's tons of them everywhere. Or there were, I guess. Voting was the first Tuesday of the month, wasn't it?"

"For the regular elections, yes," he told me. "But the office of sheriff is a special election that will be held the week of Thanksgiving."

"Okay," I said, because I was pretty sure I figured it out. "Do you need me to watch your kids? Are you working at the polling place or something?"

Mal's wife was one of two pediatricians in town, and since both of them seemed to be involved in lots of community events, perhaps they needed a favor. They had four boys, the youngest was six, like Olivia, the oldest ten, so that would be six for me in all, but I could take them to the indoor trampoline place and let them jump until they wore themselves out.

"No, I don't need you to watch my kids," he said, squinting at me.

"Then what's going on?"

He coughed softly. "You probably don't know this because you haven't been here that long, but two years ago, there was some vote tampering."

I crossed my arms to try and keep in some heat. "Listen, Mal, I appreciate the town history lesson you're about to give me, but could we maybe go inside where it's—"

"The sheriff's race was tampered with two years ago."

"All right." I squinted up at him. "Can I ask why this is so important first thing on a Saturday morning?" And then I had a thought. "Did you rig the election?"

"No, I didn't rig the election," he snapped at me.

"Are you running for sheriff?" Maybe that was it.

"No, I'm not run—" he growled, which was weird, clearly frustrated with me. "I'm a councilman, you idiot."

"Like I would know this if you didn't tell me," I groused at him. "And why you're growling at me when I've had no coffee is beyond all logical comprehension."

"You know, Jules said she should have come with me, but I said no, I said it would be fine, I said Brann's my friend, he'll get it, but now I realize that I'm gonna fuck this up, and—"

"Spit out whatever the hell is going on, will you please?"

He exhaled sharply. "Part of my job is to work closely, at election time, with Barbara Madden, the county clerk who's also the election administrator, and with Danny Powell, the recording and election office manager, to ensure that we never have the issue we were faced with two years ago."

"The vote tampering, right?"

"Exactly."

"Okay."

He crossed his thick brawny arms across the brick wall of a chest and glowered down at me. "So that explains why I'm here. Now, tell me, did you happen to notice the ads for the guy running against Reed for sheriff?"

"No," I drew out the word, indulging him. "Who is it?"

"It's Shawn Barr, the guy who you put down on the soccer field, the first day you were here, for going after Emery."

I scowled at him. "Really?"

"Yeah."

"That guy?"

He nodded.

"Mal, that guy would *not* be a good choice."

"I agree. But there's been a development on a third candidate."

"Oh, good." I sighed, rubbing my arms because I was getting colder by the second. He wouldn't notice, of course, as he was swaddled up in the same kind of layers I usually wore, a zipper-front fleece hoodie under a heavy leather jacket. I, on the other hand, was in socks and sweats and a sleep shirt. "But let's go inside and have coffee, all right? The caffeine is necessary for life. Plus, I'm starting to freeze to death."

He shook his head. "Here's the thing, Brann," he began, almost wincing. "Remember when you told me that you thought it was kind of weird how nice Thomas was being to you all the time, even from day one?"

"Sure," I agreed, inching toward the front door.

"And how he took you all over Ursa with him almost every day?"

"I remember mentioning that to you," I said, my hand on the knob. "How 'bout you just let me grab a—"

"Listen," he said, exhaling before running a hand through his thick, wavy, black hair.

Mal was a handsome man, built like a tank, and with his square jaw, piercing blue-black eyes, and a full beard, he looked like some kind of hot mountain man that you wanted to wait out the winter with. I knew, from more than a few overheard conversations, that many women in town thought Julia Jezic was a very lucky woman. "It seems like Thomas had an agenda that no one knew about."

"Agenda?" I asked irritably. Man, did I hate to be cold. That was the one thing about serving in the desert—that had never been an issue.

"Are you listening to me?"

"I'm seriously freezing to death, Mal," I apprised him. "In Chicago, I'm in my car or on the L, I don't just stand around outside turning into a fuckin' Popsicle."

"Fine, let's go in, but so you know, from the write-in ballots we've already counted as well as the absentee and mail-ins, the mayor wanted me to give you a heads up that you're more than likely going to be the new sheriff-elect of Ursa, Montana."

I had no idea what he was, or could, be talking about.

"Brann?"

One of us was on some really good drugs, and it certainly wasn't me.

"Of course, we won't have an official count until the twentieth, but since you already have more votes than we've had in the last two elections... the chances of you not winning are practically nonexistent."

And then my hearing switched off, and all I heard was white noise. There was good news, and there was bad news concerning that. The good news was, I wasn't cold anymore. The bad news was, he was talking to me, he had to be, I was the only one out there with him, and I could see his lips moving, but... there was no sound.

Nothing.

It was like someone put him on mute.

What was strange was that I could remember having snow blindness years before. I hadn't been able to see anything, not a sliver of color, or even a trace amount of light under the wrappings covering my eyes, but I recalled that it had nearly split my skull in half. Then later, once the molten lava of cluster headaches receded, there had been nothing at all, not until my vision returned.

I could remember the ringing in my ears the time I'd been blown up and suffered cracked ribs along with a concussion and a busted clavicle. I had felt like I was in a fugue state, constantly vibrating, never able to get my bearings. I'd never been so nauseous in my life, from what seemed like the constant movement, the relentless motion-sickness nearly driving me over the edge until the damage to my inner ear was repaired and the world stopped its continual quaking.

This was different from both of those, and I had to figure out why.

I wasn't the guy who freaked out. I ran toward the fight, always, my whole life, never away. I was the guy who everyone counted on to watch their back. You could turn around, whenever, and I'd be right there like a faithful golden retriever. In the zombie apocalypse, I was the guy you wanted. But this wasn't about me and being brave or not, protective or not, or anything else. This wasn't fixing something like that day with Jenny Rubio's ex-husband. This wasn't me carrying someone out of a firefight, dead or alive. This was me, physically safe yet emotionally lost, totally losing my shit.

Because I'd heard Mal's words. He was saying I could stay in Ursa and have not just *a* job but *the* job that would be perfect for me. I could stay and have a life and everything I'd ever wanted—if Emery actually wanted me. If Emery and his girls and his dog wanted me.

But he didn't want me, so that wasn't going to happen. It couldn't, it wouldn't happen, and to have what I yearned for suddenly be within my reach, for it to be possible because the good people of Ursa wanted to give me a job... that was a bit too much at the moment.

If Emery had wanted me, my life could go from pretty good to great in the blink of an eye. It was thinking you won the lottery only to realize you had the right numbers on the wrong day. It was a bit too much strain on my heart, and so my brain shut down because it was taking care of its good buddy.

There was no pain; I was simply in a bubble of static.

Even when Mal put a hand on my shoulder, opened the front door, led me through the house to the kitchen, and sat me down on the bench, still it was like the volume was turned way up on one of those sound machines, and all I could hear was white noise. Mal knelt in front of me, one hand on my knee, the other on my cheek, and seemed to be checking for signs of life. After a few moments of studying me and looking pained, he stood and walked away. I sat there frozen, panicked, and suddenly exhausted, zapped of strength, staring at the sink and the avocado pit held up by toothpicks that Olivia was trying to sprout. When April appeared in front of me, she put her hands on my face and smiled at me, her eyes lighting up like they hadn't done when I first arrived.

"Are you in there?"

"Shit," I gasped, startling her, grabbing her wrists and holding on.

"It's a bad word; I told you," Olivia stated, shaking her head as she joined her sister, smiling as well, pleased with me, as evidenced by her climbing onto my lap.

"Hey, buddy," Mal said slowly, kneeling in front of me. Emery was there now as well, next to Mal, his hand on my knee. And it hit me like a freight train that even though I was the center of a storm of concern, the girls and Mal, the only presence I truly registered was Emery's. Because when he touched me, *whenever* he touched me, I felt it down deep.

"What's going on?" Emery asked, cupping the side of my neck, listening to Mal but holding on to me, his thumb smoothing over my jaw, again and again, as I tried really hard not to lean forward into him.

It was back in an instant, all my stupid instincts that said things like *stand up, press your body into his, and wrap him in your arms.* Every day, all the time, I wondered what it would feel like if he'd just yield to me. If he just... gave... in. Because yes, I loved his kids *apart* from him, but I loved them more because they were his and *part* of him.

It was a mess.

"Who is that again?" a man asked, a stranger in what I thought of as my house.

"He's their nanny," Shelby told him, her voice seductive and snide at the same time. "Can you imagine?"

I refused to be on display, and since I couldn't go with my first instinct—to order everyone out of my house, as it wasn't, in fact, my house—I had to get out of there.

Standing quickly, I set Olivia down gently and would have bolted for my room, but Emery barred my path.

"You gotta let me—"

"Stay," he commanded, scowling at me before turning to Mal. "I need a huge favor, if you would."

"Of course I would," Mal said, glaring back at Emery. "You know I would. You know me."

After a moment, Emery nodded. "I do."

"Then," Mal growled, "act like it and talk to me."

Emery shook his head and looked at the floor, almost like he was trying to gather up pieces of himself before his gaze was back on Mal. "I'm sorry."

Mal was shocked. I read it clear as day on his face. His brows lifted, his lips parted, and he couldn't stop staring.

Emery exhaled sharply. "I am. You know I am."

"So am I," Mal said quickly, moving to take a step forward but stopping himself, holding himself in check.

Emery squinted at him. "What do you have to be sorry for? I'm the one who pulled away... after."

"But I let you because I thought you needed space. Jules did too."

I was so lost. Since when were Malachi and Emery friends? Mal had never said a word to me, and I hadn't been talking to Emery enough to ask him.

"Yeah," Emery barely got out. "I did. Need it."

"But it was too much," Mal said solemnly. "And it went on too long."

"That's hard to gauge."

Mal cleared his throat. "So you know... Jules wants you back almost desperately."

Emery sighed, and there was a trace of a smile that he had not given Lydia, but now, a bit for Mal. "Does she?"

"You know she does."

They were silent for long moments. "I worried about her too," Emery told him. "It was so hard, and I know I wasn't the only one grieving."

Mal gave him another warm smile. "I know. She knows. She's Jules, after all."

Emery's smile was wan, but he agreed. "Jules knows everything," he said as though it once upon a time had been an oft-repeated mantra.

"Yes, she does."

They were having a quiet moment, communing, and I was overwhelmed with the enormity of it, seeing it for what it was.

Change. There was change happening right in front of me.

I glanced over at Lydia to see if she was noticing, to see if she recognized it as well, but she wasn't paying any attention to Emery or Mal or anyone else. She was engrossed instead in whatever Shelby was showing them all on her phone.

"We all had to reconfigure our lives, to the way things looked after," Mal explained. "It wasn't easy."

"No."

He shrugged. "But it's been long enough, don't you think?"

"I did. I do. I wanted to... reach out," Emery said hesitantly, and I could tell from looking at him that it was hard for him to say what was in his heart.

"So did we."

Emery cleared his throat and then spoke under his breath so Mal had to take a step closer. "Lydia didn't want to try and compete with what Andrea had been to you guys, especially to Jules, so... you know."

"That's what she figured," Mal choked out, clearly a bit unmoored by the conversation at the same time April slipped her hand into his. I had no idea she knew Mal well enough to simply take his hand like it was the most natural thing in the world. There was so much history here that I had not been privy to.

Emery chuckled, but it sounded sad. "I wish we'd been talking so I could have discussed things with her." After a moment he added, "And you."

"Same," Mal said gruffly, taking a breath. "So, favor you said?"

He coughed softly. "Yeah, could you take my girls with you and feed them? Brann and I will be over there in a couple of hours to pick them up."

Mal nodded. "Will you talk to us when you pick them up?"

"Yes."

"There's more I need to say to you too," Mal said to me.

"Whatever you want," I conceded, too overwrought to say anything but yes to him.

Those dark eyes of his were back on Emery. "So then, can I tell her... lunch?" He asked the question like he was tip-toeing through a minefield, as though one misstep would cost him everything. "It would mean a lot."

Emery nodded.

Mal tipped his head ever so slightly to his left, indicating Lydia and her friends. "Even though you didn't like it at the town meeting last year—it's still a valid alternative to this."

"I know," Emery said grudgingly. "I spoke to Anne last week."

Mal's brows rose again. "You did?"

"I did."

Whatever they were talking about, Mal was now wearing an expression I hadn't seen before. It was like his guard came down, though I'd never realized he'd had one up. It was as if I hadn't seen the real guy until right then. Totally at ease and open, Malachi Jezic looked like a completely different animal. The transformation was really something.

"So, then, you're not going to—"

"No, I'm not," he admitted softly. "I'm sorry. I've been such an ass."

"You weren't alone there," Mal said, nodding quickly, and that grin went from sweet and kind of goofy to almost blinding. "And Jules wasn't the only one who missed you."

Emery tilted his head up, and I realized it was because his eyes were filling and he didn't want to cry.

"What the hell did I miss?" I said to the two men, my own meltdown forgotten as I watched them struggle through what certainly sounded like an epic reconciliation.

"Ancient history," Emery told me, putting his hand on my cheek for a moment, enough to stun me, as well as the rest of the room, into a silence that buried us all alive.

"Okay," Mal said awkwardly into the sudden deafening calm, addressing the girls. "We've got a zip line between the tree houses now. You guys wanna come see?"

They screamed out the *yes*.

"And your Aunt Jules is makin' chocolate pancakes."

They both jumped him, and he picked them up, a girl in each arm, because the man was massive, and walked them out of the kitchen toward their rooms. It wasn't lost on me that he knew exactly where he was going.

"Emery?" Lydia said sharply, and now, of course, he had everyone's full and complete attention as he stepped close to me, his hand solidly on the small of my back. The gesture was protective and signaled the grinding halt to our silence and separateness, but most of all, it was overtly possessive. There was no mistaking that.

My knees nearly buckled.

"Emery?" Lydia repeated, terse and barbed, glancing between us. "What's going on?"

He exhaled slowly and then he smiled at her, and it was so kind, so loving, that I saw her sort of unlock, un-bristle. She was ready to throw down with him, but that wasn't going to happen. He wasn't that kind of man.

"It's not fair." She passed her purse to Shelby and walked to the kitchen table. He moved away from me and joined her there, standing at the other end. "You deserve better," he said flatly.

"What?"

"You know you do," he insisted.

"Oh, screw you, Emery. Don't you dare blame whatever this is on—"

"No," he agreed quickly, which shut her down. "This is all on me; none of it is you. I'm just telling you truthfully that you *do* deserve better. You *do* deserve more." He sighed, smiling sadly. "I've been married, you haven't, and it's not fair of me to rob you of standing up in front of everyone who means something to you and doing it for real."

"It would be real," she assured him. "Our marriage would be very real."

"It wouldn't, and we both know it," he contradicted her, and there was a deep, resounding echo of certainty in his voice.

"That's not true."

He shook his head, and it was almost patronizing. It was like he was doing her thinking and not taking her feelings into consideration. Until I realized he was right, because in this instance, he did know more. He'd been there, been married, and she hadn't. "You'll regret it, Lydia. You will."

"We both decided that—"

"Here's the thing, if you wanted to just go to city hall, I'd have known you were telling the truth. I'd have believed that marrying me meant the same thing to you as it does to your father—a simple business transaction—if the ceremony itself was of no consequence."

She was biting her bottom lip, and no one in the room was missing that Emery was speaking the absolute truth.

"We both know that's not what happened."

"But, Emery, I—"

"Some people dream about their weddings. I know I did," he said softly, kindly.

"Yes, but—"

"Stop. We both know better. You want everything to be just so."

She caught me in her gaze. "Is this about the capes?"

"You know the capes were merely the latest in a long line of signs that we should have been paying attention to," he said pointedly as her focus returned to him. "You want a lavish day, and why shouldn't you? Why wouldn't you want that?"

"I—"

"And why in the world would you want to waste that on me?"

Her bridesmaids behind her gasped, and the men looked like they'd all rather be anywhere in the world but in Emery Dodd's living room.

"I thought it would be all right," he admitted, gripping the back of the chair I'd come to think of as his, the other, on the other end, as mine. "I thought, Lydia is marrying me to help the town, and I'm doing the same thing. Aren't we wonderful people because we're more concerned for others than our own happiness? We could pat ourselves on the back all day long."

She crossed her arms, gazing at him, but not sad or

angry, merely listening. "And," she began, taking a breath, tipping her head as she regarded him, "since you didn't love me, you wouldn't be cheating on Andrea."

"Without question," he confessed, looking her directly in the eye, not flinching, not sugarcoating the truth.

"The memory of her being the love of your life would remain intact," she acknowledged, and it was impossible to miss the melancholy.

Was she actually in love with him? No, I didn't think so. But she was extremely fond of the man. Not hard to see why. Everyone I met—except the sheriff's deputy—thought the world of Emery Dodd.

"Yes," he agreed, looking at her so fondly that she couldn't help but sigh and smile at him. "If I married you, Andrea's legacy stayed the same. I could say things to my girls like, the only woman I've ever truly loved was your mother."

"Yes, you could," she agreed, and I saw her eyes glisten with unshed tears and her chin wobble a bit.

"Most of all, I could hold on to my insistent sadness and never allow you to comfort me or laugh with me or let you anywhere near my heart. It would be a marriage of convenience, only and ever."

"You're certain?"

"I am. One of the reasons I agreed to the marriage was that I knew I'd never fall in love."

Her eyes began to overflow then, a few stray teardrops.

"It was business, nothing else."

The Godfather went through my head then, and it was stupid, but it did.

She was staring at him, really looking, trying to see all the way down into his heart. "It was," she finally agreed. "Yes."

"Yes," he echoed.

They were silent, and so were the rest of us, her friends and me, all of us waiting to see what Emery and Lydia were going to do next.

"What now?" she asked him.

"Well, now I tell you that I don't want to get married and I'm formally calling off the engagement."

She nodded quickly. "I'll talk to my father."

"I'll call him after you—"

"No. I'll tell him."

"I'm still going to call, Lydia. It's up to him if he wants to speak to me or not."

"Perhaps Darrow and Cahill can still become business partners."

He was about to answer when Mal walked back into the room. Both girls were dressed in their polar bear gear, as they had to be whenever they left the house once the weather hit freezing and never rose above it. I was surprised to see that April was holding Winston in her arms.

"Sorry, sorry," Mal said quickly, stopping in front of Emery and me.

I kissed Olivia while Emery kissed April and then we switched, and we both pet Winston, and I darted to his bin in the pantry to get his dog sweater for Mal.

"Really?"

"Yes, really," I said, scowling at him. "He's a small dog."

He made a face like I was nuts, then hurried out of the house and put both kids down outside the front door so he could close it behind him.

Lydia turned to Emery, slowly, and I saw her shoulders slump. "When did you decide on breaking off the engagement?"

"You all," Shelby interrupted, "don't you think you should be alone for the rest of this?"

Everyone started talking at once then, offering their thoughts on the matter, and I took that opportunity to bolt for my room.

It was the strangest thing; my face was hot and my skin was flushed. I was flying inside, and I shut the door behind me and leaned back against it, needing a moment to replace my façade. I'd been fun guy, happy guy for weeks. I could be him again as soon as I figured out how to separate *could have* from reality. I had to stop thinking about forever and ever with Emery Dodd and how sure I was that I could make him happy, and fit seamlessly into his life, if he could see past me being a guy.

It was ridiculous. I had to leave. There was no excuse for staying. Daydreaming about me with a husband and kids and a dog and the sweet little house was slowly eating my heart out.

It was time to go.

FOURTEEN

Emery had been worried that Olivia would get attached and then, later, April as well. What he didn't understand was that I was the one in utter peril. I was the one with nothing else, no foundation, no base, and no people who were mine.

I wouldn't recover if I left my heart with them when I drove out of town.

It struck me again that there wasn't all this uncertainty and dealing with awkward personal choices when people were shooting at me. In life-and-death situations, the concern over one's emotional health didn't come up. When I was deployed, I'd never been asked how I *felt*, only if I'd lost too much blood to go on. It would be so much easier if I went back to the Navy, things no longer gray; instead, simple black and white, good or bad, kill or be killed, go where they tell me.

I had made a mistake when I'd left, but I could fix it. I had driven my CO nuts, but I knew he would recommend the Navy reinstate me in a second. I was good at being a soldier. It was the transition from military to civilian life I was failing at.

The knock wasn't a surprise.

"Just gimme a sec," I said, swallowing down my heart and then muttering the rest under my breath so whoever was out there couldn't hear. "I'm not quite done figuring out my life yet."

"Open the door," Emery demanded from the other side.

The hell? "Why aren't you—"

"Did you hear me?"

"Of course I heard you, but you need to go back out there and—"

"Stop," he said, simple but firm.

As though that was going to work. "Have you lost your mind?"

"Actually, the opposite is finally true, so open the door," he insisted.

"Emery," I sighed, taking a breath so I could say what was best for him and not for me. "I'm fine; you don't need to check on me. I just needed a minute."

"Open the door," he repeated, lower, almost guttural.

I felt the sound in the pit of my stomach.

"Now, Brann."

I cleared my throat. "I'm okay. I was…. Listen, I know you and Lydia need to talk and figure everything out and make plans to—"

"We've done all we're going to do today."

"Emery—"

"Open the door!"

"You should—"

"I'm so sick of you telling me what I should and shouldn't do that I could puke."

What? "I don't tell—"

"You say what you think I want to hear, and it's driving me nuts. You're—" he rasped, almost choking on the words. "—driving me nuts."

I took a breath, girding for what I had to say. It was time to sever the tie. "I'm really sorry. I was thinking that I should probably go, because I'm making you miserable and I don't want to keep feeling like crap either, and—"

"Please, baby, just open the door," he pleaded.

If he'd gut-punched me, the air would not have left my body any faster. Yes, the endearment was surprising, but mostly because I couldn't ever imagine him ever using it to refer to me. Locryn Barnes, on the other hand, if he'd ever called me anything but my name, I would have died of shock. He wasn't that guy. His brain didn't move to soft places of the heart, because that wasn't the part of his anatomy that drove him.

But, Emery Dodd had already shown me that his heart, his gentle, vulnerable though sturdy heart, was where he lived. It was evident in the way he talked to the students we ran into around town, to his parents and siblings when they spoke on the phone, and, of course, with his girls. I knew the man was tender to his core. What I'd never expected was that any of that compassion or affection could ever be turned on me in any but the most generic way. He cared for me, but like a colleague and nothing more.

Except that wasn't what he'd said. He said *baby*, which was not something I'd ever heard him utter before. I jolted, bumping the door, the word running through me, the ache in his voice, the yearning, setting my whole life on fire.

"I've been so stupid," he confessed hoarsely. "You've been nonsensical, doing the opposite of everything I know you wanted, but I've allowed it because I thought it was the right thing even though I knew better the whole time."

I had no idea what to say.

"Putting myself through hell is one thing, but allowing my girls to be eaten up with fear and watching you turn yourself inside out—that's unforgivable."

"What?" I asked, turning around, facing the door now. "I haven't been—"

"Yes, you have," he heaved out the words, and it sounded like he hit the wood gently with his fist. "I see how you look at me, but I told myself it wasn't what I thought, though I knew better from day one."

"Emery—"

"I've been so fucking selfish," he spat out, the self-loathing clear. "I allowed this to go on because facing it— the fallout of it—was going to be hard."

I was back to not knowing what I could say to offer him comfort.

"I'm so sorry, Brann."

"What? No. You don't have—"

"Oh, the hell I don't. I listened to your words instead of your actions."

"No, that's—"

"You die a little every day."

I did, it was true. Without question.

"This isn't working, Brann."

My heart sank, and I found I had barely enough air to breathe.

"We're walking around each other, the two of us, here, in this house, neither of us wanting to do anything irreparable... unforgivable... both of us treading water until it's time for you to go."

He was right. I would die before I let his girls down. I got up every day and said I could do it. I got up every day and performed an internal pep talk. For one more second, one more minute, one more hour, and one more day... I would pretend I didn't care a fraction about Emery Dodd. I would ignore his presence to be there for Olivia and April. I could and I had, but it was, without a doubt, hollowing me out inside.

"But you can't just stay for them."

I put my hands on the door and levered back, my head slumped forward between my shoulders.

"And I hate Mal Jezic, even though I sent my kids off with him."

"What?" I gasped, scrambling fast, throwing open the door to have him almost fall in on me. He'd been leaning hard and had to correct quickly or hit me.

I ended up catching him, my hands on his hips, making sure he didn't fall.

We stood there, both of us at six-two, eye to eye, neither of us flinching or making excuses or running away.

"I said," he murmured, as he eased from my hold, turned, closed the door, and locked it, "that I hate Mal Jezic."

I stared at him, watching him, mesmerized, as he turned to face me after having made sure no one but the two of us could get into the room.

"Don't you need to go back out there?"

He took a step forward, and though normally—or the new normal that we'd established—I would have taken one back, I couldn't bring myself to move.

"Emery, I—"

"Brann." He said my name, husky and deep, the sound of it, the feeling I could hear as my name tumbled off his tongue, rolled through me, snapping and crackling over my skin. "Don't you want to know why I hate him?"

I nodded, unable to speak, drowning in the way he was staring at me, hearing my own breath start and stop.

"I hate him because you like him and trust him and you're so relaxed when you're with him," he murmured, smiling at me. "I've seen you two together, along with his wife and his kids. You're yourself when you're with him, like you are with the girls, and not at all how you are with me. Not anymore."

What could I say? It was the truth; I'd been perfect with Emery since the day I'd kissed him. No one could have asked for a better caregiver for their children, but I'd checked out when it came to him. I was more robot than human.

He stepped closer, making the space between us nonexistent, and I couldn't stifle the moan of having him there, against me, his thighs pressed to mine, his groin, his abdomen.

I was afraid to do anything, not wanting to wake up, to break the spell.

"I want you to be real with me too, Brann," he whispered, his breath ghosting over my face. "Say you will."

But how could I?

I went to move, but he cupped my neck, holding me still as his left hand slipped under my sleep shirt to slide over my hip.

The answering shiver was involuntary. "No, don't touch me," I groaned, the exact opposite of what was in my heart coming out of my mouth.

"But I want to," he assured me, leaning in to press his lips to the side of my throat.

I caught my breath, and I heard his satisfied male rumble, and for the first time I realized something important.

All this time I thought I was the one in charge. I thought I was the one making the decisions, holding myself back, in check and not pushing. But it hit me that Emery had been playing along. He hadn't been participating before, but now he was. This was what Emery Dodd looked like when he was engaged.

"You have people in the living room," I ground out, because it killed me to remind him, but it was the right thing to do.

"No," he said hoarsely, his voice thick, like poured molasses, as he kissed up to my jaw, his hand fisting in my hair, holding tight, the other sliding back to my ass. "Everyone's gone. We're the only ones here."

We were?

"Lydia and I have a few more things to hash out, but we're done, which I needed so I can concentrate all my energy on you."

I recovered then. Instantly. Like a drunk sobering up from shock. And even though I was already painfully hard, that fast, I shoved free and stared at him.

"What?" I yelled at him.

He looked me up and down and then sighed deeply. "You should see yourself with your hair all sticking up and the flush on your skin and your beautiful blue eyes."

"I—"

"You take my breath away."

"Emery! What the fuck is going on?"

"Come here," he said, gesturing for me. "I want to kiss you."

"You're gonna turn me into a crazy person if you don't start talking."

He moved fast, and I did too, but I only succeeded in bumping up against the wall, because the room was only so big.

Pinning me there, he put a hand flat on my chest, and

reached down inside my sweats, under the elastic band of my briefs, and took hold of my already leaking cock.

I bucked into his grip, eyes closing, lips parting, as he stroked me from balls to head. It felt amazing, and every nerve ending in my body sparked to life.

"Emery," I moaned, my voice cracking as he milked me, the pressure, the rhythm, the way his thumb slid over my crown all perfect. "The fuck are you doing?"

"You thought all the wrong things that night you kissed me."

I did? I had?

"And that's on me," he said solemnly as he leaned in, inhaling deeply. "Because it's been so long since anyone has asked me what I wanted… that I'm out of practice."

What he wanted?

"Look at me."

My eyes fluttered open, and I was lost, stunned by the dark depths of his gaze, pupils blown wide as he bit his lip, stroking my flesh in his warm fist.

"You wanted me the night you kissed me," he said roughly, both his voice and breath ragged. "Do you still?"

There was only the truth now, no more lies. I couldn't bear to tell him one more, and I wasn't sure if it was even possible with his hand on my cock. "Oh, yes," I ground out.

"Good," he growled, and the sound of him, all gruff and sexy, sent sizzling heat down my spine. "Because I'm dying to touch you."

He wanted me, and I wasn't proud of the whimper that came out of me, but he must have liked it, because I got a smile that was wicked, one I'd never seen before, and then he kissed me hard enough to make me open my mouth and groan.

I had no idea Emery Dodd could deliver a kiss that

would nearly send me to my knees. I felt it, like a pinball bouncing around under my skin, lighting up everything it touched, every part of me, and I understood that I'd never been kissed like that, ever, even once before in my life.

The last time I'd kissed him, in my rush to lay claim, I'd missed that he wasn't responding to me, wasn't kissing me back.

This was not the same.

He devoured my mouth, his tongue rubbing over mine, tasting all of me, and I could feel his yearning, his desire, and the surprise of absolute possessiveness. The demand was there, in the kiss, for *me* to give in, for *my* submission, in his hand up under my t-shirt, torturing my nipples, in his thigh pressed between mine and the weight of him pushing against me as I arched my hips against him.

I shuddered as his hand slid down my abdomen, mapping my skin, his touch and his lips making me boneless and aching and needy before he broke the kiss and went to his knees in front of me. His eyes lifted to mine as he dragged my sweats and underwear to my ankles slowly, holding my gaze.

"Emery," I choked out his name as my straining, already dripping cock bounced free, and he took hold of me, stroking tenderly but firmly.

"Oh, Brann," he moaned, "this is as beautiful as the rest of you."

I'd been told I was thick and long, but never beautiful, and I felt my face heat because it was embarrassing and hot at the same time. When he swallowed me to the root in one smooth, fluid motion, no gagging, just sucking my cock as though there were nothing in the world he'd rather be doing, my brain finally made the connection that Emery Dodd certainly knew what he wanted.

I reached for him, my hands buried in his thick, silky, brown hair that curled around my fingers, following his lead, his motion, slowly fucking his mouth.

Holy God, he felt good. The suction and his tongue with the barest hint of his teeth, his fingers wet with saliva, squeezing my balls and sliding under them and back, slowly, maddeningly, until he was there at my entrance, fingering me gently but deliberately—almost brought me to climax far too quickly.

"Emery," I rasped, my voice sounding thick and labored to my ears.

He swallowed around my cock, wedged there in the back of his throat, and another finger joined the first in my ass, pushing and stretching, the assault tender but unremitting.

The message was clear, his agenda obvious. He wanted inside of me.

It was a surprise. I'd never bottomed. It had never occurred to me. All my life I'd been in bed with men who expected me to take charge, expected me to hold them down and deliver the rough or gentle fuck they begged for. I had assumed if I was ever lucky enough to get Emery into my bed that he'd be shy, unsure, and I'd have to be gentle and patient with him as I showed him how amazing sex with a man could be. Apparently, though, Emery already knew. And Emery wanted something from me I'd never given anyone before—my submission. What surprised the hell out of me was how much him knowing what he was doing, knowing what he wanted, was turning me on. That, and his mouth. I'd never been so close so fast.

"Stop," I begged him, tugging gently, wanting us together in my bed so I could hold him after. This too was a surprise because never before had having someone in my arms when the fucking was over even crossed my mind. "I want you on the bed. Please, Em."

He eased back, and I gasped at the loss.

"Where's your lube?" he croaked out as he rose in front of me, still completely dressed as I stood there bare from the waist down.

"In the drawer in the bathroom," I managed to get out. "There are condoms in there too."

The way he suddenly focused on me, squinting, was a surprise. "Why would we need those?" He asked sharply, and I felt the air change in the room. "I know what your status is; it's in your records from Torus."

I could only stand there and stare at him.

"I'm the father of two small children who lost their mother; I would never be so reckless as to have unprotected sex with someone I didn't know and trust."

"Of course not, but you don't know who I've been with."

"Has there been anyone since you've been here?" His tone held a trace of anger.

"No," I snapped, almost angry myself because I couldn't see anyone but Emery Dodd. "Absolutely not."

"Well I haven't been with anyone since Andrea," he informed me. "But even so, I was tested before Lydia and I were engaged."

"You and Lydia never—"

"No," he said flatly.

"Why not?"

"We were going to wait until after we were married."

"How come?" I pried, needing to know, my hand slipping to his cheek, my voice coming out silky, soothing so he'd answer and not bristle. "Tell me."

"Because we hoped the marriage would at least have that," he replied with a huff, sounding defeated.

"Heat and desire," I whispered, my thumb sliding over that lush bottom lip of his. "You hoped you two would at least enjoy fucking since you weren't in love."

"Yes," he gritted out, the confession ugly.

"And because you needed that to be a possibility, you held off."

Quick tip of his head told me I was correct before his lips parted around my thumb, and his tongue traced over my skin.

"You must not have wanted her, if you could wait."

He sucked my thumb into his mouth.

"I could be wrong," I teased him, breathless, "but I feel like me, you want."

"There's no question," he rumbled out, and the sound of him, gravelly, ragged, made my cock swell almost painfully. "But so we're clear, we don't need protection."

"No, we don't," I agreed, loving how his eyes ate me up, his desire palpable.

"Step out of this," he demanded, kneeling to help me untangle my feet from my sweats, and then as he stood, he dragged my sleep shirt up over my head before taking my hand to pull me after him to the bed.

"There have been other men?" I said faintly, wanting to know and, at the same time, not.

"Yes," he said, letting go of my hand. He darted into the en suite connected to my bedroom, then emerged moments later with my tube of lubricant. I hadn't moved, unsure whether to get in the bed, because usually I was the guy going for the lube. After a second, I realized that again, like earlier, his gaze dragged over me, from head to toe, missing nothing, I was self-conscious, but when I tried to get into bed, he stopped me, moving fast to take my face in his hands.

"I never thought I'd get to see all of you, even though it's all I've wanted since you stepped foot in my house."

"You have?" I wanted that so badly it was too hard not to sound hopeful, my breath hitching with the heat I saw in his dark eyes.

"Oh, yes," he husked, yanking off his jacket and making quick work of his waistcoat, dropping them onto the floor, uncaring, as he toed off his wingtips and began struggling with his dress shirt.

"Lemme help you," I soothed him, stepping in close so I could smell the soap on his skin and the trace of after-shave, a citrusy bergamot mix that I already associated with him.

His hands went to his belt and zipper as I chuckled, because it was hard to work open buttons while he was contorting in an effort to take off his jeans and underwear.

"Tell me about the others."

He shoved me back, toppling me over onto the bed, and I watched, splayed out under him, as he drew the still half-way-buttoned shirt up over his head, and let it join the rest of his clothes on the hardwood floor.

"I had two boyfriends and one girlfriend in college before I met Andrea," he informed me, shucking down his jeans and then sitting on the edge of the bed to pull them off. His boxer briefs were last, because he left his socks on. "I knew she was the one." He sighed, smiling sadly. "The same way I know about you."

I scrambled up off the bed so we traded positions, with him now sprawled out and me standing. "What about Lydia?"

His scowl was dark. "Just so we're clear, I would never have come in here after you if there was anything at all left between me and Lydia Cahill," he said, and I loved the gravelly, strained sound of his voice, like he was having trouble focusing as he stared up at me with molten eyes.

"You're sure?"

"I am."

"And why is that?"

"Because it turns out that no matter the reason," he said, never looking away from me, "I can't make a vow to someone I don't love."

"But you didn't love her from the start, so what changed your mind?"

"You did."

"How?" I asked, unsteady and scared at the same time because he felt so close to opening up to me and I didn't want to lose him for any reason.

"You changed my whole life when you came through the front door," he confessed, sitting up, taking my right hand in both of his. "And it sounds like overly romantic drivel, but I swear to God, it was like the sun came in with you."

It turned out that drivel was my thing.

"Everything about you is kind and gentle and soothing and... hot."

I exhaled sharply. "I think all the same stuff about you."

"You do? Even the hot part?"

I chuckled because he sounded surprised. "Especially that."

"That's so... good," he told me, sounding stilted, nervous, the catch of breath betraying him if the slight tremble had not.

"Why?"

"Are you kidding?"

"No. I wanna know what you're thinking."

He gestured at me. "I'm thinking about you, Brann, like

always. You're all I've thought about for months... all I dream about."

I am?

His brows furrowed, and his jaw clenched as he struggled for a moment, glancing away from me, concentrating before his head lifted and he was again staring up at my face. "Having you all to myself," he said levelly, "is the only thing I'm missing in my life."

His words, the weight of them, the concern on his face, and how tight he was holding on to me told me everything I needed to know.

He wanted me.

He wanted to keep me.

He wanted me in his life.

"It won't work anymore without you," he whispered, easing me down beside him and then pushing on my chest until I was flat on my back. He rolled over on top of me before sitting up, straddling my thighs.

I bowed up off the bed, oversensitized after only seconds, his warm, smooth skin sliding over mine. It was more than I ever imagined I'd have.

"Jesus, Emery," I groaned, staring up at him, admiring his wide, solid chest, smooth belly, and long, toned legs. The man was covered in hard, sculpted muscle, and I realized even though I was more powerfully built, he was not as lean as I'd thought he would be under his clothes. "Look how beautiful you are."

I was marked with too many scars to count, from my time in the service. I was not the stunning creature that Emery Dodd was.

"Oh, no, make no mistake," he said with a husky growl, curling over me, hands down on either side of my head, and his lips hovering over mine, "it's you with your broad shoulders and those amazing muscles in your back, those sexy veins in your hands and that hair that won't stay out of your eyes. You are an utterly devastating work of art."

I couldn't help smiling. "I didn't think you noticed anything about me."

"I may be an idiot, but I can see you clear as day," he said with a wolfish grin. "And you are the most beautiful man I've ever seen."

It didn't matter that he was seeing me through the lens of caregiver for his kids and his home; I didn't care. It didn't matter. What did matter was his desire to claim me that stirred a flutter way down deep.

Slowly he bent and buried his face against my neck, kissing before sucking, humming as he did it so the sound and vibration combined made me squirm under him.

I wanted to ask how he had just changed the entire direction of his life on a Saturday morning, but if thinking would lead him away from my bed, I could wait for my answers. The part that was important was that he was no longer engaged. He'd ended that before he reached for me. We would deal with the fallout together.

His mouth slid to my collarbone, kissing and suckling the whole way, and I wanted more, so I reached for his cock.

"Wait," he stopped me with garbled words, clearly loving the taste of my skin. "Take this," he directed, passing me the lube. "And touch us both."

Quickly I snapped open the bottle and squeezed some lube into my hand before letting it fall near my pillow. He groaned as I palmed our cocks, stroking us together, tight, the feel of him twitching in my hand, full and hard, making it impossible not to lift my knees and cage him between my thighs. I didn't want him to move.

"Brann," he said, breathless and strangled, as he leaned

all his weight on his left arm so he could grab the lube with his right. "Tell me I can have you."

I opened my mouth to answer as a lube-coated finger pressed, again at my entrance, this time so much slicker, slipping all the way inside without resistance.

"Oh God," I said instead.

"That's a yes," he rumbled, taking my mouth, kissing me like I was his, no question about who was in charge now, as his tongue dueled with my own.

I moaned loudly when his hot, leaking cock slid over mine, and then gasped when he broke the kiss to lift my right leg over his shoulder. Two lube-coated fingers pressed inside of me, and he scissored with that same deliberateness from earlier, relaxing the tight ring of muscle before recapturing my lips.

The man could kiss. It was like being worshipped, as though he was savoring the contact, my taste, and the feel of me under him. Heat rolled inexorably up my spine as I tried to take those fingers in deeper, needing more, ready as I thought I'd never be.

When he withdrew his fingers, I arched up off the bed, and he lifted my left leg over his shoulder before the wide head of his cock notched against my entrance.

"I've never," I whispered, needing him to understand as I met his narrowed eyes. "Just so you know."

"I know," he murmured, and I was struck by that confirmation. Not by the words alone, but by the look in his eyes, as if I were already beloved, and then he pushed forward, slow and steady, without pause but with more restraint than I could have shown. "I know this is a gift."

The stretch and the burn started off dull, but the pain brightened and blossomed, and I was caught between wanting him more than life and not wanting him lodged in my ass, splitting me apart. It was torture, wanting him both in and out, but then he did something totally unexpected. He bit my bottom lip. Not hard, it was more a nip than a bite, but still, it jolted me, altered my focus, and the tugging and sucking, like he wanted to eat me, was really fucking hot. The sexy, languorous grin he gave me before he kissed me again, this one desperate and devouring as he took hold of my cock in his slippery fist, roiled through me like a stormy sea.

I roared his name.

It was lucky we were the only ones in the house, because everyone would have heard. If his neighbors were home, they probably did.

My muscles relaxed, and the solar flare of pain, hot and engulfing, eased with each stroke of his hand and each ravenous kiss as he slid his long, hard length into me.

His name came from deep in my chest then.

"Jesus, Brann," he choked out, his forehead pressed to mine as he panted, sweaty, not moving, just there, buried all the way inside of me. "I don't even think I can move, that's how tight you are."

"I need you to try," I entreated, wanting him somehow deeper, shivering now, flushing hot and cold, so close to the orgasm I could feel flickering near the base of my spine, my balls drawing up tight, the all-consuming clenching that told me I was ready. "Please."

"God yes. Beg me to fuck you," he growled, easing out a fraction only to screw himself back inside, grinding into me. "It's only what I'm dying to do, what I was made to do."

I lifted my ass off the mattress the second time he withdrew, and he shoved a pillow under my hips so when he pounded back inside me—deeper, faster, harder—I felt it, like ripples of pleasure throughout my body.

"Do you feel me? Because I feel you, all of you, wrapped around all of me," he said, his voice spiking, almost frantic, as he found his rhythm, thrusting deeply in and dragging slowly out, over and over.

I turned my head and reached for my pillow, pressing it to my face, trying to muffle the sounds he was pulling out of me.

"No," he ordered, snatching the pillow from me and tossing it aside. I looked up at his face, at the dilated pupils, his swollen lips and flushed skin. "I want to hear all your noises; I want to know them all."

"You will. There's time, right?"

"Oh," he said like I'd struck him, changing position, rolling forward, tighter, bending me in half. "There's all the time, nothing but, because you're the only one who's ever going to work in my life... fit in my life. It's all you, Brann. Just you."

Reaching up, I took hold of his shoulders for leverage as he ground down into me, changing his angle on the descent, which drove his heavy cock over the place I had touched in others but never experienced myself.

I tightened my hands knowing I'd leave bruises, but I was done caring, too lost in what my body was doing, the hurtling rise right before the crest. I checked out, all of it, all of *him* more than I could bear. And then at last, when he hit the spot that triggered my climax, I held nothing back. The orgasm hurtled up my spine, and my flexing muscles clamped down around him, holding him there as I came apart, splattering his belly and chest.

His head fell back as he came, nailing me to the bed, filling me, the pumping deep inside washing me hot, from the inside out, his cum spilling around his cock and seeping between the cheeks of my ass.

It was like being at the top of a mountain and then freefalling, and there was a moment where I was me, then I was not, and then I was me again. And I was under him, still, and there was air and I could see, though I couldn't hear anything over the pounding of my own heart.

Emery fell forward, on me, into my waiting arms, and I wrapped him up as he buried his face in the hollow between my neck and shoulder.

After a moment, I realized he was laughing, and I nudged him to no avail.

"What's so funny?" I grumbled. Hand buried in his sweat-soaked hair, I tilted his head back to expose an illicit grin. His eyes were closed and I took that moment, those small but precious seconds, to drink him in. I'd heard the phrase 'my heart was full to bursting' before but it had never meant anything to me. Until now.

"We're both covered in sweat and semen," he said dreamily, licking his delectable lips, puffy and red from mauling my mouth and sucking my dick. "It's sexy as hell, my cum leaking from your ass, yours all over my chest, and in my hair."

He sounded drugged, or drunk, and I loved it. The grin grew into a smile as he opened his eyes and looked at me.

"What?"

Slowly, gently, he eased free of my body with a slight groan as my muscles fisted his length, milking him that last little bit.

"God, did you feel that?" he asked as he rolled to his back beside me. "You didn't want to let me go."

"You seem quite proud of yourself."

"I feel like a pirate."

I grunted, turning away from him so he couldn't see my smile.

Ridiculous man.

"I ravaged you."

"Shuddup."

"I pillaged you."

I buried my face in my pillow.

"What are you doing?" He grabbed my shoulder and tugged until I was on my back again. "Come here."

I rolled my head so I could see him.

"Brann," he said my name like it was magical. "Please."

My grin was just as cheesy as his, I was certain. "You're covered in cum, like you said. You should shower."

"Baby, come here."

I rolled over into him, and he ran a hand up my back and into my hair, burying it there, staring into my eyes the whole time.

"Olivia's right, you have pretty hair."

"Speaking of," I said, exhaling, feeling my body get heavy, lulled by his warmth and closeness and the hand now carding through my hair. "What are we gonna do?"

"*We* is right," he said hoarsely, kissing my temple. "And *we* will go over to Mal's and have a talk with the girls."

"Okay."

He was quiet then, and I almost nodded off.

"I know things," he whispered.

"What things?" I asked, not opening my eyes, happy to still try and doze with him talking to me.

"Well, for example, I know you love me, you love my girls, you love my dog, and you love my house."

I stayed quiet, though now I was wide awake.

"Right? Don't you? Love all those things?"

I knew what he was asking. "Yes," I said honestly, because this was us, together, in my bed. We had no more time for lies on either side.

"Hey."

Leaning away from him, I opened my eyes so I could see him. The smile was gone; he was dead serious now.

"I told Lydia I couldn't marry her today, and the only reason for that is because it turns out you can't choose when you're going to fall in love."

"No, you can't," I agreed wholeheartedly.

"And just so we're clear, I am totally and completely in love with you."

The words took me a second to process because they were big and life-changing, and I'd never heard them before. "Oh, yeah?" I said, feeling the happiness spread slowly over me, infusing every cell in my body, filling me up and making me smile like an idiot. "You love me?"

He nodded.

"A lot?"

"Yes."

"Like you'd marry me?"

"I would."

I pounced on him, clutching him in my arms and burying my face in his shoulder as I squeezed the life out of him.

"You knew we were supposed to be together," he prodded, and I could hear the need in his voice. "Didn't you?"

I nodded fast, a bit too choked up to speak.

"You wanted me to love you."

"And you do," I barely got out.

"And I do," he declared with so much feeling that I felt it like a buzz under my skin as he hugged me tighter.

WE HAD to clean up and go get the girls so I rolled out of bed, even though it was the last thing I wanted to do.

As I walked into my bathroom and looked at myself in the mirror, I noticed that the bites he'd given me were now smears of dark wine against my skin. It was amazing. This was what being claimed was, the marks, my mauled lips, the stubble burn, my tousled hair, and the blotchy flush over my chest and throat.

That was the outside.

Inside, the changes were bigger, broader, painted on my soul like a lush, overgrown garden teeming with life and sweetness and hope. So much of that.

Under the warm water, I felt the tempest beneath my skin trying to erupt, to escape, to pierce my flesh and show the world that he and I were joined, and together there would be a whole new life built on the solid foundation of the first. I would take care of what Andrea Dodd had begun, be caregiver and lover, father and husband. I'd never felt anything but love in the house, comforted by it, enveloped and accepted. And I knew I was out of my head, vulnerable and joyful, but there was a solidness too, a weight, and even as I clutched for balance in my sudden new life, there was an engulfing peace as well.

Because he saw me.

Emery had the ability to see me as I truly was, with all the flaws, all the shortcomings and selfishness, but all the good parts too. He saw my heart and how it belonged only to him. And now there was the quiet after the storm, and so I was reverent of what had been and what would be.

Wiping the fog from the mirror, I saw myself again and I felt it, how settled I was in my skin, and I smiled back thinking this was what being crazy in love looked like.

He walked behind me, on his way to the shower, but stopped and stared.

"What?" I asked, almost breathless all over again from his unwavering attention.

He shook his head, pressing his chest to my back, brushing his lips over my ear, and spoke so I shivered from his warm breath. "I fall fast, you know," he confided to me in a whisper. "I saw Andrea on a Friday, and it was like walking outside in the warm summer sun. I knew she was supposed to be with me, so I asked her to move in with me on the following Monday." His sigh, like he remembered it so very clearly, made me smile. "After she died, I thought... well, a lot of things, but most of all, that I'd never feel that way again."

I waited because the way he was staring at me, standing beside me, touching, smoothing his hands over my skin, told me there was more.

"When you walked in the front door that Saturday morning, I saw it again, and then I felt the same bright-ness and sense of peace." His voice cracked on the last word as his hand slipped over my flaccid cock and lower to my balls. "I was stunned," he said, his warm breath tickling over my damp skin. "And I thought I was wrong. That maybe it was an illusion, that I was seeing things that weren't there. Because I was sure my life was going to be a certain way after my wife died, so I agreed to a marriage that had nothing to do with love."

Everything felt different. Being in the house, being in his space, I was lighter, my life irrevocably complete with an outcome I could have never imagined. We were the same, he and I.

"But there you were," he said, his voice sultry, rich, stroking me gently as I hardened slowly in his hand. "Your first instinct not to please or flatter, like everyone else tried to do, but to protect, which is what we all so desperately needed."

I pushed into his hand, hearing my breath go raspy and ragged.

"You've been a confidant and a champion. You've become the parent both the girls needed," he said, leaning me forward over the counter, his hand on my ass, rubbing and massaging as my eyes drifted closed. "And I saw you the whole time, and the amazing thing is, you saw me too."

He went to his knees behind me and when he parted my cheeks, I gasped before bucking against the counter as his tongue slid into my hole.

"I'll be so gentle," he promised before he licked and pressed, the spearing and suction and endless laving turning my bones to liquid so, guided by his strong hands, I sank to the floor on my hands and knees.

He left me there to retrieve the lube from the bed, back before my skin chilled, kissing down my spine, the delicious rimming starting all over again. When he replaced his hot tongue with two lube-covered fingers, pushing in deep, I moaned his name.

"If this isn't all right, you tell me," he said, and I could hear the seduction as well as the sincerity there as he took hold of my hip with one hand and positioned the head of his cock to my entrance with the other.

In answer, I pushed back, craving the feeling of fullness, but more than that, the connection with him. He was gentle, and I felt my body stretch around him, open, take him in as he groaned, husky and low, pressing inside me.

"When you want this from me, Brann, when you want to be inside me, put me down on the bed and I'm yours, you understand? I want this too."

"But not as much as you want to be inside me," I said,

shivering as I rode the line between pleasure and pain, the pinpricks of sharp, overly-sensitized flesh contrasting with the desire to have him fuck me into the floor.

"I love having you under me," he growled, pushing, filling me, inch by inch, his movement a slow, steady glide until he was fully seated and I was impaled on his hard length. "And the idea that such a strong, sexy man has my cock buried in his ass is making me stupid."

I turned my head to look at him over my shoulder. "I could ride you."

"Oh fuck," he groaned, reaching out to clench his fingers in my hair, tilting my head, bowing my back, sliding in and out, hard and fast, the sound of slapping flesh a steady tempo until he faltered as the primal urge to rut took over. "Grab your cock, because just imagining you bottoming from the top is going to make me come."

"Is it better than this? Now?" I teased him with my last cognizant thought before there was only the deep stroking to my core.

"Nothing is better than you right now, at this moment," he said, panting, lost to his own body thrusting, pumping, and above all else, staking his claim. Again.

I'd never been wanted, needed, as I was by Emery Dodd, and as my muscles clamped down along his length like a fist, I came spurting on the floor beneath me, amazed that there was anything left after the first time.

He was seconds behind me, falling across my back, replete as his orgasm washed over him, shuddering with the aftershocks.

"I feel good, huh?" I rumbled, loving his hands sliding all over me before his arms wrapped around my chest, and he clunked his head down between my shoulder blades.

"You feel so much better than good, and I find myself

compelled to put marks on every square inch of your beautiful skin."

"Compelled, huh?" I snickered, loving how ridiculous he sounded.

"Don't make fun of me."

"Absolutely not." I couldn't help teasing.

"Just... I want you to stay here and belong to me," he murmured. "You need to be mine for the rest of my life."

He was postorgasm, so not all of what he was saying could be counted on to come from his heart. "Is that right?"

"Yeah, that's right," he said, voice low, throaty and almost somber. "I mean, I know I just had really great sex, so you might infer that I'm not terribly credible, but I assure you that I am. Don't leave me; I won't survive."

The chances weren't much better for me, and as I exhaled the last shred of uncertainty in me, I realized he was it, the only man who would ever do.

"I'm heavy," he yawned. "I'm sorry."

But he didn't move, and when I chuckled, I felt him smile against my back. "You're not sorry one bit."

"No," he agreed, lifting up but not pulling out, instead reaching for my chin to turn my head so he could kiss me. "Not one bit."

FIFTEEN

I drove toward Mal's, smiling like an idiot because Emery had his hand on my thigh the whole way, like it was the most natural thing in the world.

"I need to ask you a question," I began hesitantly, pulling over and parking, but leaving the car running, turning in my seat to face him after I unclipped my seat belt.

"I'm sure you need to ask me a million." He sighed, tucking a strand of hair behind my ear, sliding the back of his knuckles down my cheek. "I'm ready when you are."

I took a breath. "You touched me all the time."

"Yes, I did," he admitted gravely.

"And you're a high school teacher, so... you should be very aware of boundaries and touching and what that all means."

"Which, of course, I am."

"And yet with me...," I said, letting the words trail off, waiting on him.

"And yet with you, all that flew out the window," he finished my sentence for me, his breath a defeated huff. "I touched you all the time, and I couldn't help it even though it only made everything worse for me."

"For me too," I confessed.

"I know," he said thickly, dragging his hand through his hair. "You should be so angry and…. It's not fair, what I did."

I held his gaze.

"I don't deserve you," he rasped, "but I will."

I grinned at him. "We covered that in bed, didn't we? Me belonging to you?"

"I thought so, but you're sitting here scaring the hell out of me, and I don't know what I need to say or—I mean, how does one go about holding on to a retired Navy SEAL? How do I keep you without making you feel trapped? We're in the middle of Montana, for God's sake. Is there something, anything, I can do to make you want to stay?" He asked me, sounding a bit unhinged. "What do I––"

"Your heart will do it," I said, then kissed him until he stopped trying to talk and melted against me.

"Whatever you want," he said when I finally leaned back in my seat after easing free of the kiss, "it's yours."

All I wanted was the forever with him, and he'd already promised that. "Good."

His sigh was long and deep, and I put my seat belt back on and slowly eased my Toyota back onto the road, headed again toward Mal's. "So tell me, is your school still going to let you teach if you live with me?"

His scowl came fast. "Are you serious?"

"Of course," I said, affronted, glaring at him.

His snort of laughter made me smile in spite of myself.

"Listen, I—"

"Yes, Brann," he soothed me, leaning in to kiss the side of my neck. "I can be married to a man and still teach AP and Honors English, drama, and be the yearbook advisor. I told them I was bisexual when they hired me nine years ago, because I never wanted to be anything but truthful even though it's none of their business."

I exhaled the breath I'd been holding.

"I'm sure there are schools that care, but Ursa High isn't one of them."

"I was worried," I said gruffly. "I don't want you to lose anything because of me."

"You're a gift, Brann. There's only what you're bringing to my life, to my girls' lives. There's nothing bad that could ever come by way of you."

My eyes prickled with tears as I turned away from him to look out the side window for a moment.

"We probably should have stayed in bed a bit longer and not rushed right out."

My eyes were back on his face.

"I mean, I know how I feel, how you feel, and we've basically been co-parenting since the day you showed up, but we have to find our footing together too."

"You're saying that we've got the 'taking care of the girls' part down cold, but the *us* piece needs some work?"

"Not work," he said thoughtfully, brushing my hair out of my eyes. "I simply need to tell you, a lot, until you believe it as an absolute truth, that I don't want to just live with you."

"Oh yeah?" I said as I parked my Toyota in front of Mal's rambling three-story American Queen Anne-style monstrosity of a house, which stood out from all the others on his street.

It was actually a mix of a bunch of Victorian styles, and I really hoped Mal and his wife, Jules, never wanted to move, because it was one of those things that looked kind of cool but was overbuilt and a bit too quirky. The fact there was a widow's walk the length of the third story next to a spired sunroom was one of the first things I noticed. It turned out Mal had inherited the house from an eccentric aunt. He told me the homeowners association had begged him to tear it down and build a ranch house on the land or a Foursquare or a Craftsman, but instead, Mal had renovated it, painted it pale green with red trim, and built a pergola in the backyard for his wife as well as planting an extensive vegetable and herb garden.

"Look at me."

I turned in the seat to face Emery. "I'm looking at you."

He unclipped his belt, took my face in his warm hands, and leaned in and kissed me. Unlike the earlier kisses, this one was gentle and coaxing, his tongue stroking over mine as he tasted and lingered, and I forgot about anything else but the slow, sensual heat building between us. When he turned into me, tipping my head back, hands slipping under my heavy, zippered cardigan and t-shirt to my skin, I jolted with the contact.

"Shit," he gasped, breaking the kiss and opening his door at the same time.

"What're you doing?" I murmured, staring at him.

"Get out of the car where it's safe," he ordered brusquely.

"Are you mad?"

"Mad? Are you kidding?"

I waited, not moving as he stared in at me from where he was standing on the curb.

"Brann, I was *thisclose* to attacking you right there in the driver's seat," he said indignantly. "Mad at you? Brann, honey. I want to wrestle you into the back seat and screw your brains out. Again."

I smiled slowly.

He made a noise like he was dying, and I got out as well, closed the door, and came around the front to stand beside him as he shut his door too.

"You want me more?" I asked, waiting, staring at his lush lips, thinking about how great they had felt stretched around my cock earlier. "Em?"

He looked like he was in pain, squinting at me.

"Maybe in your bed next time," I whispered, moving closer, my gaze locked with his. "Do you want me there? In your bed? In your room?"

His exhale was sharp, halting, as he watched me move closer.

"Emery?"

"That's what I was trying to say before—I don't want you to live with me. I want you to marry me. I want you there, with me and the girls, always."

His eyes were glassy and dark and deep, and I wanted to be there, like that, be the guy he wanted to fuck and eat and hold down. I never before in my life had anyone desperate and hungry and consumed with a need to keep me. It was an altogether brand-new experience that I wanted to savor.

"I want permanent with you."

"So then I shouldn't go back to Chicago?"

He shook his head. "No."

"You're sure?" I barely got out as I reached him.

"Let's go home and get in bed, and we'll come back later."

I broke into a huge grin. I could feel it on my face, and he groaned loudly and bent over, hands on his knees, taking deep breaths.

"I feel like I'm drunk or underwater or…. It's like I need the normal to start right now."

"Because this doesn't seem real." I said what we were

both thinking, my hand on his back as he straightened up and stared at me.

"It doesn't, not yet."

We had moved so fast, from sex to the forever, and we both knew it didn't work like that. There were supposed to be relationship milestones, and we'd hit them all, but backward. We learned how to be a family before we learned to be the two of us.

"But it will," he promised me, taking my hands in his. "There are so many things we know already; give it all a chance."

"I have no choice," I assured him. "I want to be part of your family."

"But not just for my girls. You don't just love them."

"No, you're right," I confirmed, chuckling. "There's the dog too."

I wasn't surprised that he lunged at me, arms wrapping around my neck, yanking me close, crushing me against him.

"He's a really cute dog," I murmured, loving how tight I was being held. His muffled laughter made me smile.

"Don't tease me anymore. Just profess your undying love," he demanded hoarsely.

"Consider it done," I growled before I captured his mouth and kissed him until he was breathless and panting, his fingers digging into my back. "You're not the only one who's dying to have his life begin."

"Good to know," he croaked, still clutching at me.

It took us a few minutes to get it together enough to go to the door and knock.

Julia Jezic hurled open the front door, and before Emery could get a word of greeting out, she flung herself at him so he had to scramble to catch her. Normally, Jules was a whirlwind of activity. She directed a booming pediatric practice by day and co-parented a household with four growing boys by night. I had never seen her slow down, never seen her quiet or still, and never, ever, seen her weep. At the moment, she was doing all four. Also, the woman with the honey-blonde hair and peaches-and-cream complexion, who wasn't in any way short at five-seven, seemed tiny and deli-cate and breakable as she trembled in Emery Dodd's arms. It was clear to see that she had missed him very much. It was also apparent from the way his eyes closed and he held her, protectively, tenderly, that she'd been missed just as dearly.

"Holy crap, are you people lucky I came to town," I announced as Mal walked up behind Emery and his wife, still hugging furiously, and leaned around them with a cup of coffee for me.

"Yeah, we are," he agreed, smiling. "Without question."

The girls had come to greet us, quickly, out of obligation, because they needed to get back to playing with the boys in the adjacent room. Olivia and Luke, who was also six, and Romeo, who was seven, were playing Mario Kart, and April and Danny, who was April's age, and Liam, the oldest at ten, were playing some role-playing game that I missed the name of, but that Jules informed me would most certainly give April nightmares.

"There's blood and demons and—"

"She's played it a million times," Emery assured her. "We all know the only nightmares April's ever had were about how her mother died."

"It sounds like she's doing better with that," Jules said, turning to smile at me. "She told me all about her therapist and I understand you have a friend who's a surgeon in Chicago."

I gestured at her as I sipped the amazing French roast Mal had given me. "You could have done the same thing."

"And I told her that today when she told me. I said if she had more questions, with Emery's permission, I could answer them." Jules sighed, reaching over to slip her hand over my forearm and squeeze gently. "If Emery and I had been talking, I could have helped."

"So maybe don't not talk anymore," I said softly, patting her hand. "You all should make certain you stay constant in each other's lives."

"I agree a hundred percent," Mal said, standing at the stove making huevos rancheros, which was, he told me, his specialty. From the whimper that came out of Emery after Mal revealed what was on the lunch menu, I was guessing it was pretty good.

It was nice when Jules leaned over out of the blue and hugged me, and then smiled at me like I was a gift she couldn't believe belonged to her.

"So," she said tentatively, wincing, turning to face Emery. "How was the breakup scene with Lydia Cahill?"

He groaned and clunked his head down onto the table in his folded arms.

"That good, huh?"

"It was horrible," he muttered, speaking into the table so his voice was muffled.

She cleared her throat. "You'll remember at the town meeting that your friend, the councilman, did suggest an alternate path."

"Shut up."

Her eyes flicked to mine, and she widened them for a

moment before returning her gaze to him. "So what exactly is your new plan here, Mr. Dodd?"

He lifted his head up off his arms. "To do what your husband suggested."

Her smile was evil as she waggled her eyebrows at him. "It's all right, Em. What fun would life be if we actually took good advice the first time it was offered? Then we would never have to live and learn. We could simply bypass pain and misery."

Her sarcasm wasn't lost on any of us.

"Yes," he sighed, bumping his knee with mine under the table. "That wouldn't be any fun at all."

Mal picked that moment to serve Emery as Jules dissolved into relieved laughter.

It turned out that Anne Stratton, Grant Cahill's companion, was, in fact, a real estate developer who specialized in resorts. As Whitefish was already a scenic travel destination for people who wanted to hike and fish and hunt and spend the winter in a cozy cabin, Anne had suggested that the town of Ursa, and, in particular, Emery and Darrow Holdings, step up and add a luxury ski resort to that mix.

Since ski season in the mountain town of Ursa was typically between December and March, falling off sharply by mid-April, there would be peak times when every room would be full, and during nonpeak times, there would still be that which drew nonskiing visitors year-round. But what Anne had pushed Emery to see was the possibility to capitalize on the one hundred and forty or so days that the ski season offered. And she knew what she was talking about.

Anne Stratton had built some of the most exclusive, high-end ski resorts in Vail, Colorado. More importantly, she knew what amenities people wanted, what they were looking for in a romantic getaway, family vacation, or corporate retreat. She had made the offer to Emery and Darrow but not Grant because Cahill Lumber was a thriving business that already employed hundreds of people in the town of Ursa. Emery's land was used for grazing, but only the area in the lower valley. The rest went unused and untouched.

Initially, Emery had been concerned about the indigenous wildlife, but Anne had explained that there was quite a lot of federal land between Darrow's parcel and the Canadian border, not to mention the fact that the resort itself would be big, yes, but not ten-thousand-acres big. Anne had made him an offer for three thousand acres of overall skiable terrain. The resort would be built and managed by her company and owned by Darrow Holdings. It was, she said, that once-in-a-lifetime venture that was a sure thing. They would make money hand over fist. People wanted more options, and Ursa could offer one. It would also be a boon to the community.

Sitting there, gazing at the man I loved, I was compelled to reach across the table and smack him on the side of the head.

"What the hell was that for?" he snapped at me as Jules scowled at him and Mal carried two plates over, serving me and his wife.

"Are you kidding?" I asked him, staring, hoping I appeared as annoyed as I felt. "You had the option of building a resort instead of getting married, and you went with door number two? Are you high?"

He glanced at Jules and Mal, both of whom also seemed concerned over his mental capacity, and then exhaled a deep breath of frustration. "The resort doesn't just get built in a day, and there's a lot of work to do before you even break ground, and—"

"You were worried it wasn't a sure thing," Jules offered

before starting to eat.

"That and everyone loves Cahill Lumber, and it seemed like the perfect fit, and the biggest factor of all was that the girls would have someone besides me to love and care for them."

"But then?" Mal prodded, taking a sip of the mimosa he'd made for himself.

Emery's dark eyes flicked to me. "Then Brann walked in the door, and marrying Lydia instead of seeing where instant attraction and natural chemistry went seemed really stupid."

"Aww," Jules cooed, her eyes filling.

"He's talking about lust ya know," Mal informed her, rolling his eyes.

"Not anymore," she whispered and grabbed hold of my hand.

We were all quiet, enjoying Mal's amazing food, the fresh fruit as well, and, of course, the mimosas and coffee.

"So you called Anne?" Mal asked Emery.

"I did, yes. Last week."

"What'd she say?" I inquired, because it was my whole life's happiness he was talking about.

"She said it was about damn time I pulled my head out of my ass, because allowing the sham of a marriage to progress any further when I clearly had feelings for my nanny was the epitome—and this is a direct quote now—of stupidity."

I grinned at him. "She thought you had feelings for me?"

"She didn't think; she knew."

And it hit me, then, all at once, so I took a breath and drained the mimosa in three gulps before reaching for Jules' and drinking hers as well.

"Shit," Emery groaned under his breath before getting

up fast and coming around the table to crouch down beside me.

I wouldn't run. I didn't do that. But it hurt to know that even though he'd had an option, even when he knew he had feelings for me, and that his girls did too, he'd still allowed plans for the wedding to move forward.

"I told you it was unforgivable," he said, his hand sliding over my cheek, turning my head so I had to look at him, into his eyes. "I told you I'd been a coward."

Yes, he had told me. And yes, he had been a coward.

"I was afraid that if you didn't want me too, then I'd be out of the deal with Cahill and have no one for my girls."

It was very logical as well as cynical.

"But it had nothing to do with love or faith or hope, and everything to do with me being comfortable with my life, complacent and wanting a quick, easy fix."

"Makes sense," I said, my voice brittle, pained.

"No, it doesn't. Anyone with half a brain knows that there are no quick fixes when it comes to love and big, reckless hearts. You showed up, fell in love, and were there, being you, the perfect thing for me, more than I deserve or would have thought to ever ask for, and still I was scared."

"Would you have still reached for me if Anne Stratton had said there was no deal on the table?" I asked, scared of the answer.

"What? Oh, no, it's not—there's no deal yet. It's all up in the air," he explained, hands cupping my face, holding me still. "I have to see the board, with Anne, and they'll review the proposal. Hopefully they'll move fast on it, but they could turn her down like I did at first."

I turned in my chair, facing him, and he made room and then went to his knees in front of me, hands on my thighs to keep his balance.

"But please don't think that I waited to reach for you before I knew I had a plan B in place, because nothing could be further from the truth."

I nodded, my eyes blurring as they filled with hot tears.

"I reached for you because it was the only way I could make sure that my life wouldn't be total shit."

"Oh, you romantic you," I teased him, but I was so very pleased with the man who had killed me minutes before only to restart my heart with his confession.

"Whatever else happens, Brann, you're the best thing for me, you're the best thing for my girls, and our life together starts right now."

I bent to kiss him, and he lifted to meet me halfway, and it was tender and claiming, and I felt it warm all the places inside that had grown cold when I thought he made a safe choice with me instead of the scary, death-defying, no-net decision it truly was.

"So did you happen to tell Emery that you're going to be the new sheriff?"

"What?" Emery asked, his voice guttural after breaking the kiss to stare up at me. "You're going to be what?"

I grunted.

His eyes widened. "Brann?"

"This is a funny story."

He rose slowly, staring at me the whole time. "Tell me now."

"Well, see, apparently there were some write-in ballots."

His mouth fell open in disbelief.

"And from what Mal says... I'm gonna be the new sheriff," I said cheerfully. "Isn't that great? So you don't have to support me 'cause I'll have my own job." I cleared my throat because he still hadn't reacted at all. "Yay," I added, smiling big.

"Sheriff?"

He was louder than I thought he would be.

"Sheriff!"

I had no idea his voice could travel like that. He would have given my old CO a run for his money.

"Have you lost your fuckin' mind?"

Mal coughed. "You know there are kids in the other—"

"I forbid it!"

"I'm sorry, you what?" I asked him, standing so we were eye to eye.

"You could be killed!"

And it hit me that he had lost Andrea and so of course, he'd be scared of losing me too, so I had to clear that up fast. "I won't be killed. Think about it a second," I soothed him. "Take a breath and remember where you are."

He started to pace in front of me, but as I watched him, I saw his logical mind kick in, and he growled a bit even as he nodded.

"It's Ursa, Montana," I reminded him.

He continued with the pacing, but the sharp exhale followed by the furrowed brows let me know he was getting closer and closer to wrapping his brain around the truth. That not only was I going to do a job I suddenly really wanted, but one it turned out I was going to be excellent at as well. But more important than me being sheriff was his visceral reaction to the news.

He couldn't lose me.

"Hey," Jules said, grabbing Mal's hand. "I need to talk to my husband really quick, we'll be right back."

It wasn't subtle, the way she gave us our privacy, but I appreciated it.

Moving fast, I grabbed his bicep and yanked him forward, into me, into my arms, and wrapped him up, one hand in his hair, the other in the middle of his back, pressing him close, holding tight so I could whisper into his ear.

"I love you back," I said because that was what all his yelling translated to, after all.

He shivered hard, a full-body one, and I could feel how terrified he was.

"Nothing will happen to me."

"You can't promise that," he whispered hoarsely. "I can't —if you're going to do this, then I can't have—"

"No," I soothed him, tilting his head back, kissing his throat, up to his chin and taking his mouth, kissing him until he was boneless in my arms, his coiled around my neck, holding on like he would drown if he didn't.

When I lifted my lips from him, his eyes, glazed with blown pupils, told me that he was in a place to hear me.

"Don't throw me away because you're scared. I know full well that neither you nor the girls can go through losing me, and I promise that I will be vigilant about my safety. I'm actually pretty well-trained, right? I know how to keep myself safe in more adverse conditions than this."

He gave me a slight nod.

"I won't take my life here, with you, for granted, because I was terrified it was never even gonna start."

His jaw clenched as his eyes filled, and he didn't say anything because, I was guessing, he couldn't at the moment.

"But we all take chances every day, and the idea of being the sheriff in this town, where the girls are growing up and you teach school and where our home is—" Suddenly I couldn't speak either, momentarily overcome with having everything I ever wanted all at once. It was like being hit with a wave you never saw coming, and it was scary for a second before you found yourself spitting up warm salt water on a white sandy beach on the perfect sunny day.

"All right," he murmured, slipping his hand around the back of my head, easing me down, my lips hovering over his. "I'll be brave, you'll be careful, and we'll do this together."

I kissed him to seal that promise between us.

"Daddy, why are you kissing Brann?"

SIXTEEN

We took the girls and Winston home, because the talk was going to be a long one. I was ready for hard questions and tears, time needed for them to adjust to the change, and perhaps anger. They might be so scared of what would happen to them at school, the repercussions there, that they would want Lydia back and not me.

I feared that outcome the most. I was used to being loved now. I didn't want that to go away. I was terrified it would.

The four of us took a seat in the living room, the girls on the couch, Emery and I sitting on the coffee table in front of them.

"All right," Emery began, taking a breath. "Let me begin by saying—"

"You kissed Brann," Olivia told him.

He nodded. "Yes. Yes, I did."

"Does that mean you're going to only kiss him now and not Lydia?"

"Uhm, well, yes," he answered, squinting at his youngest. "That's exactly what that means."

"So are you still going to marry Lydia?"

"No, I'm not."

"And do we get to live here?" Olivia asked, hands in her lap, waiting.

"Yes, but—"

"Will Brann live here too?"

"Well, honey, Brann lives here now."

"That's not what she asked," April clarified, almost sharply, eyes boring into her father. "She asked you if Brann would live here, and what she meant by that was, would he live here with us, instead of going back to Chicago?"

He turned to me. "Is that what you got from that?"

I smiled at him before I leaned forward to give Olivia my undivided attention. "I would very much like to live here with you and your sister and your father and Winston forever, if that would be okay with you."

Her grin was instant before she scrambled up off the couch, stood, and then launched herself at me like a missile.

I caught her easily, stood up and hugged her tight, and the feeling that came over me, that she belonged to me, that now she was my daughter too, made it hard to breathe.

"So will you get married?" April asked Emery.

"Yes."

"And Brann will sleep in bed with you like Mommy used to?"

"Yes, he will."

She was quiet a moment. "And we can just keep calling him Brann?"

"You can call him whatever you want as long as it's not dude or jerk or—you get my meaning," he informed her, being as serious as she was.

"Will he adopt us?"

"Why would you ask that?"

"Because I listened when you talked to the lawyer, and you made sure that Lydia couldn't adopt us. Will you let Brann?"

He coughed softly. "I would very much like Brann to adopt you and be your legal guardian just like I am."

She nodded. "I would like that too."

"Me too," Olivia said, her hands on my face as she stared at me. "Do you want to be my legal guardian?"

I nodded quickly, voice gone.

"Brann wants to do that too," she said authoritatively, speaking for me.

"Can we still have a wedding?" April asked her father.

"I would like that."

"But only in the backyard maybe, and just us... and Mom."

Emery gasped. "Mom?"

April nodded. "I think Brann was right when he said that a part of her was still here in me and Ollie and you, and I think she would like it if you got married 'cause I think she would like Brann."

My eyes overflowed, and Olivia wiped away my tears and told me not to cry and then hugged me again.

Emery bent and April stood at the same time, and he wrapped her up in his arms so tight she made a noise like he squeezed out all her air before she started laughing.

After long moments, I passed him Olivia and sank down in front of April.

"You didn't like me at first."

"Only at the very first," she corrected me, sliding her hand up on my shoulder. "But it went away superfast."

"It did. You're right."

She was studying my face, checking for something.

"April, honey, I—"

"I love you, Brann," she said, stepping into me, arms around my neck. "I was going to be really sad when you left, so this is way better. And Daddy has really warm blankets on his bed, better than the ones in your room, so you're gonna like sleeping with Daddy."

Of that I had no doubt.

"And I think I should go to Chicago with you when you go and get your stuff so you don't get lost on your way home."

"I think that's a great idea." I sighed, squeezing her tight.

"Brann, I can't breathe."

I let her go just a little.

"Liam heard his Daddy talking to somebody on the phone, and they said that Brann was going to be the new sheriff. Is that true?"

All of us were staring at April.

"Well? Is it true?"

Hedging, I said, "Possibly."

"I hope so. That would be awesome," April said excitedly.

"It would be so badass!" Olivia squealed.

"Pardon me?" Emery said to his daughter. "What did you just say?"

"Ohmygod, Dad, I'm taking karate, and the sheriff is one of my parents!" She cackled evilly, and I, for one, had no idea she could make a noise like that—it was a little scary.

I exchanged a quick glance with Emery, who cleared his throat. "You guys wouldn't be worried that Brann might get hurt? I mean, what if somebody shot at him?"

Olivia squinted at her father. "In Ursa?"

Even a six-year-old knew there was nothing to be worried about. And yes, famous last words and everything else, and we'd all heard about people coming back from some of the scariest places in the world only to be killed five blocks from home. But this wasn't the same. A sleepy mountain town in Montana was a place to be careful in but not paranoid.

"Besides, Dad," April soothed him, giving him a look of sympathy, "Brann is a retired Navy SEAL. Now, I don't know if you know what that is, but I'll go get my laptop and show you."

I lost it, because she was so very serious.

Olivia trailed after her sister, spouting question after question at her about what a SEAL actually was, and what had she missed, and how come nobody ever told her anything!

Emery went after the girls, promising me he'd be right back. The soft knock on the door stopped me from following him.

Answering it, I was only a bit surprised to find Huck Riley.

"Holy crap," I said, so happy he was there, lifting my arms in welcome. "Good to see you, brother."

He didn't say anything, just walked up to me, into the waiting hug, and wrapped his arms around me tighter than he had in a while. Instantly I was worried. When he leaned and gave me his weight, I was terrified about what he could have done.

"Did you use?" I asked quickly, hoping to God the answer would be no. In the past, when he'd said yes, it was the start of the rehab process that I would be there to see him through, again. This time, it would be different, because this time, now, if the answer came back in the affirmative, I'd have to send him back to Phoenix. I couldn't have a drug user near my kids.

"No," he said, his voice ragged. "I got on a plane to come see you instead."

"Oh thank God." I almost whimpered with relief, tightening my hold, willing some of my strength into him, so pleased with the choice he'd made.

"Brann?" Emery said hesitantly.

We both turned to him, and I saw Emery deflate when he got a look at Huck. If I were him, if the roles were reversed, I'd feel the same, so I understood. He was basically gazing at a perfect specimen of the male form, and seeing Huck all over me probably wasn't making him happy. Our thing was a minute old, and here was Huck in all his disheveled glory.

"Hey, Em," I greeted him softly. "Come meet my buddy."

His head lifted, and he went from looking dejected to looking more like himself—confident, charismatic—as he rushed across the room to take the hand Huck held out for him.

What was even more interesting was that the moment Emery was close enough to see Huck's face and eyes, his own brows furrowed with concern.

"Nice to meet you, Mr. Dodd," Huck said, his voice a husky rasp. "Brann speaks so highly of you and your girls, and I don't mean to intrude, but Brann invited me out, so—"

"Oh, no, I'm so pleased you decided to visit, and hopefully it can be quite an extended one. We have a very comfortable guest room that has just become vacant."

"Really?" Huck asked hopefully, glancing from Emery to me and back.

"Absolutely," Emery said, squeezing Huck's shoulder as he held on to his hand.

"That sounds great."

. . .

AN HOUR LATER, Huck was sitting on the floor in the living room, Olivia on one side, April on the other, and the three of them were playing what looked like a cooking game, where they had to work together. Emery and I were in the kitchen.

"How come they never had me play that with them?" I asked Emery.

"Are you jealous?"

"What?"

"Oh God, I love that your voice went up about three octaves there. Poor baby."

"I'm sorry?"

"That's what happens, love," he teased me, slipping his hand around the side of my neck and easing me close for a kiss. "Once you become a parent, you slip in the hierarchy. I had to take a back seat to you; now you have to step aside for Huck."

"No," I groused at him, shooting him a glare as he chuckled and kissed along my jawline. "They don't like him better."

Apparently I was very amusing, and the kisses grew languorous as I watched my friend in the living room, watched Olivia touch his mane of hair, saw April put on his hoodie that he had taken off and then feed him popcorn that she had made for all three of them. They could tell he was delicate, that he needed care and nurturing, and they were ready to treat him like the brother they never had. And for Huck's part, he didn't want to think about himself or be in his own head, so video games after walking the dog, snacks, and sitting in front of the fire were likely his idea of heaven.

Emery and I had quickly moved all my stuff into his room, and I stripped the bed we'd wrecked earlier, and he made it up fresh and put new towels in the bathroom. It was strange, but it looked like I'd never been in there.

"Hey," he said softly, and I heard the teasing in his voice, in the seductive chuckle, "I need to show you something."

I allowed him to steer me out of the kitchen, grumbling as I walked. "He's not gonna be their favorite, I can tell you that right now."

Emery's rumble of agreement didn't help my mood.

"I'm the one who goes on all the field trips and stuff," I told him.

"Yes, you are," he conceded, pushing me into the master bedroom that I had to start thinking about as mine, and locking the door behind him.

"I'm the one who's been here," I declared, as he came around in front of me and sank to his knees. "I'm the fun one."

"I know, baby," he promised, staring up into my eyes as he rucked up my Henley and splayed his hand across my abdomen, then worked open my belt, the snap of my jeans, and finally the zipper. "You're loads of fun."

I gasped as he shucked my jeans and briefs to my knees and took my cock greedily down the back of his throat before letting it slide from between his lips so he could speak to me.

"Or should I say, your load will be fun."

I groaned over the pun and he swallowed me back down and laughed around my dick, which made me jolt with the vibration of it, the ripple of sensation on my skin.

He sucked hard and voraciously, and I lost track of where I ended and he began, the movement perfect, his rhythm and the pressure all blending into an arc of arousal, rise and fall, until I pulled free of Emery's sweet, sinful mouth and collapsed face-first onto the bed.

I was surprised when he rolled me to my back. I felt drunk, dazed, watching him climb over me, dragging his already lubed fingers over my shaft.

"What're you—Em?"

His fingers disappeared behind him as he smiled at me, decadently, eyes hooded, and then his hand was back, stroking my cock, smearing it with lube before he lifted and pressed the head to his entrance.

"No, you don't have—"

"But I want to," he said, gravelly and low, his breath catching as he sank down over me just a fraction, both hands anchored on my chest, digging into my pectorals like claws. "You have no idea how much I need to."

"Go slow, and—Em!" I cried out, not meaning to because Huck and the girls were still playing games in the family room, but the tight satin heat of him opening around me, stretching in tiny increments, was almost more than I could bear. "Fuck, you're gonna make me come before I even get inside."

"Don't you dare," he warned me, and I was surprised at his face, at the ache I saw there, the need. He wasn't in pain; there was no clenching, no hesitancy. He was working himself on the end of my cock, pushing, rutting, taking more and more, and when I reached out and took hold of his dripping cock, stroking him, tugging, his head fell back as he moaned out my name.

I filled him slowly, and he leaned forward to kiss me, bite me, lick my lips, lick into my mouth and suck on my tongue. I took firm hold of his hips and arched up inside of him, fucking him from the bottom, thrusting gently until he shoved down onto me, seated fully, impaled on my shaft.

His muscles clamped around me, and the grin he gave

me, wicked and wanting, sent a flush of heat prickling over my skin.

"You were all power earlier, completely in charge, and you fucked me hard both times, showing me who was in control."

"Yes," he agreed, riding my cock, lifting up only to grind back down, his fingers pinching my nipples, painfully but good, before he curled forward to take my mouth, a whine escaping his throat at the same instant, betraying his absolute hunger for me.

There was no way I could wait a second longer, I had to have him.

Showing him my strength, I wrestled him off me and manhandled him down onto the bed, shoving his face down and lifting his ass in the air. I didn't ask permission, I drove to his core, burying myself inside of him in one heaving thrust.

They would have heard him in the living room if he hadn't screamed my name into the pillow. His hands scrabbled in the blankets as he shuddered hard, turning his head so I could hear the garbled sob. "Don't stop," he begged me, his words choppy, halting, each one torn from his chest, punctuated with a sharp gasp. "Please. Brann... Brann...."

I fucked him hard, my hand on his shoulder, holding tight, shoving inside to an endless litany of filthy pleading.

"Grab your cock and make yourself come," I growled into the back of his neck, my lips there, my breath, and it was enough, because he clenched around me so tightly, lost in the throes of his own body as his climax roiled through him, loud enough that I had to slip my hand over his mouth to muffle the howl.

My own orgasm wrung me inside out, and I emptied inside of him, pumping all there was, everything, and my mind turned off, oblivion washing over me as I collapsed across his back, sated, replete, and aware of only his silky skin covered in sweat.

I had to catch my breath, and he was trembling beneath me.

"Sorry," I rumbled out, lifting, trying to move. "I'm heavy and I'm—"

"No," he whispered, taking hold of my right hand and dragging it across his chest, his fingers sliding through mine so our fingers were splayed together over his heart. "Stay. Please. I'm not ready yet."

I wasn't either, so I let him be my anchor just as I was his, and we breathed together until we could breathe apart.

I GOT to the kitchen first, and it took me a moment to realize the living room was empty. Checking the guest bedroom that was now Huck's, I didn't find him, and both girls' bedrooms yielded no kid in either. Even the dog was gone. I was about to call Huck when I saw the note on the back of the front door. It said they were all hungry, and that shakes had sounded awesome. And they were taking Winston too.

I growled to myself because the man was already starting to horn in on things that the girls and I did together. I was growling when I went in to complain about it to Emery.

He just leaned out of the shower, cupped my neck, and pulled me into a kiss.

"Don't kiss me. I'm mad," I told him before I kissed him back, feeling the now familiar bloom of yearning in my chest, the desperate need for him. Again.

"We should probably go stay at a hotel for, like, a week." He sighed as he eased back, me leaning with him, only his hand on my chest stopping me from joining him under the water. "I don't see this dying down... ever."

"That's good," I said, chuckling, palming his semi-erect cock. "I like you all hot for me."

"It's not hard," he admitted, smiling at me. "The whole town's hot for you. Do you have any idea how jealous I've been of everyone?"

"I'm jealous of Huck," I confessed. "I don't want you to think about trading me in."

"What are you talking about?"

"You saw him."

He snorted out a laugh. "I promise you that you're the only one I see, the only one I want. You're perfect for me in every way, utterly made for me."

It was stupid on my part, but I needed the words. It was necessary. "Same. You, for me."

"Again. I'm sorry it took me so long. I'll make it up to you."

"No. I'm perfect right here, right now. I want to go forward with you, no looking back."

"Okay," he said, nodding fast, his voice deserting him.

I kissed him again, and that time I got eased under the water, jeans, t-shirt, and all. We both laughed over socks in the shower.

EMERY WAS OUT FIRST the second time, and because it had started to rain—the icy, stinging kind—and Huck and the kids had walked, he said he'd drive over to the restaurant, order us some food too and then bring everyone home with him. It was a good plan.

I was washing dishes, cleaning up the popcorn and bowl and the glasses that had been left for the maid, when there was a knock on the door. Bolting to the door, thinking maybe Emery forgot his wallet, I threw it open only to find David Reed there, holding a gun.

"What the hell are you doing, Deputy?"

"Get in the house," he ordered, and when I took several steps back, he came in, followed quickly by Anne Stratton, Mr. Duvall, and Grant Cahill.

"What's going on?" I asked sharply.

"You," Cahill said through gritted teeth at the same time shoving Anne toward me.

I realized she was unsteady and off-balance because her hands were tied, but I caught her easily before lifting her chin, checking her over, having noticed instantly that her normally elegant appearance was marred by a split lip, a bloody nose, and what would soon be a black eye along with some bruising on her throat.

"Are you all right?" I asked her.

"Oh, Brann, I'm so sorry," she said shakily. "This is all my fault."

"Yeah, I'm betting not," I assured her. "Stay behind me," I ordered, stepping in front of her, shielding her with my body. I faced Duvall then, who had a gun as well, much bigger than the deputy's Glock 17. He was holding a Beretta M9 on Anne and me, as Cahill began pacing back-and-forth behind the couch.

"Aren't you going to check the rest of the house?" I asked Cahill.

"No," Duvall answered me. "We waited until we saw Emery go out."

Of course they had.

I heard my phone ring in the other room, which was probably the man I loved checking to see what I wanted for dinner since he'd forgotten to ask before he left.

"You ruined the wedding," Cahill announced, eyes on me, glaring, flushed and sweating, looking like he was about to have a heart attack.

"I did," I conceded with a shrug. "And I get why you'd be pissed about that," I said to Cahill. "But I figured you'd be thrilled," I said to Reed.

"Why would he be happy?"

"Because he's in love with your daughter," I said matter-of-factly, answering Cahill.

He shook his head. "David wants to be rich, as does Allen"—he nodded toward Duvall—"as do I."

I focused on Reed. "So that was all crap you told me?"

"No," he said, squinting, looking uncomfortable as he tugged on the collar of his shirt. "It's just... even not marrying Emery, she's not going to look at me. It'll be another of those rich entitled assholes who jets off to Paris or Rome."

"Okay, so you need Emery's land," I said, turning my attention back to Cahill. "And you know about that because of the geologist."

"There's nothing on my land," Cahill explained to me. "It's all on Emery's."

"You mean on the grazing land."

"No, I mean on Andrea's private land, on the land where Emery wants to put the resort."

"There's no way that Emery Dodd knows that his wife's family had any private land. He thinks it all belongs to Darrow."

"I know that," Cahill snarled at me. "But he's wrong. I had Duvall remove all those records that show the exact property lines between what belongs to Darrow and what belonged specifically to Andrea's family the night she died."

"You cheating son of a bitch," I rebuked him. "It's Emery

who will actually take care of the town when the resort goes in, not you, and not Darrow."

He was fuming, utterly enraged over the turn of fortune.

"And when Emery called Anne to talk about the deal, as any good builder would, she went to City Hall to look at the deeds and see where the property lines were."

"Yes," Mr. Duvall answered me, lifting the gun. "So now, unfortunately, we have no choice but to eliminate both you and Ms. Stratton."

"And what about Peter Bannon? Why kill him?"

"Because even though we hired him," Duvall explained, "he wasn't comfortable with not providing Emery with the same information he gave us."

"Poor guy, killed for being ethical," I quipped, hearing my phone ring again, hoping Emery would find it odd I wasn't picking up and not annoying enough to just get me a club sandwich and a strawberry shake. "So who did the honors there?"

"That was me," Duvall said, shrugging, making a face. "Why does it matter? You and Ms. Stratton will have a similar accident, and then everything can go back to the way it was."

"Meaning?"

"Meaning that Emery will marry Lydia, and once that's done and he signs over the company to the third-party just as Mr. Cahill will sign over the lumberyard, once it's one big conglomerate, the mining can begin."

"Because the third-party joint company is actually one of yours."

"You're smarter than you look, Mr. Calder," Duvall told me.

"Yeah, I get that a lot," I said, exhaling, starting to worry about how I would keep Anne safe while moving as fast as I'd need to. Reed would be first, of course, and I was concerned at that point about Duvall killing Anne. "But tell me, Mr. Cahill, was your daughter in on any of this? Does she know about the land or Darrow or the dead geologist?"

His disgust for my suggestion was evident in his glare. "Don't be absurd."

"So you had Lydia ready to throw away her whole future, her shot at finding love, to marry Emery, and all you actually needed was his land."

"I—"

"What kind of a father are you?"

"Oh, please, Calder. I would have had Lydia divorce Emery before their first anniversary."

"So the prenup they signed, that protects Lydia's money from the mill, and Emery's kids, but the land, that's all joint property?"

"Exactly."

"But not Emery's land; that's not part of the pot."

"Of course it is," Reed snapped at me.

"No. That land doesn't belong to him. He's only the trustee. The land belongs to April and Olivia."

"That's the holding company," Duvall argued.

"No," Anne said, leaning sideways from behind me. "The way the land is zoned, just as you said, it's separate and owned exclusively by him. But Brann's correct, even Emery isn't the actual owner; the land belongs to the girls."

"And the girls are his alone," I explained to the men in the living room of my home. "The prenup states that Lydia can never adopt them."

"Which means that anything we find on their land, is theirs," Duvall said, staring at me blankly before turning to Cahill.

"You should know," I said to Duvall. "You're the one who told me about it the very first day I hit town."

"Fucking, Calder," Reed swore, lifting the Glock, levelling it at me. "Now you're going to make us kill Emery's kids!"

"Oh, you're not going to hurt anybody else, and as the new sheriff of this town, the first thing I'm gonna do is make all three of you pay for what you did to Mr. Bannon."

"Sheriff!" Reed yelled at me. "Have you lost your—"

The large picture window to the right of me exploded, glass and wood flying in every direction as Huck flew by me, landing in a crouch, gun drawn.

"Anne, get down!" I roared at her as Huck fired.

I leaped toward Duvall, who pulled the trigger as I hit him. Both of us fell in a scramble of limbs, but Duvall was slammed against the floor first, with me coming down on top of him, and the force winded him and knocked the gun free.

Rolling to my feet, Duvall's Beretta in my hand, I yelled for Huck. "Clear!"

"Clear," he echoed me, picking up Reed's gun before walking to the kitchen, working his bad shoulder as he moved.

I heard Reed moaning, figured he was fine, and then looked down at Duvall. "If you get up, I will shoot you in the head. Are we clear?"

He nodded from where he was spread-eagle near the front door. Mr. Cahill was in a fetal position near him, hands over his head, not moving. I walked over to him, checked for a weapon, found nothing, then darted across the room to Anne, who was crouched behind the coffee table.

"You okay?" I asked, easing her up. I brushed her hair out of her eyes and made sure she was steady on her feet.

"Yes, I—Brann are you—where's Reed?"

"He's fine," I assured her, tipping my head to Huck, who was back from the kitchen with a dishtowel that he bent and pressed to Reed's shoulder before moving the man's other hand to apply pressure. "You can't die from that."

She nodded quickly, looking at Huck as he reached us.

"You all right, ma'am?" he asked gently with that whiskey-sounding voice of his that reminded everyone of sex.

"Oh," she sighed, staring at him, all doe-eyed and vulnerable. "Yes. Thank you."

He made a face. "It was fine. Brann had it. I wouldn't've even come in, but he might've taken a bullet protecting you, and I can't have that."

"You have glass in your hair," I told him, "and you probably tracked it all the way to the kitchen. We're gonna be vacuuming for hours."

"Blame the assholes with the guns," he groused at me. "So since you're not the law in this town yet, who am I calling to pick these guys up?"

"Who told you about that?"

"Emery and the girls."

I nodded, arching an eyebrow for him.

He squinted at me, looking bored.

"What's happening right now?" Anne asked us both.

"Is that what you want?" He was staring at me, his blue-green eyes steady, unwavering, waiting for what I would say.

"Of course that's what I want."

He sniffed once, pulling his phone from his back pocket. "That means us, here, and you might be the one stuck with me long-term 'cause I'm not going again."

Translated from Huck into English, it meant that if I wanted him here, then Ursa would become his new home, but I had better not change my mind because this was it and I was stuck with him. Forever.

"Good," I said simply, giving him a quick pat on the shoulder. "We're all set."

"I get no hug?" he said, holding his phone to his ear.

"What part of 'covered in glass' don't you get?"

"This is fuckin' Colombia all over again," he muttered with a roll of his eyes.

"How much coke were you covered in?" I snapped, scowling at him. "We had to hose you down for hours."

He wasn't listening to me anymore, instead talking to whoever was on the other end of his call. "Yeah, I've got the former deputy of Ursa here bleeding on the floor of my friend's living room. We need an ambulance, and we've got two more guys ready to go to jail."

"Tell 'em not to kill themselves getting over here."

"You heard him. The new sheriff of Ursa says you can take your time. We've got this."

SEVENTEEN

By the time Emery and the girls got back from the diner with Winston—they had run into Mal and Jules and their boys—there was a maid service completing the cleanup of the house, and I was finishing up with Sheriff Thomas and Sergeant Tavares from Whitefish.

Tavares had brought twenty of his men, all of whom, along with Tavares, were very pleased to hear I would be taking over the sheriff duties from Thomas, earlier than normal, in the first week of December. Starting off my tenure by closing a homicide investigation was impressive, to say the least.

"It will also give Mrs. Bannon some closure."

I was glad about that.

"Brann!" Emery yelled from the sidewalk, where the Whitefish officers were holding everyone, not letting anyone through to the house unless they got Tavares's okay.

"Oh, that's Mr. Dodd and his children, isn't it?" Tavares asked me.

"Yes," I said, smiling at him. "They're my family now."

"Well that's wonderful news, even more ties to the

community," he said, turning to face Emery and the girls, extending his hand. "I'm Sergeant Tavares from the Whitefish Police Department; I met you once, Mr. Dodd, as you recall?"

Emery shook the man's hand, glancing at me, then Huck, who had changed into cargo pants, his combat boots, and a thick Navy-issue sweater. The gun holster he was wearing was not to be missed.

Olivia said hello to Tavares, remembering him, and then scrambled up the steps to reach me. Flinging her arms around my waist, she leaned her face into my belly. "Are you okay? Did somebody shoot at you?"

"I'm fine," I soothed her, hugging her back as April joined her sister, wrapping around me, her face higher, jammed into my abdomen.

"Why are there people cleaning the house?" Emery asked as he reached us, taking a breath, hands on the sides of my neck, checking me over before he joined his girls and pressed in against me, holding on, taking deep breaths.

"I really am fine," I reiterated. "And think how clean the house will be."

"And they already boarded up the window," Huck explained, pointing inside. "All we have to do is order a new one."

"Why do we need a new window?" Emery asked, pulling back to look at my face.

"Huck had to come through it 'cause he didn't have a key, which reminds me, did you get the key back from Lydia?"

"She left it yesterday, and—why would Huck just crash through a window? Does this have something to do with why he left the diner so fast?"

It certainly did. "We should probably get it rekeyed," I said to Huck. "Don't you think?"

"It'll be the sheriff's house now, so yeah, I think so," Huck agreed, then yawned before turning to Emery. "And I had to go through the window because that deputy—what was his name?"

"Reed," I supplied, patting Olivia's back. "You better have brought me something to eat because I'm frickin' starving."

"Yeah, so Reed, he was holding a Glock on Brann, and the other guy—Duvall, yeah?"

"Yeah," I confirmed, even as I glowered at Olivia.

"I picked you out a meatloaf sandwich and curly fries and a chocolate shake," she explained, smiling up at me.

"I see no shake. I see no bag. I see nada. Where's my food?"

"Duvall," Huck explained to Emery, "he had a Beretta M9. It's what those Air Force douchebags carry."

"Don't say douchebags in front of the girls," I scolded, turning to look at him.

His face scrunched up like I was insane. "What? Why?"

"It's a bad word."

He didn't appear convinced.

"And that's not fair," I said, correcting his earlier statement. "Those guys who picked us up in Caracas that time were great."

He grunted.

"They were."

"I think you're overly sentimental because you were in jail again."

"I don't recall that at all," I said, making a face at April, whose eyes got huge. "And it wasn't that kind of jail."

"Huck," Emery prodded him.

"Sorry. So, Mr. Cahill was here, talking to Brann, and

Duvall had the Beretta, and Reed had the Glock, so because Brann wasn't holding, I came through the window and put a bullet in Reed's shoulder, and Brann rushed Duvall."

Emery rounded on me and almost yelled. "You rushed Duvall and he had a gun?"

"You're not getting it; he had the Beretta," I corrected him, taking hold of his shoulder and drawing him close, nuzzling my face in his soft, clean hair, loving the feel of it on my face.

"I don't… I'm not—"

"Every carry or duty handgun has a trigger-pull weight," Huck explained to Emery. "It's basically how hard you have to squeeze to get a shot off."

"Yes," Emery said woodenly, listening, even as he remained leaning into me.

"So the Glock, I wanna say with a factory stock trigger, it's gonna be like what, five pounds give or take?"

I nodded.

"But the Beretta, with the double-action on that, that's gonna be more like thirteen, fourteen pounds."

"I don't understand what—"

"There was no way unless Duvall was specifically trained with that gun that he could shoot Brann before Brann could get to him."

Emery stared at Huck in disbelief.

"I know on TV, all the guns shoot the same—fast—and everyone holds the gun straight out and squeezes off the shots," he explained patiently, being better, gentler, than I'd seen him be with anyone in ages. "But in real life, that's not the case, and when you're a Soldier, they teach you to not only read the man but his weapon as well. So I can tell you with absolute certainty, that the only person in the room that could have hurt me or Brann or Ms. Stratton, was Deputy Reed. He had the gun he knew how to use. Duvall bought that gun probably because he thought it was cool, but he wasn't trained to use it."

"You're certain of that," Emery pressed him.

Huck nodded. "Absolutely." And then he qualified, "Now, that Beretta in the hands of someone who actually knows how to use it, is deadly. I mean, once you get that first shot off, it's just like firing the Glock. The second through however many shots, the hammer is always back which gives it the same pull. The first shot taking longer though, that's the one Brann was banking on."

Emery was studying my friend, unsure, trying to make sense of what he was being told.

"Anyway, that Beretta is a combat pistol; it's not something you take to scare a SEAL in his home."

Emery turned into me, arms around my neck, holding tight.

"You're not helping," I snarled at Huck under my breath, rubbing Emery's back, clutching him against me.

Huck shrugged. "I tried."

Glancing away from him, I stared daggers at Olivia. "Food?"

"On the way home, I saw Mariah and her mom, and they both looked kinda sad, so I gave them your food and your shake to cheer them up, and they were happy and said they could split it and that it was super nice of you."

"Of me?"

"I said it was from you."

I growled at her.

"Daddy said he would make you an omelet."

"Yeah?" I said to Emery. "You're gonna cook?"

He didn't respond, just continued to hug me. Not that I

was complaining. He could hold me for as long as he wanted.

"Are you mad?" Olivia asked me, her eyes searching my face.

"Do I look mad?"

She shook her head.

I smiled at her. "It was a nice thing you did for your friend, Livi."

She took a breath. "I told Daddy and April to start calling me Livi again, and I told Huck to call me Livi too."

"Oh, I'm real glad," I admitted, easing her close to me so I could hold her.

April, who hadn't left my side, huddled close as well.

Easy to see I was loved.

As soon as the Whitefish PD cleared out, people started coming by the house. Mal and Jules came over to meet Huck, thank him, and check on me. Mal and Huck were still talking an hour later, and Jules was with the girls, going through pictures of Andrea that she'd brought over.

Anne Stratton, bruised but hardly broken, came back to speak to Emery so they could formalize a date for her to make him an offer on officially building the resort. They disappeared into his office to hammer out the details.

Cahill Lumber moved quickly, removing Grant Cahill from the board of his own company, and Lydia took over as the interim CEO, pending an investigation into involvement on her part. I let the reporters who came by from news stations in Helena, Whitefish, and Ursa's local paper know I had every confidence in Lydia Cahill's innocence. Emery got an email from Lydia a couple of hours after that, informing him that she would not be seeking any monetary restitution for lost funds due to his termination of their engagement. There were, her letter went on to say, new extenuating circumstances.

"Like the fact that the entire marriage was a sham from the beginning, since Cahill was only trying to defraud his new son-in-law out of land that was rightly his!" Jules finished hotly, and loudly, arms crossed as she'd read the email over Emery's shoulder.

Emery and I both turned to look at her.

"But that's just a guess."

Cahill and Duvall were driven to Helena by the Whitefish PD, who formally took jurisdiction of the case as the findings of their ME pertaining to Peter Bannon would be used during the prosecution of the case. Huck turned over his findings—the hacking he'd done—to the Whitefish PD. Both he and I would be deposed at a later date as witnesses.

David Reed would spend the night at the hospital for no good reason. It was a shoulder wound that both Huck and I had been through on more than one occasion, but he would be transferred to Helena the following day. Taken to the hospital in Whitefish, he was cuffed to his bed, with one officer in the room and two at the door. The chief of police there was taking no chances with his continued health or custody.

Taking a break from talking to everyone, I went into my bedroom and called Jared Colter. He answered on the third ring.

"Calder," he greeted me. "To what do I owe the pleasure?"

"Did I wake you, sir?"

"Chicago is only an hour ahead of Ursa, Calder," my boss said snidely. "It's only eleven here, not three in the morning. I'm not quite that old."

"No, sir," I replied quickly.

"Don't treat me like I'm a fossil."

"Yes, sir." I sighed, smiling, because I realized, with only those few words passing between us, that he was treating me differently. He already knew I was quitting. "I called because I wanted to thank you for the opportunity you gave me. I enjoyed working for you."

"For someone who didn't want to commit to law enforcement, you certainly changed your mind quickly."

"I was asked to serve by the people of Ursa, sir. You can't say no when you're asked."

"I'm not arguing," he said solemnly, his deep baritone rumbling over the other end of the line. "And I'm certain you'll make a fine sheriff."

He wasn't using *fine* in that mediocre way either. He meant it as a true compliment.

"May I ask you something?"

"Of course."

"There's no mutual friend, right? I mean, Harlan Thomas is your friend, isn't he?"

"Sheriff Harlan Thomas is the oldest brother of my partner who was killed a very long time ago."

I had no idea what kind of partner he was talking about, and there was no way to ask any more questions. I was amazed that I got that much. "I'm so sorry, sir."

"Thank you, Calder."

Quiet a moment, thinking how to frame the next question, I took a breath to dive in.

"We both know that you going to Ursa was not our usual kind of job."

"Yessir," I said, so relieved he was talking.

"I send you guys out to protect kids or retrieve them, not

normally make them grilled cheese or drive them to school in the morning."

"There's normally a lot more shooting and bullets flying and a greater capacity for peril."

"Yes, there is," he conceded, and the warmth that came over the line made me smile, because this was the best and last conversation I was ever going to have with Jared Colter as my boss. It wouldn't be the same after this. I wouldn't be one of his guys anymore. "But that wasn't the job in Ursa. The job there was to find the perfect mix of commitment and pride, protectiveness and empathy. Harlan's been trying to find a man he could trust to take his place for a while now, but no one who wanted to transfer to Ursa, who was running from an old life, was what the town needed."

He was telling me that I alone had been the best fit, and to have Jared Colter think so much of me, when I'd thought the exact opposite was the case, caught my heart in a vise.

"Harlan's been the sheriff there for twenty years, and two years ago, when Cahill tried to rig the election to put his man in instead, it still turned out to be Harlan."

"May I ask why Sheriff Thomas even wants to retire?"

"He told me that the town is changing and they need a sheriff who is engaged with the community, someone everyone can pick out in a crowd and feel safe with."

"He just means younger than him."

"No, he means calm under pressure, well-trained, capable, persuasive, and more than anything else, trustworthy," he said, and the list, his list, was a lot of good to hear all at once. "And you look the part too, Calder. You're tall and strong, you smile a lot, which puts people at ease, and you have a hefty ego because you know you can handle yourself in most situations. But, you stop and listen, and Harlan said he knew right away that you were the right man when everywhere he went and everyone he talked to already knew your name. This is the best outcome for everyone."

I had a thought. "I wonder if folks who come to Torus now will think you're running a dating service."

"Calder—"

"Like pick the fixer you might wanna keep 'cause you never know, you just might."

"All right, we're done talking now."

I chuckled. "When I come clear out my apartment, should I call you to meet me for lunch? I'm thinking I might bring my family and show them Chicago."

"I would love that. Make sure to call."

"Yessir," I barely got out. "Thank you, sir."

When he hung up, I let my head fall back and simply breathed, letting my life settle in around me.

I was still standing there when Emery came into the room, walked up behind me, and wrapped me in his arms.

"What are you doing in here alone?" he whispered, his breath warm on the back of my neck before his lips pressed against my nape.

"I called my boss and quit so I can live here with you now."

"That's good because I wasn't letting you leave. Not now. Not ever."

"I like it when you say scary possessive things."

"I know," he rumbled, turning me in his arms for a kiss.

EIGHTEEN

Emery's parents, who had only occasionally visited since Andrea passed, and had never accepted an invitation to be away from their home during any holiday, happily said yes to Olivia when she said they should come see her for Christmas.

Emery nearly passed out.

"What's the big deal?" I asked him, watching as he paced from one side of our bedroom to the other.

"Are you kidding?" he asked, eyes wide, arms flailing, absolutely sputtering with words that were all trying to get out at the same time.

"What's the worst that could happen?"

The answering whimper was pretty damn funny.

November had been busy.

On Election Day, I officially became the new sheriff of Ursa, and in a surprise move, Sheriff Thomas said he was resigning immediately. He was ready to be done, I was ready to take over, and his son and daughter-in-law wanted him moved in with them before the holidays. I suspected he would enjoy living on Maui. He gave all his winter coats to charity.

Even though I already had a home, I bought Sheriff Thomas's one-bedroom Craftsman bungalow and moved Huck in. I told him if he liked the place, he could make payments until it was his. Since it was love at first sight for him—I think it was the sunporch that did it, and the view of the mountains—he was fixing it up and paying me a little each month. Originally I told Emery that I was going to give it to Huck, but he cautioned me against that.

"Having only known Huck for a short time, I can still tell you that his pride is a serious thing."

He was right, it was.

"What's your point?" I asked him.

He ran his fingers through my newly cut hair, liking how it was short on the sides and back but still longer on top. I didn't think a sheriff should look like a hipster, and he had agreed.

"I think you should let him make payments for, say, six months, a year, and then tell him it's paid off and sign over the deed. That way his pride is protected, and the two of you are on equal footing instead of him owing you for not only his life here but his home as well."

As I valued the man's insight, I acquiesced to his plan.

The change in Huck was great for him, annoying for me.

He was healthy, eating regularly, working out, teaching self-defense classes at the dojo with Sensei Ozumi and, of course, since he was already certified to teach Krav Maga, he took the spot that had originally been offered to me. The part that agitated me, however, was the daily visits from women all over Ursa.

Somehow it had gotten out that Huck had a bit of a

sweet tooth, and suddenly the office was inundated with baked goods. There were always women popping by to bring Huck a pie or some cupcakes or banana bread or cookies. So many goddamn cookies. Our office smelled more like a bakery than a jail.

"Why is that a bad thing?" he asked, stuffing a macaroon into his mouth. "I think it's awesome," he teased me, talking with his mouth full.

I threw up my hands in disgust.

We had to hire two new deputies because the resort Anne was building on Emery's land was approved by a unanimous town charter, and Ursa had a whole influx of construction workers who had nothing to do at night if bingo at the Episcopalian Church didn't do it for them. In response, two new bars and a brewhouse went up on the edge of town. I liked Ironwood, the brewhouse, but the bars were a bit skanky, and we got a lot of complaints. Huck and I took turns driving out there and stopping in at the bars, and the two new deputies, Simone Keller, who also volunteered with the fire department and had a serious round house kick, and Garret Nakama, Olivia's teacher's husband, who, it turned out, had been an EMT in Denver before they moved to Ursa. I offered to talk to the Fire Chief for him, but he said he preferred to be in law enforcement instead. Stop the blood before it started was his new motto.

As paperwork was not my strong suit, I hired Jenny Rubio to be our receptionist and clerk, and she took to the job quickly. She was especially understanding with the women, and men, who came in to report altercations with spouses, domestic partners, or estranged lovers.

Sadly, there was an influx of restraining orders to be served, and I got to be on a first-name basis with the district court judge in Whitefish. The only good part of that was Huck and I in someone's home, man or woman, explaining the pitfalls of testing us, reinforced our already powerful bond. I had always liked him, loved him, but I realized almost immediately that he was more my brother than anything else. The first time I introduced him like that, I saw how quiet he got and how shiny his eyes were. When his mother visited, checking up on him, dragging Huck's sister along, they were thrilled and relieved to see him so healthy and happy and engaged with the community. Both women were charmed by the never-ending array of desserts as well.

"No wonder you work out all the time," his sister said to him, eyeing the assorted tins and decorative canisters and ribbon-wrapped pans. "I'd be as big as a house in days."

Interestingly enough, the only person I saw him have dinner with or go to the movies with or attend the harvest festival with was Anne Stratton. It was unexpected—the stunningly elegant older woman and the rough-around-the edges retired SEAL turned deputy sheriff. I didn't pretend to understand their dynamic, but it was a pleasure to have Anne over for dinner with him the few times she accompanied him, because she was amazing with the girls, and Emery always enjoyed talking to her about the resort.

Emery and I had a new routine where he dropped the girls off in the morning and I picked them up after school. They enjoyed getting into the cruiser, and I would do it until the novelty wore off. I suspected that as soon as April hit middle school I was going to need to change it up.

After school, I was still in charge unless there was an emergency, at which time Huck was on deck or Mal or Jules, and even Anne when it was time to pick out a dress for April for the winter song contest. Each grade sang, and April had been chosen as a soloist.

In the back of my mind, I had worried about me being an openly gay sheriff in a small mountain town in Montana. But there weren't any whispers about it, as far as I could tell. Emery had one parent who wanted his daughter moved out of his AP English class when he disclosed that he was going to be marrying the sheriff, but when the principal called the young woman into the office with her parents to explain what was about to happen, she lost her mind about college credits and her GPA and basically explained to them that Yale didn't accept classes from her school not taught by Emery Dodd. He was published in scholarly periodicals, did they know?

There was no more talk about moving kids out of any of his classes after that.

April and Olivia had some questions from kids they knew but nothing ugly, just confused, and the one boy who thought to take out his father's homophobia on Olivia ended up with his face in the grass at recess. She already had a blue belt in karate.

I went with Olivia to the boy's home to meet with the single dad and ended up inviting them over for dinner with all of us, including, as usual, Huck. I made arrangements to get the guy's son into karate with Olivia, and Emery got the father some grief counseling over the loss of his wife from breast cancer the year before. The boy, Crew Markham, soon became one of Olivia's best friends. Emery said I needed to put that in the win column.

When I visited Chicago with Emery and the girls over fall break, I took them to Navy Pier, to the Field Museum and Shedd Aquarium, and to Chinatown for my favorite dim sum. We had dinner with my buddy Anthony, and April was thrilled to see him in person, and when he offered to give her a behind-the-scenes tour of the hospital the following day, Emery did that with her while Olivia and I had lunch with Jared Colter. It was amazing the questions Olivia got away with asking him, things I would have never had the balls to bring up, like was he ever in the military like I was? He was exceedingly patient with her and explained to her about black ops, and what the CIA did to protect her freedom, and why it was important to vote when she got older and ran for office.

"What should I be?" she asked him brightly.

"I think you'd make an excellent prosecutor, because it seems like you enjoy digging for the truth."

Like everyone who ever met Jared Colter, she took his words as gospel and went on a fact-finding mission to see if that could truly be her life goal at six. I told her she had some time to consider all her options, since the day before her plan had been to be an astronaut.

I got a strange call from Locryn Barnes, who asked to see me the last night we were there.

"You could have gone, you know," Emery told me that night as we lay in bed together, the girls in the adjoining room, our door closed and locked, theirs open on the other side.

"What?"

"Locryn Barnes," Emery reminded me, slipping his hand across my chest, touching me like he always had to. "You could have gone to see him."

"I know that."

"And I wouldn't have insisted on going with you," he imparted quietly, leaning close to kiss over my pectoral as his hand slid down over what he called my bumpy abdomen.

"I know that too." I sighed, my breath catching as his hand slipped lower under the blanket to my cock. "But

Locryn Barnes and I are not friends, which is why we had dinner with Cooper tonight and not him."

"I liked Cooper. I hope he visits for that fishing he wants to do."

At the moment, the only thing I cared about was Emery and his hand under my balls lazily fondling me until he fisted my already hardening cock. "Yeah, he's great," I muttered, pushing up into his somehow always perfect grip. The man had hand jobs down to a science.

"I'm just telling you," he whispered in the darkness, stroking me, milking me, his thumb smearing leaking precome over the head of my cock, "that you're free to see anyone you want."

"You don't have to—fuck," I moaned, choking down the sound, glancing at the door, checking again to make sure it was closed on our side. "Are you sure that's locked?"

"Yes, it's locked."

We could hear them, though, and they could hear us if we were speaking normally, hence the heated whispering and swallowing down the noises that could be very, very loud when we got lucky and girls both had sleepovers at their friends' houses on the same night.

"Brann?" he husked out my name, as he flung the blanket back and slipped between my legs. "Bend your knees."

I did as I was told, and I was rewarded with first his tongue on the weeping end of my cock before he slowly, steadily, deep-throated me, swallowing around my length until he had every inch.

It was heaven.

I had no idea he had lube until a finger speared inside my opening, and I gasped, spurting a bit down the back of his throat.

When he added another finger, pushing both deep while sucking my cock, I bowed up off the mattress, words lost because they had to be, the only begging I could do was the arching of my hips and panting breath.

Emery Dodd was a beautiful, sexy man, but unless you shared a bed with him you'd never know that his skin felt like hot silk when it slid over yours, or that his lean muscles moved fluidly, languidly until he wanted more. And then there was strength and power and the delicious manhandling as he bent you in half and held you down and took what he wanted—your submission, his pleasure.

His hands were behind my knees as he curled over me, predatory and unyielding, the wide head of his cock against my entrance, pressing inside, my muscles stretching around him, straining, legs trembling in his grip as I whimpered, the stifled sound somehow even more lewd and desperate. Not that I cared, all my pride abandoned. He took it from me, the façade, the control I presented to everyone, stripped it away when we were in bed, and when he had all my armor removed, then he fucked me, like he did now, thrusting home, all of me utterly his.

I bucked against him, pushing him deeper, and his eyes glinted in the darkness before they narrowed to slits, too hard to see.

"Brann," he whispered, shoving inside me only to roll his hips back, sliding him almost free of my clasping hole before he drove in again and again, relentlessly, without hesitancy, the message clear—I belonged to him.

I reached for him and only then did the punishing rhythm falter as he curled over me, bending to deliver a brutal kiss, mauling, devouring, one hand fisted in my hair as he ground into me, dragging over my gland as I came in a heated rush, splattering his belly and chest, twitching and trembling beneath him.

He was sheathed in my body, and he came like that, buried, anchored, making everything inside hot and slick as he sank against my chest, the sound of his low, husky chuckle swimming through my veins before he kissed me again, this time gentler but with the same demand of his lips, tongue, and teeth. I had to turn my head to breathe.

"You're always so thorough when you're jealous," I whispered against his glistening skin, smiling, satisfied body and soul, ready to sleep in his arms.

"What are you—what do I have to be jealous for?" he asked, easing from my channel as he always did, slowly, gently and with the utmost care.

"I dunno," I snickered, watching him pull the covers up around us, neither of us caring that we were sticky with cum. "Why are you?"

"You made love to him."

"Correction. I fucked him. There's a difference."

"I don't want you to fuck anyone but me."

"Don't worry about it. It ain't ever gonna happen." I pulled him down to me as I said it, tucking him against my chest and squeezing him tight. "I'm smarter than I look, you know."

"I want to get married when we get back. I don't want to wait until January. City Hall here we come."

"The girls wanna have their party," I teased him, my eyes dipping closed once, twice, before I simply forgot to open them. "And all the flowers. We promised we'd stand in the kitchen by the chandelier."

"This is a serious conversation," he informed me. "Open your eyes."

I whined, but it was a quiet one.

"Now."

I did as I was told.

"We can have everything the girls want and still do it next weekend. I'll tell Mal when we get home. You tell Huck."

"The ring won't make me anymore yours than I am now," I promised him.

"I know," he agreed, kissing me deeply before he stopped to look into my eyes. "But then I won't need to fuck you through the mattress every time I get jealous."

"I knew you were jealous."

"Yes, you're very smart."

I scoffed and he smiled.

"I want you to always know who loves you, and I feel like if I imprint it on every inch of your skin, then there's no way you could ever forget."

"I could never forget, so I'll take the power fuck without the double helping of fear and jealousy next time, all right?"

"It's a deal."

We got married when we got home, and I never saw Locryn Barnes.

AND NOW, as I stood at the kitchen counter, drinking coffee, having changed into jeans, a gray t-shirt, and the blue zippered cardigan Emery loved me in, showered and shaved in preparation for the imminent arrival of Emery and his parents from the airport, I should have been nervous, but I wasn't. I hoped they liked me. I would bend over backward to get them to, but if they didn't, that was okay too. Emery was head-over-heels crazy in love with me. I saw it in his face when he looked at me, felt it in his hands when he touched me, and heard it in his voice whenever he said my name. I felt the same.

The girls loved me, even though I drove them bonkers, and Winston was on the fence about me since I took over brushing his teeth with an electric toothbrush. It was so much easier and faster.

My best friend loved me, plus all the new ones I'd made in Ursa, and I felt like I had Andrea's blessing too since, when we got married, the light came through the window and hit the chandelier, showering the room in a rainbow of color. It didn't get much better than that.

I heard the car coming up the driveway, headed for the garage behind the house.

"They're here!" Olivia yelled, running by me toward the back door.

"Wait until your father parks the car," I warned her.

"Oh, Brann," she whined, because clearly I was ridiculous. "You worry too much."

"I can't ever worry too much," I told her as she reached the door. "I love you."

She turned and smiled at me over her shoulder as April walked up beside me and took hold of my hand.

"I love you too, Brann," Olivia told me. "But you know that."

"I do."

"I love you too." April sighed, squeezing my hand, not moving from my side.

"Me too," I said, having to take a quick breath because they were messing with me, making me all…. "What the hell is going on?" I groused at them, rubbing my eyes.

"Just wanted you to know," Olivia snickered before she threw open the door and darted outside. I heard a woman gasp her name.

April gave my hand a last squeeze before following her sister.

I took a breath, saw the prism of color on the ceiling from the chandelier, and headed out to meet the rest of my family.

"There he is," I heard Emery say.

It was all I needed.

A NOTE FROM THE AUTHOR

∼

Thank you so much for reading No Quick Fix, the first book in the Torus Intercession series. I hope you enjoyed Brann and Emery's story, and if you did, please consider leaving a review on Amazon for my guys. It would help so much with the book's visibility. There are more books yet to come, including Croy's book, *In A Fix*, which is up next.

Want to stay up-to-date on my release? Join the mob!

Thank you so much for joining me for my new series, I hope to see you soon!

ALSO BY MARY CALMES

By Mary Calmes

Published by DREAMSPINNER PRESS

www.dreamspinnerpress.com

Acrobat

Again

Any Closer

Floodgates

Frog

The Guardian

Heart of the Race

His Consort

Ice Around the Edges

Judgment

Just Desserts

Kairos

Lay It Down

Mine

Romanus * Chevalier

The Servant

Steamroller

Still

Three Fates

What Can Be

Where You Lead

You Never Know

CHANGE OF HEART

Change of Heart

Trusted Bond

Honored Vow

Crucible of Fate

Forging the Future

L'ANGE

Old Loyalty, New Love

Fighting Instinct

Chosen Pride

THE VAULT

A Day Makes

Late In The Day

MANGROVE STORIES

Blue Days

Quiet Nights

Sultry Sunset

Easy Evenings

Sleeping 'til Sunrise

MARSHALS

ABOUT THE AUTHOR

~

Mary Calmes believes in romance, happily ever afters, and the faith it takes for her characters to get there. She bleeds coffee, thinks chocolate should be its own food group, and currently lives in Kentucky with a five-pound furry ninja that protects her from baby birds, spiders and the neighbor's dogs. To stay up to date on her ponderings and pandemonium (as well as the adventures of the ninja) follow her on Twitter Facebook, Instagram and subscribe to her newsletter.

Made in the USA
Middletown, DE
14 April 2019